"You've got to stop thinking of me as your nephew," Charles said in dead earnest. "I want you to think of me as a man."

I almost laughed but he was so serious I couldn't. What exactly was happening? Was my ten-year-old nephew actually about to romance me?

In a moment I had my answer. He leaned across the hamper and kissed my lips. As his face left mine, I sat there speechless.

"Say something," he demanded.

"This is silly," I blurted out, making a joke of it.

"I won't always be a kid, you know."

"Oh, honey," I said, trying to repair the damage. "I love you . . . I do love you, but this is silly. I'm your aunt and I'm forty-one years old. You're just all mixed up because of what we've been through these past weeks . . ."

"I'm going to marry you someday," he said soberly. "There's no sense in arguing. When I'm bigger we'll discuss it again."

"Very well," I answered innocently. *The pact had been made.* Charles would be bigger sooner than I had dreamed possible, and I would be beyond discussing anything . . . rationally.

Also by Bob Randall

The Fan

Published by
WARNER BOOKS

THE NEXT

Bob Randall

WARNER BOOKS

A Warner Communications Company

ACKNOWLEDGMENTS

The author wishes to express his
sincere thanks to Bernard Shir-Cliff,
Jeff Brown and Consuelo Baehr
for their generous advise.

WARNER BOOKS EDITION

Cover art by Dario Campanile

Book design by H. Roberts

Warner Books, Inc., 75 Rockefeller Plaza, New York, N.Y. 10019

A Warner Communications Company

Printed in the United States of America

First Printing: February, 1981

10 9 8 7 6 5 4 3 2 1

For Bessie

Q.   *Why did God make me?*

A.   To love and obey him in this world and be
     happy with him in the next.
                              A Child's Catechism

THE
NEXT

KATE

We are not here to decide our fates, merely our nomenclatures: Defilers of small children, faithful lovers, lunatics, heretics, innocents. Our fates are quite sealed, my sister's and mine. We shall spend the remaining years we have, sitting here, in our father's house, shuffling our guilts and regrets like cards in an endless game of solitaire. Metaphor number one. Others will follow, I assure you, but I will try, for your sake, to avoid my usual metaphoric self-indulgence.

Now then, to understand what happened to us during the past summer, or at least to see it fully, since Solomon would be at a loss to understand it, I think I'd best tell you something about Molly and me. We were raised in the forties in one of those immense and utterly useless houses prosperous merchants built around the turn of the century before social awareness and income tax. Father bought the beige elephant shortly before I was born and in the following two years devoted himself to furnishing it and filling it with offspring. The furnishing went rather better than the filling, however, for the year after Molly was born he promptly gave up his baronial pretentiousness by way of dying.

Now, as to mother. Suffice to say that when we were small and braided, dear mother did something writers of detective fiction might call *nasty*. Very nasty, indeed. The outcome of which was that Molly and I were raised by a large black woman named Sissy, who spent half of her time trying to find us and the other half praying to her favorite saint that mother's predispositions hadn't been passed on to us. Until this summer I was sure they hadn't been.

So there you have it. Two small girls, pretty if I say so myself, bright, surrounded by modified opulence, nannylike devotion and not a bad trust fund to boot.

We flourished.

During adolescence, after a somewhat extended obsession with masturbation, I discovered the delights and joys of that appendage nature has seen fit to bestow on men alone. Once discovered, it quickly became the focal point of my life. I recall keeping a journal which was nothing more than a comparative list of such appendages, on whom I had found them, what I had done with them and, most deliciously, what they had done with me. I was, to understate it, promiscuous.

Molly on the other hand was Rebecca of Sunnybrook Farm, Margaret Mead and Eleanor Roosevelt rolled into one. I can still see her curled up behind that morocco-bound Edna St. Vincent Millay, thrilled with the discovery of Feelings, Thoughts, Moods,

Vapors. While big sister was away somewhere doing her own research.

At any rate, so we grew, became educated, goal-oriented and finally, mercifully, women. Molly became a sculptress and I an actress. Very arty indeed. And we set the world, if not exactly on fire, at least on hold.

And eventually we married. Oh, sweet God, did we marry! George, Molly's husband, was an old beau of mine and I gladly handed him over. Not because I didn't appreciate him, I adored him, but I knew that George and I could never have that breathless passion he could have with Molly, and I wanted them both to have it. I know I sound too noble for this world, but then, perhaps I am. At any rate, it worked out brilliantly. Molly and George fell in love, talked poetry at each other *ad nauseum*, levitated, hand in hand, through every art gallery in New York, married and quickly gave birth to our darling Charles.

It was soon after that George died. He died as he had lived, quietly, sweetly, considerate in his haste, lest anyone else suffer. He was the second most attractive man I've ever known.

Which brings me to the first. Alan. *My* dead husband. We do seem to have a curse in the old family, don't we, Molly? We meet, love, marry and bury with ferocious rapidity. Perhaps that's why we're here now, asking perfect strangers to judge us. Perhaps we're not real at all, merely figments in some ancient Greek playwright's imagination. If so, I hope the gang in the odeum throws stones at him for putting us through this. And I, for one, will not satisfy him by railing against the gods. My toga will remain intact and my speech filled with hyperbole, but calm.

Back to Alan. I have always been attracted to

gentle, dangerous men. An odd combination, I know. The fist that might strike but opens to stroke. The painless rape. How I loved it. How I missed it. And how I thanked God when I found it again. But I'm ahead of myself. I first saw Alan at an off-Broadway audition. There, in the midst of the cattle call, was the most beautiful man I'd ever estrogenized over. I tossed my auburn locks till near dizzy to attract his attention but his eyes wouldn't leave his script. I mused on their color. The blue of late June skies surely. No, blue green with brown specks, like autumn leaves floating in a pool. Excuse the hyperbole, I was young, excessively romantic and hadn't been to bed with anyone in weeks. I can't imagine why not; it certainly wasn't like me. Well, between tossing my head, clearing my throat and humming like a banshee, I finally managed to catch his eye. I'm sure he thought I was suffering from Parkinson's disease, but he smiled at me nonetheless. And then, with the door open, I swooped down on him like a 747 landing on a door-step; my poor Alan didn't have a chance. He was bound, gagged and with muffled screams led to a coffee shop near the theater. Has anyone out there in this ancient amphitheater ever consumed fourteen cups of coffee at a sitting? The effect was double; my bladder assumed the proportions of the Goodyear blimp and I was in love with Alan. No, not in love. In obsession. I was virginal once again, untried, trembling, frightened, desperately in need of being touched. And he touched me. I thank Apollo for that. That night, in his horrendous apartment he touched me until I thought I'd faint and wake up reciting the *Decameron*.

From that moment on, Alan was lost. Struggle though he tried, the hook went deep. We were married two years later, several months after George died. I remember standing in the backyard of our father's compulsion, Sissy trying valiantly to keep Charles from toddling into the preacher, Molly weeping softly next to me, Alan in his white suit looking like a visitor from paradise.

We would have been married nine years this winter. Would have been.

I was not there when he died. Alan died alone, sliding in his own blood toward Molly, who lay unconscious near him.

I want you to know about his death. Tell them about his death, Molly. Please.

MOLLY

All right.

But before I do, I want to tell you something. Kate's the romantic, not me. I don't believe in curses, ancient Greeks or any of that crap. I believe what happened happened. I'll be damned if I know how, but I sure as hell am not going to go metaphysical over it. There's another thing you should know. I love my sister. If I didn't, I swear there was a time I would have ripped her heart out, and let me tell you, I'm just the cookie who could do it. So now you know who the romantic is and who the slob is.

It happened a few months ago, on Charles's

tenth birthday. Kate was taking him out for the day.
Christ, all I heard all morning was "What time is it?"
"When's Aunt Kate getting here?" "Is she taking me
to a show?" He was in a sweat, like he always got
when Kate showed up.

So, anyway, Kate and Alan got to the apartment
around noon, she told Charles she was taking him to
a magic show, he ran up and down the walls the way
he does ... the way he used to ... and they left. I had
a sculpture I had to get out to a gallery in Nyack and
I conned Alan into driving me.

It was on the way back, on the West Side Highway that it happened. I don't know whether it was
our fault, the other guy's fault—it all happened too
fast. All I remember was suddenly seeing this car
nose to nose with us. I could see the expression of the
woman behind the wheel. It was almost funny. Like
she was saying, "What the hell are you doing right in
front of me facing the wrong way?"

I heard the sound of the impact, though I didn't
feel it. I must've stayed conscious for a moment because I saw Alan break through the windshield. I saw
a piece of glass go into his throat. And that's that. The
next thing I remember was waking up in a hospital
with more broken bones than unbroken, a face like
ground round and a body pumped full of morphine.

As I look back on it, it was the best I've felt in
months.

KATE

After the show, I brought Charles home and we settled down to wait for Molly and Alan. I recall he was unusually kinetic that afternoon, even for Charles. He seemed plugged into some emotional electrical outlet. No game could keep his attention more than a few minutes. No story assuage his need to move. I finally forced him to lie on the couch in my arms, but I could still feel the nervous twitching in his body as he pressed against me. I assumed it was the excitement of his birthday. I assumed wrong.

The phone rang a little after seven. I don't know who it was who told me. Perhaps the police, perhaps someone at the hospital. He was delicate, evasive and oddly soothing, which of course terrified me. The next time I hear that tone of voice I shall know who it is. The angel of death: "Kate? Kate, dear. Come here. I've something beautiful to show you."

It wasn't beautiful.

Alan had slid across that broken windshield and was eviscerated, like one of the chickens Sissy used to disembowel on Friday afternoons while Molly watched, fascinated, and I pretended to gag or faint or whatever would make them laugh. I don't know why they let me see him. I suppose it was because I insisted. It remains one of the many times in my life I wish to God I had kept my mouth shut. And the one time I actually did faint.

I wish to digress, as much for your sake as mine. Besides which, fainting reminds me of a story that might give you some insight into what I laughingly call my character.

It was on the occasion of another piece of grievous news, concerning dear mother. Molly and I were in the playroom doing damage to what we later found out was a valuable Sheraton table when Sissy came in, her black face swollen from crying. She sat down and said nothing for a long time. We merely stared.

"Your mama done something," she finally said.

"Our 'mama done' what?" I mimicked.

"Something bad."

I for one was shocked. Not by the fact that mother had done something wrong, but that Sissy, mother's virtual handmaiden, was tattling on her. That was *verboten* in our house.

"Your mama done something real bad."

"Shit," I recall Molly saying.

"Don't cuss, sweetheart," Sissy said, and took Molly in her arms. "Don't never cuss, my little sweetheart."

She remained that way for a while, holding Molly, reaching out her hand for me to join the embrace. I held back, for fear that if I joined them Sissy would go on with the bad news.

"Where is she?" I finally asked.

"Gone, honey. She's gone."

"Gone where?"

"Just gone."

"You mean dead, like daddy?"

"No, honey. She ain't dead. She's gone."

"Damn you, nigger," I said, having no idea what-soever why I said it. Surely mother was gone because she had done something wrong. Sissy wasn't to blame. "Damn you, nigger."

"Come let me hug you, Katie," she said.

"Damn you, nigger!"

It was then I pretended to faint. Again, I have no idea why. Perhaps to capitalize on the drama of the moment, to take stage center, to be the object of the pity, the applause. I must have smirked in my mock unconsciousness, however, because Molly kicked me. Hard.

Later that afternoon we watched Sissy pack mother's things. Neither of us said a word as we watched her dresses, so familiar I can still recall their scent, being sent away for the last time. Her red shoes that we had taken turns wearing when she was out of the house. Her pearls that we had bitten on to see if they were real. It seems to me now that in some peculiar way our mother's possessions were more real to us than she was. I'm sure I missed them more.

That night Sissy put mother's things in the car, told us to stay in the house and not get into any mischief and drove off. We immediately went to our mother's room and divided the residue.

"What do you think mama did?" Molly asked.

"Murder, mayhem, sacrilege," I said, delighted to find Sissy hadn't packed mother's long blue silk scarf, which I twirled round my shoulders.

"I still think she's dead," Molly said.

"Dead, gone, what's the difference. I'll choose you for her evening bag."

And so the Santini sisters carted their loot off to their rooms and had them secreted away by the time Sissy returned, even more swollen from crying, to the now nearly empty big house. The point of this digression is that I have fainted twice in my life. Once for pleasure, once for need. And that second time, when I saw Alan, I don't think I fainted as much as tried to die, quickly, before anyone could interfere. The point is that I had loved twice in my life. First Molly, then Alan, and that no matter how flippant my speech patterns may be I loved him deeply and profoundly.

They wouldn't permit me to die. Not then, not after I saw Molly, not in the hallway, holding Charles, frightened and silent in my arms. Later, I thought. I'll die later when Molly is well and Charles protected.

Death is a member of our family. Father started it, by buying a dead house and forcing us to live in it. And as the virus of the house killed him, he infected our mother. Molly passed it to George and I to Alan. But you must believe one thing of me if nothing else. I want to be free of this plague I bring to others. I want, more than life itself, to be *good*. As mother begged me to be. As I have never been. My, that does sound like self-pity, doesn't it? As well it might, for I do pity myself. And you, Molly. I don't think we ever had a chance, growing up in this house, clinging to each other against the madness all around us. The quiet, upper middle-class, socially approved, go-to-church-on-Sunday madness. Do you remember . . . no, of course you wouldn't. You were too young. I must have been only five or six myself. Mother was having a luncheon in the garden to which we were definitely not invited. Sissy had to do double duty that afternoon; amuse us within the house and serve the guests outside. It occurred to me that the reason I hadn't been invited was my age and so I set out to alter it. I put one of mother's dresses on, smeared my face with her makeup, threw a mink stole over my shoulders and arrived, charming and totally disguised at the party.

Mother wept.

No, not out of happiness or pride. She wept because I had ruined her party. I had disgraced her in front of the ladies of the town.

Madness.

Honestly, I do wander, don't I? The point I was trying to make was that I wanted to die, but of course, I couldn't. There was Charles to be cared for while Molly was mending, the funeral, a thousand things to do—death being such a busy time. Has my flippancy become an irritant yet? It's what we in the theater call playing *against* the scene. Much more effective. Besides which, I can't speak more directly. The last few days have drained me of all human emotion. There's nothing left but facade.

I won't bore you with the particulars of the next three weeks. Suffice to say, Charles and I managed to get through them. That was the beginning of June, and private schools being what they are, the school year was already over. So there we were, faced with the long, hot summer ahead, Molly incarcerated in that loathesome hospital for at least another month, Charles languishing in the apartment, and me, with a list of summer stock leads in the offing. Well, what could I do? I could take the stock job . . . drag Charles, kicking and screaming, behind me through what would doubtless be a summer to kill us both, or we could stay in town, visit Molly an hour or two a day and live in the local Loew's. Either alternative loomed liked a radioactive cloud on the horizon, so with Molly's consent, I decided on another plan. We two stricken children would spend the summer at father's obsession. After all, be it ever so ostentatious, there's no place like home. I hadn't been back to the house in years but there was land, air and a pond complete with turtles to nip Charles's toes. And of course, Sissy, now rounding seventy, to wait on us. It seemed the best choice. Molly would join us, knitted bones permitting, in the middle of the summer. So, that was that. Off we went, over the hills and through the woods to the house where mommy and aunty had spent so many carefree minutes.

On the drive up, something happened, which in retrospect seems important, though hardly so at the time. Charles was sitting in the front seat beside me, against the far door. Between us was a small cage in which, heaven help me, resided Charles's pet guinea pig, much against my will. It seemed to be having an attack of car sickness, by the sound of it, and I suggested that Charles put it next to the window where it might get some air. He did, and ended up sitting directly beside me. As we drove I became aware of Charles's pushing into me. I thought he might be frightened, going to a strange place without Molly.

"Are you okay, honey?" I asked him.

"Uh-huh."

"Just feel like snuggling, huh?"

"Yeah."

He pushed into me harder, so that I had difficulty driving.

"Sweetie, don't do that. The old lady's driving."

"You're not old."

"Bless your heart. Honest, Charles, move a little, huh? I may need to use my arm."

He moved away slightly.

"You sure you're okay?"

"What's the house like?"

"Don't you remember it? The big tan house? You once peed on the living room rug."

He frowned at me.

"Sorry, did I embarrass you?"

He nodded yes and pushed into me again. Harder.

"Charles, please . . ."

"I love you."

"I love you, too, honey, but I'd like to get us there in one piece, okay?"

Harder.

"Charles, I'm not kidding. Now give me some room. Move!"

He acquiesced reluctantly and put the cage between us.

"You mad?" I asked after a moment's silence.

"No."

"Sad?"

"No."

"Truculent, despondent, cycloid, bemused, any of the above?"

He looked over at me and smirked. "You're not old," he said.

And that was that.

Sissy was getting senile. After we put Charles to bed in Molly's old room we sat across the kitchen table from each other, pretending not to be strangers.

"I'm sorry about George," she said.

"Alan."

"That's right."

Senile and old. Her hair had been gray for as long as I could remember, but now it was coming in pure white, like a fake Santa's beard. And there were deep black circles under her eyes.

"Have you been all right?" I asked.

She was startled by the question, as if no one had ever asked about her health before. And grateful. She took my hand in hers.

"I'm fine, Katie. I'm just fine. Don't waste your time worrying about me."

I suddenly felt guilty, for the truth is, I don't think I ever worried about Sissy. She had always been made of some mystical black marble to me, impervious to the plagues around her. But now, there she was, old, frail, grateful if someone asked how she'd been. I held her hand and felt the roughness and strength that years of cleaning father's possessions had given it.

"We'll take care of each other this summer, Sissy, you and I. And Charles. He'll need us both."

"Don't worry, Katie. You're both home now."

I hoped she didn't notice my shudder.

Several days later . . . no, I won't do this. I was going to skip an embarrassing essential, but if you're to be any help to us at all, you may as well see it all, degrading step by degrading step. I fled Sissy shortly after that and went upstairs to unpack. There were four suitcases in my room, three of which housed my clothes. One of which was filled with . . . this is difficult; I've always despised self-betrayal . . . well, damn, the fact is I had packed a suitcase full of Alan's things. Don't ask why. It was maudlin and neurotic and Lord knows self-indulgent, but nonetheless, I did it. I opened the suitcase and melodramatically looked over its contents. Alan's watch, a T-shirt from the hamper that still had his blessed perspiration stains around the underarms . . . I am getting mawkish, aren't I? Well, full steam ahead, I say. If you're going to be mawkish, go whole hog. I wept. I wept for Alan. I wept for Sissy. But mostly, I wept for Kate. There's a kind of selfishness that comes, I suppose, from early starvation and, my dears, I've got quite a case of it. Show me a television commercial with a crippled child pleading for donations and I'll show you a woman complaining that her agent hasn't gotten her a commercial. Tell me of your pain and watch me interrupt with mine. Did I say I despised self-betrayal? I do. But you're the surgeon and if I withhold the wound, how will you repair it?

I do adore a good metaphor.

I replaced Alan's things and, still playing the mad scene from *Streetcar*, put the suitcase in the back of my closet where Sissy wouldn't find it. And then, in true Southern-decadent-heroine fashion I *insinuated* myself into a hot tub.

Charles adjusted to the country better than I did. He even found a playmate down the road. A little girl, at least I think it was a girl, country children being so androgynous. And as for me, during those first few weeks I wandered. Down one country road, up another, round the pond, into town, wherever Alan and I could be alone. Yes, alone with Alan, for my obsession with his loss had taken a new turn. I had become an internal dramatist, inventing a thousand dialogues between us. At times I'd chastise him for leaving me and promise to forgive him upon his return. It had been a mistake. The body wasn't his. It was necessary to keep the truth from me. Sealed orders from the Federal Bureau of Investigation.

"But my God, didn't you know what you were putting me through, Alan?"

"Of course I did, darling, and it killed me but what could I do?"

"What could you do? Jesus, Alan, I'm your wife!"

"Sweetheart, I know. I begged them to get in touch with you but the president himself couldn't intervene. Baby, enough. I'm back."

"You're back. Big deal."

"It is a big deal. Come here."

"No."

"Come on. Make love, not war."

"Creep . . ."

"Come to papa."

"Some papa . . ."

"I love you."

All the dialogues ended that way, with Alan saying I love you, and with me, in one of hundreds of moods, melting into him.

You see, I choose to suffer. I enjoy it. Pleasure is intangible but pain is concrete. I define my existence through pain. And my little playlets allowed me to lose Alan daily. To suffer on the way to the post office. To die a little while picking up the groceries. To mourn afresh over the most pedestrian activity.

I frequently, and with no false modesty, make myself sick.

It was during one of my flights of self-abusive fantasy that I almost allowed Charles to be harmed. We were walking into town for a movie, Charles going on endlessly about his little unisex friend, while I sat in an imaginary airport lounge weeping softly into my daiquiri, Alan consoling me over his bourbon neat. We came to a road, Charles and I, not Alan and I, for we were still in the lounge, and a car that had the right of way yelped to a halt. I apologized for not having looked in either direction and we walked on.

"That was a close one," Charles said.

I put my arm around him as we walked, but this time I didn't think of Alan. I thought of Charles and how my monstrous self-indulgence affected him.

It was somewhere in the middle of the movie that I resolved to let Alan die, to let him decay in the ground, to let his dust be blown away. Finally. Mercifully. *Hopefully.*

That evening, over dinner, I left the table and went to my room. I took the suitcase from the back of my closet and opened it. I withdrew Alan's watch and replaced the suitcase. Downstairs, Charles was seeing how much sherbet he could spill while still getting some in his mouth. I handed him the watch.

"A little present for you, kiddo. It was Uncle Alan's."

"Hey, neat!"

"It cost a bloody fortune, so no dunking it in the sherbet."

"Don't worry, I've had watches before. How much did it cost?"

"Two C-notes, just about."

"What's that?"

"Two hundred bucks to you."

And then, as if someone had lowered a movie screen between us, I saw myself give Alan the watch, a Christmas before. I saw him in his short robe, his hairy legs stretched out in front of him, his silly long toes wiggling in delight at it. I saw him put it on his left wrist, then his right, then an ankle. And I saw him hand me a small red box from beneath the tree. I watched as I opened it and withdrew the garnet ring.

Then, once again sitting across the table from

Charles, the screen mercifully lifted, I felt the tears start and went outside to the pond. He was already there, waiting for me.

So much for letting Alan die.

I don't want to continue this. There's a difference between seeking advice and letting your blood for the amusement of others. I won't go on with this . . . but of course I must, if Molly and I are ever to have any peace.

I was standing there in the darkness beside the pond, and at the same time entering my apartment to see Alan's suitcases sitting there in the hallway. I heard noises from the kitchen.

"Who's there? Who is it?"

He came out of the kitchen wearing a dish towel tucked in the waist of his trousers.

"Hello, darling," he said.

I stared at him, not understanding.

"I'm home."

He came to me and put his arms around me. I said nothing, felt nothing except the emptyings of a small gland somewhere in my body which was working at a fever pitch to prevent shock.

"I should have written you," he said.

"Yes," I answered, not knowing what I was saying.

"At first, in the hospital, I couldn't write. Then, when I could, I knew you'd come to see me and I didn't want that. I wasn't exactly a pretty sight, baby. So I waited till they put the pieces back together. And here I am."

I turned away from him, planning how to continue the fantasy. And then I felt his hand on my arm. But it wasn't Alan. It was Charles.

"What're you doing?" he asked.

"Nothing, honey. Just listening to the bugs."

"Which bugs?"

"Charles, I'm not an entomologist. Just bugs, as in crawly things."

"Don't be mad at me, I didn't do anything."

"Oh, sweetheart, I'm not mad at you."

He put his little arm around my waist and we started to walk around the pond. Charles was silent, probably straining to hear my imaginary bugs. I put Alan's suitcases out the service door, hoping they'd be carted away, and all remained silent. That heavy oppressive silence I had fled the country to escape.

And then, a buzzing.

"What's that?" Charles asked. "A bug?"

"No, dear. It's the watch. You wound it?"

"Yeah."

"It's the alarm."

He stared at it in the darkness but couldn't see it. "You mean it's got an alarm clock?"

"Right."

"Oh, neat! God!"

"You won't think so after awhile. Uncle Alan used to say I gave it to him so he'd be responsible for getting us places on time. He said it was a sneaky way to make him take over."

"I don't mind taking over," he said and his voice was so loving it startled me.

"You don't, do you, sweetheart?"

"No. I'll take over from now on. You'll see."

"You'll be my little man?"

"Yes."

"My darling little man," I said. "That's a deal. I don't have anybody else, you know."

"You don't need anybody else," he said, and we turned back to the house.

That night at the pond was my first demonic act, though I hardly knew it. I had invited the first rain drop in a torrent that would sweep us all away and drown any chance of redemption. God, I love melodrama.

Charles was as good as his word. The next morning he woke me early by pulling at my arm.

"Get up, get up, get up!"

"God, Charles, what time is it?"

He proudly consulted the new watch. "Eightthirty. Will you get up?"

I put a pillow over my head.

"Katie, get up!"

"It's *Aunt* Katie to you and beat it. I'll see you around ten."

"But everything'll be ruined!"

"Charles . . ."

He tugged at the pillow. "It'll be ruined!"

"What in God's name will be ruined?"

"Breakfast! I made you breakfast! It'll be ruined!"

I moaned and sat up. "Goddamnit, Charlie, what'd you have to go and do a nice thing like that for? Where's my other slipper?"

"Hurry, will you!"

The slipper refused my big toe admittance, my robe buttoned itself on the bias and I stumbled downstairs, mumbling curses after my little locomotive. He turned toward the back door.

"This way."

"Old chum, the dining room's *that* way."

"We're eating by the pond. I said I'd take over."

"Oh Lord . . ."

Will someone please tell me how corn flakes, still in the box, can be *ruined?* There we sat, dining alfresco, my little man and his chilled-to-the-bone aunty, on cold cereal, cold milk, cold oranges and cold toast. That, at least, *was* ruined. But teeth achatter, I smiled at him over the wilting flakes. He was so pleased with himself. So delighted to have planned this breakfast all by himself. His love almost, but not quite, warmed me.

"Charles, I love our picnic and I don't want you to get the wrong idea, but darling, I am freezing my ass off out here."

He laughed.

"I know I shouldn't curse in front of children but I think I just lost the use of my right foot."

He laughed again.

"So, what do you say, sport. Shall we repair to the hearth?"

We did and Sissy, ever the realist, was waiting with coffee for me and hot chocolate for my little Eskimo.

"I told him it was too cold, but try to change that one's mind," she said, tousling his hair.

"Don't do that," Charles snapped at her.

"Why, since when can't I touch my baby?" she smiled.

"Since I'm not your baby or anybody else's. Keep your black hands to yourself."

"Charles!" I woke to the situation. "Apologize at once!"

"No."

"Charles . . ."

"All right," he said. "I'm sorry. I just don't like being touched."

Sissy went back to her sink, the hurt obvious, and Charles avoided my eyes.

"Now what was that about?" I demanded.

"I just don't like her hands on me," he whispered.

"Why?"

He took my hand in his and suddenly became so earnest it was as if he were pleading.

"We don't need her here, Kate. We should be alone, just the two of us. Fire her, please. Please!"

"Don't be ridiculous. And don't call me Kate."

Offended, Charles pushed his cup of hot chocolate away from him, got up and left the room, proclaiming in a voice filled with anger and surprisingly adult, "I'll see you at dinner, *Aunt Kathryn.*"

I sat there stunned.

Four weeks later to the day, Charles had his way. I dismissed Sissy.

After forty-two years in our house, after raising Molly and me single-handed, after polishing father's silver hundreds of thousands of times, after comforting us and nourishing us and protecting us, I dismissed her.

"You serious, baby?" she said, sitting down slowly at the kitchen table.

"I'm serious."

"Where will I go?"

"I don't know."

An envelope with her name on it sat in front of her on the table.

"Open it," I said.

She did and withdrew a cashier's check for ten thousand dollars. She looked at it as if it were a death notice.

"Where will I go?"

I started to weep and she came to me. *She* came to *me*.

"Don't, baby," she said, holding me. "Don't cry."

"Oh, Sissy, I wish it could be different . . ."

"It can. Stop this evil thing, Katie. It ain't right. You gotta stop it now before it gets any worse . . ."

"I can't, Sissy!" I pulled away from her. "I can't."

She moved to the sink and stroked its edge, perhaps getting comfort from its familiarity.

"Then I will," she said in a voice as hard as the porcelain she was holding to.

"And how will you do that?"

"I'm going to tell Molly. I should've done it a long time ago but I let you and that devil talk me out of it."

"He's not a devil, Sissy."

"Then what is he, child? What is that *thing* upstairs?"

"I don't know."

"Maybe his mama will then," she threatened.

"It won't make any difference, you know. By the time Molly gets here, we'll be gone."

She turned from the sink to face me and I saw that she, too, was crying.

"Baby, I beg you. Don't do this evil thing. Don't be like . . ."

She hesitated.

"Like my mother?" I asked.

"Yes, like your mama."

She went to the table and sat down wearily.

"It's time, sweetheart," she said. "After all these years, it's time you knew about your mama. Come, sit down."

"I don't think I want to."

It was true enough. I had always been protected

from any knowledge of what mother had done. I had tried for years to get Sissy to tell me but her black face would turn to stone at the suggestion. I could always make Sissy do anything I wanted, twist her round my finger like a ring, but I could never, never force her to talk about mother's crime. And now, with all the years of silence behind me, I didn't want to know. Whatever it was loomed over me like a bursting star, the end, the end of everything.

I sat down.

MOLLY

First of all, Sissy never said a damn word. Some kind of mammylike loyalty, I suppose. To Kate, sure as hell not to me. I had to figure it out for myself. To figure out something was happening up in that mausoleum that wasn't kosher. I don't know exactly when I first got scared that Charles was lying to me. Hell, he had always lied to me about this or that. We weren't exactly Donna Reed and family. I always tried to be a good mother, but, Jesus, you try losing a husband and being saddled with a year-old kid and see how your disposition develops. But I did love him. I still do, God help me.

Anyway, he used to call me from the country once a day at noon. Talk about your obligatory calls. All I ever got out of him was that he and Kate were on their way somewhere and he had to hurry up. I bet their phone bill to the hospital for the whole month must've totaled a fat buck and a half. So, while you're handing out sympathy, you might throw a little my way. I mean, there I was, flat on what was left of my back, a tube in every opening, pins in every bone. And what comfort do I get from my own kid? "Gotta go, call you tomorrow."

Crap. It wasn't all his fault. I'm no honeybunch to get along with, as you can no doubt tell. But, Jesus, I wouldn't do what Kate did if they hung me over live coals and chewed on the rope. I mean, there are limits, aren't there? There's got to be some point where you say to yourself "Hold it. This is too much. Fuck this."

You may have noticed the daffodil sisters have some mouths on them. I got it from Kate. She used to give me lessons when we were kids. We'd sit on ma's old bed and she'd say—

"Today, sister dear, we're going to learn all the B's. They include, please pay attention, Bitch, Bastard, Son of a Bitch, Bullshit, Barf, Bang—in the sexual connotation—and the ever popular Buns."

I was a quick study. By the time I was six I could hand it out with the best of them. And where was our resident angel Sissy during all this? Listen, Sissy couldn't stop a caterpillar from spinning a cocoon if you gave her a stick of dynamite. No, Kate made me what I am today. Such as it is.

I don't want you to get the idea that I hate Kate. I don't. The simple truth is, the reason I'm so fucking confused at this moment is that I love my sister and, believe it or not, I know what she went through with Alan. I know what a slave she was to him. But, Jesus, there are limits.

Anyway, there I was flat on my back and there

were the two-second calls coming in regular, like
clockwork, but where the hell were the calls from
my loving sister? Sure, at the beginning of the summer she'd call. She was about the only thing that kept
me and my sanity on speaking terms. But then her
calls stopped. I remember one time I called her and
got my first brush-off.

". . . it's just not a good time, Molly. I'm up to my
neck in errands."

"So send Sissy and talk to me. I'm going bugs in
this place. You should see this new contraption they
got for stretching my legs. Christ, it's right out of the
Marquis de . . ."

"Honey, I've got to go. I'll call you later, okay?"

Shit.

"Well, thanks for nothing, sis."

"Don't be mad, I just have to go. Later."

And a big fat click for me.

Christ, I should've known. I should've guessed
the two of them were up to more than Boy Scout
hikes. Oh, did I mention that's the Bullshit Kate fed
me? Yeah, little Charlie had joined a local Boy Scout
troop, so she said, and the little dickens was spaced
out on it. Oh, jeepers, the fun they were having. The
nice innocent fun. Picture this. The two of them romp-
ing through the woods, taking little plant cuttings to
put on little bits of cardboard to get Charlie some
badge or other. Gets you right in the gut, doesn't it?

I might even have pictured her doing the bucolic
bit, but Charles? Are you kidding? And the Boy
Scouts? Let me tell you what kind of an average
American Archie Andrews I got stuck with.

When he was about seven, I took him out to
Fire Island for a week, to stay with a friend of mine.
All right, a boyfriend of mine. It was about midnight

and this guy and I were in the sack, doing it, with him competing for the world's title of dirtiest talker.

"Hey, quiet down. I got a kid in the next room."

"He's been asleep for hours. Come here you—."

Never mind what he called me. It wasn't cutie pie. Anyway, he was also after the title of slowest comer, a real schmuck, so we finished off somewhere in the wee hours. With my last ounce of strength, I reached over for a cigarette on the night table but couldn't find the pack.

"Close your eyes, I'm putting the light on."

"Okay, you—."

Another beauty popped out. Christ, what a prick. So I turned the light on and guess what I saw? Sitting over in the corner, wide awake, having listened to and watched the whole damn scene? You got it. Little Chuck, the pride of troop sixty-nine.

Look, I'm not proud of it. To be honest, I packed us up the next day and we made a beeline back to town, leaving lover boy on the dock practicing his obscenities. But what kind of kid would do a thing like that? I mean, I don't buy that primal scene trauma junk, but to sit there calmly in the dark and watch his own mother get her brains screwed out? Normal, it ain't.

I don't know, maybe that had something to do with what happened this summer. Maybe I'm the one to blame.

Christ.

KATE

It was evening, the evening of the day Charles had attacked poor Sissy. He had steered clear of the house and me until dinner and, then, entered with tail firmly between legs. It was a simple Chekhovian meal; Charles and I ate silently, not deigning to look at each other, and Sissy sniffled through the serving of the courses, mumbling about the direct relationship between hurt feelings and overdone roasts. Midway through the sodden apple pie, I could no longer tolerate the dark brown atmosphere and went upstairs to my room.

And to Alan's suitcase.

It was his old cardigan sweater that gave me solace this time.

"Katie, what are you doing wearing my sweater? I've been looking all over for it."

"What? Who . . ."

"What d'you mean, *who?* Don't you recognize your own husband? Come on, hand it over."

A knock on the door sent Alan back to his grave and me scurrying guiltily to take the sweater off.

"Who is it?" Aloud this time.

"Charles."

He opened the door before I had a chance to put the sweater back in the suitcase, which sat open on my bed.

"What is it?" I asked, haughtily as I could muster.

"I'm sorry."

"For what?"

"For being mean to Sissy and you. I'm really sorry."

I held out my arms and he entered them.

"All right, we'll forget about it, honey. Just try to be nice to Sissy, will you? She's an old lady and we're all she's got."

"Sure." He glanced over at the open suitcase. "What's that?"

"Nothing," I tried to close it.

"No, come on, whose stuff?"

"Charles, a little privacy, huh? I don't go poking around your things."

He put his hand on my cheek tenderly. "Uncle Alan's?"

I was too taken aback to answer.

"I understand," was all that he said.

I suppose that in my guilt over my insane fantasies it had never occurred to me that anyone might understand, and certainly not a child. But there it was. He looked at me so gently, so sweetly, that for a moment I forgot that I was a madwoman.

"They comfort me," I said.

"I know. Can I see them?"

I let him browse through Alan's things, almost grateful to be sharing the secret. He took out one of Alan's shirts and held it up in front of himself.

"Look good?" he asked.

"Neat."

"Can I have it?"

"No, babe."

"Why not?"

"First of all, I want to keep Uncle Alan's things

together. Second of all, it's miles too big for you. It looks like a nightgown."

"I'll roll up the sleeves," he begged.

"Charlie . . ."

"Oh, come on, Kate, what good does it do anyone in a suitcase? Besides, if I wear it, it'll remind you of Uncle Alan. It'll be our special shirt, okay?"

"Gimme," I held out my hand.

"No." Charles backed off holding the shirt.

"Charles . . ."

"Come on, let me wear it for a while. Just for a while."

"Charlie, don't whine at me and give me the shirt."

"No. It's mine."

"Charles!"

He bolted for the door.

"Charles!"

I ran after him, down the stairs, out the back door, to the pond; I caught him halfway round it and wrestled him to the ground.

"All right, Charlie, fun's fun but let go of the shirt."

He was giggling heartily.

"Let go!"

"Don't wanna!"

He was lying on his back on the grassy slope of the pond; I was on top of him, straddling him, both of us holding tight to the shirt.

"Why won't you give me the shirt?" I asked, breathless.

"Because it's mine." He took a shirt sleeve in his mouth and bit down on it, holding it firmly between his teeth.

"Don't do that, you'll rip it."

"Grrrrrr."

"Charlie, stop acting crazy!"

"I'm Alan and it's my shirt!" he growled without unclenching his teeth.

"What the hell is this, *Oedipus Rex?* Give me the goddamn shirt!"

I pulled on it quickly and heard it rip. I must have reacted in horror because he opened his mouth immediately, as much in fear as in defeat. I lifted myself off him and sat down on the ground, holding the ripped shirt in my lap and started to cry. This was the first of Alan's possessions to be harmed, the first reminder that someday everything that linked me to him would tear, fade, turn to dust, as he was doing at that very moment; turning to dust far from me in a cemetery I would never have the courage to visit again. Lost. He was lost. A million fantasies, a thousand suitcases filled with his things couldn't change that.

Lost.

I felt Charles's arms around my shoulders; he pushed his cheek into mine.

"I'm sorry," he said.

"I know."

"Why are you crying?"

"Because I'm crazy," I said. "Because Alan's gone and I can't have him back. Because I never loved my mother and can't remember my father. I'm crying because all my life I had to be strong, for your mother. And then Alan came along and he was the strong one. And now he's dead and I don't think I can ever be strong again. That's why I'm crying."

He held me while I cried and then, feeling foolish, I stopped.

"Enough of that," I said. "Come on, let's go in

the house before someone sees us and sends for the men from the booby hatch."

He helped me to my feet and we started toward the back door.

"Here," I said, tossing him the shirt. "Tell Sissy to mend the tear and you can have it. I'm tired of being crazy."

He was delighted.

"It'll look good on me, you'll see," he said.

Talk about your prophesies.

Charles's campaign to get Sissy out of the house started shortly thereafter. For those interested in the deviousness of the ten-year-old mind, I include several strategic examples of how one small boy can drive two women, one elderly and the other in her prime, to the absolute brink. Picture, if you will, a roast duck dinner, perfect in every aspect, except that the duck was stuffed with a dish towel. The purpose? To prove to me that Sissy was too old to know what she was doing. Then there was the morning Charles rubbed soil on all the carpets and then complained that Sissy had neglected to vacuum them. Or the evening he went on safari by the pond, collecting the beetles we later found crawling in her room. Oh yes, we had lots of fun around our house.

And more.

One night, quite late, I was going downstairs, I don't remember why, and I heard something from the direction of Charles's darkened room. I hesitated by the top of the staircase, listening. In a few moments I recognized what I had been hearing, it was unmistakable. The soft sighs and moans of masturbation. But surely ten-year-old boys don't masturbate! I approached his room and he pretended to be asleep. I stood there in the doorway and watched him in the moonlight. I saw his body shudder, though he tried to remain motionless. And then, his absurd parody of being awakened.

"Who's that?"

"It's me. Aunt Kate. Are you all right?"

"What?"

"Are you all right?"

"What?"

"Stop saying *what*, Charles, and answer my question."

"What?"

"Charles, I know you're awake . . ."

"I'm not. I mean, you woke me up. What do you want, Kate?"

"*Aunt* Kate."

"What?"

"Oh, for crying out loud . . ."

I went downstairs, searched the living room for a pack of stale cigarettes, lit one and sat down to think about our little Charles. Something was definitely up with the child, no pun intended. The attacks on Sissy, subtle as atom bombs though they were, his increasing tendency to hang around the house rather than go out with his androgynous friend, his constant dogging of my footsteps, and his basic mood of late, which ranged from distinctly odd to positively otherworldly. Something was definitely up.

As I sat there in the darkness, in father's old Queen Anne wing chair, possibly the most uncomfortable seat in the world, Charles crept into the room, startling me.

"Jesus, Charles, cough or something when you come into a dark room. You scared me."

"Sorry. What are you doing in the dark?"

"Just thinking. Charles . . . are you happy here? In this house?"

"Sure."

"I mean, I know it's kind of lonely . . ."

"It's not lonely. You're here."

"Yes, but your friends . . ."

"I don't have any."

He moved through the darkness and sat on the floor in front of me.

"What do you mean, you don't have any? You have lots of friends in the city, don't you?"

"No."

"Why not?"

"I don't know. Kids don't like me I guess."

He rested his hand on my knee. I felt a wave of sympathy for him and put my hand on top of his.

"Why not?" I asked.

"'Cause I don't like them. I'd rather be with grownups."

"Well, what about your friend down the road? You like her, don't you?"

"No. I don't play with her anymore."

"I've noticed. How come?"

"Don't know."

I became aware that he was gently squeezing my knee. I removed his hand and held it in mine.

"Listen, old buddy, I think part of what's bothering you is probably that you miss your mother. How about we go into town and pay her a visit?"

"Nothing's bothering me."

"Okay, if that's the way you want it, but what do you say? Day after tomorrow?"

"What about it?"

"Shall we go into New York?"

"What for?"

I became impatient and released his hand.

"What do you mean, 'what for'? To collect dog shit. Forget I said that. To visit your mother, Charles."

"Oh," he said noncommittally. "Do we have to?"

"Yes, I do think we have to."

"Why?"

"Because, old chap, being stuck out here in the boondocks with your aging aunt is no real vacation for you. I think you'd feel better if you saw your mother and I think she'd feel better if she saw you. That's why, day after tomorrow, we're packing it all in the family Model T and tooting off to town."

"Let's make up our minds tomorrow," he said, getting up and walking to the door quickly.

"*Our* minds? Since when did this become a democracy?"

"We'll discuss it tomorrow," he said rather grandly and disappeared into the darkness of the hall.

I sat there for a while trying desperately to remember what I was like when I was ten. No, Charles was assuredly another breed.

Two days later I stood in the hall calling upstairs to him.

"Charles, will you move it? I want to get an early start."

"Coming," he called back laconically.

I went into the kitchen for the basket of sandwiches Sissy had packed for the trip. It would take upwards of three hours to drive to town and I didn't want to waste time in any roadside diner pleading with Charles to finish his french fries or eat them in the car.

"What kind did you make?" I asked Sissy.

"Tuna fish."

"Oh dear, Charles hates tuna fish."

I thought I saw the hint of a smile on her face at that.

"Things better between you two?" I asked.

"No, things are not better between us two. Unless you call gettin' presents better."

She took something out of her apron pocket and handed it to me. It was a small doll, crudely made of black cloth, tied with string to make a neck and waist. Protruding from the chest was a pin. It was a voodoo doll.

"I found it in my bureau this morning," she said.

"Jesus Christ."

"*He* ain't gonna do nothin' about it. It ain't *His* job."

"I'll talk to Charles."

"Sure, honey, you do that."

"Sissy, I've forbidden him to annoy you a thousand times. Couldn't you try to . . ."

"I'm all tried out, Katie."

"All right, I'll talk to him. And I'll have Molly talk to him, okay?"

"Whatever you say," and she sulked back to her sink.

I put Charles's latest handicraft into the basket and carried it into the hall in time to see our resident witch doctor descend the stairs at a snail's pace.

"You'll freeze to a stair if you don't walk faster."

"I'm coming."

"Oh, Charles, look at your socks."

"What about them?" he asked, without so much as a glance downward.

"One is white and one is blue, that's what about them. Go change."

He turned sluggishly and then tossed over his

shoulder "Sissy rolled them up together. She's so dumb..."

"Don't start, young man. And change your pants. Those are too short. They're above your ankles."

"So damn dumb..."

"Move!"

He threw me a snide salute and wafted back to his room.

"I didn't roll no white sock with no blue one." And the kitchen door slammed shut.

At that moment I gave a silent prayer that on arriving at the hospital we would find a completely recovered Molly waiting for us with a very usable right uppercut. I put the basket in the car, waited there for what seemed a minor eternity and finally stormed back into the house.

"Charles, will you move your bloody ass!"

He appeared at the top of the stairs smiling smugly and came down, two steps at a time.

"Fast enough for you?"

"Fine, but you didn't change your pants. I can still see your socks."

"I did, too!"

"All right, all right, let's just go. Next week we'll get you some new pants."

We would indeed.

We had been on the road for over an hour when Charles reached into the basket between us for a sandwich and came out with the doll.

"What's that?" he asked, pure innocence.

"What does it look like?"

"A black penis."

My foot involuntarily moved to the brake.

"My God, Charles, what kind of thing is that for a ten-year-old to say!"

And then, unable to control myself, I started to laugh. He was right. It did look like a black penis. He started to laugh, too.

"Don't you dare laugh, you weirdo," I said.

"You're laughing."

"I'm entitled."

He tossed the doll aside and reached for a sandwich.

"No, really, Charles, what does it look like?"

"I dunno."

"Think."

"How would *I* know? Just something dumb that Sissy put in the basket. She's always doing dumb things. Oh God! Tuna fish! She knows I hate tuna fish! Goddamn her!"

I'll spare you the rest of our ride except to say that it was spent in complete silence, once I had said a few choice words to my nephew.

MOLLY

They got to the hospital about an hour after I expected them, so I was already in a sweat. I wasn't exactly blasé about their driving at that point. But finally in they walked, Kate looking terrific and tanned, Charles looking like he was in for root canal work.

"Hey, kid, how about a kiss for what's left of your mother?"

He leaned over and planted something on my cheek that felt like a hummingbird had flicked a turd at me. Par for the course; like I said, *Happy Days* we ain't. So we all sat down for a nice chat; at least they sat down, I was still flat out. We did the usual bull about how I was feeling, how the old homestead was holding up, how everybody was getting along out there in nowheresville, but all the time I had the distinct feeling that Charles was avoiding looking directly at me. Like he was hiding something. And let me tell you, when it comes to his hiding something, I'm Sherlock Holmes and Ralph Nader rolled into one. He gets this funny dead expression on his face like he doesn't want to think if I'm in the room. Like I could overhear his thoughts. Which is not so far from the truth.

"What's with you?" I finally asked him, breaking Kate off in midstream.

"Nothing."

"Never mind 'nothing'. What's up?"

"I told you, nothing." And like a shot, he's at the window, suddenly fascinated with the view of the brick wall across the hospital courtyard.

"We've been a little edgy lately," Kate answered for him.

"Is that the royal *we?*"

"It ought to be, I've earned it. Charles," she called to him matter-of-factly, "would you do your old aunt a favor and go down to the newsstand and get me a pack of cigarettes?"

"Okay."

After he left, Kate got down to business.

"Listen, I think you ought to have a talk with

49

Charles. There's something wrong, but I can't seem to get him to discuss it."

"Yeah? What's going on?"

She filled me in on his hate on for Sissy, his continuing smart-ass attacks, the whole bit. Frankly, I didn't exactly get hysterical. Drama is my sister's middle name, so I tried to add a little calm to the proceedings.

"Listen, what he needs is not to hang around that house all the time. Is there any kind of day camp up there we could put him in?"

"I think the Boy Scouts has one in Water's Edge."

"That's our best bet, then. Also, it wouldn't hurt if once in awhile when he's acting up, you'd give him a smack on the ass instead of enjoying it so much."

"Enjoying it? I don't . . ."

"Come on, Kate, you know you love it when he opens that little sewer mouth. You get a big kick out of it."

"Not lately, I don't. And while we're tossing blame around, maybe if his mother didn't talk like a sailor, he wouldn't."

"Don't yell at me. I'm an invalid."

"Well, don't yell at me. I'm a widow."

Then we laughed, God help us. When Charles returned with the unwanted cigarettes, Kate took off for the apartment, another unnecessary trip, but it gave Charles and me a chance for an overdue mother-son chat.

"So what's this I hear about your giving everybody a hard time?" I asked his back, since he was at the window again.

"I didn't do anything."

"That's not what I hear. What's with you and Sissy?"

"I hate her guts," he said, studying the radiator.

"What are you talking about? You're crazy about Sissy."

"*You're* crazy."

Terrific. Just what I needed. A little lip.

"Watch it, I can still manage a smack with my good arm. Come here and sit down."

"Don't wanna."

"I didn't ask if you *wanna.* Come here."

"You come here."

I was about to hit the roof, but there was something small and lost about him standing there playing with the radiator valve.

"Hey, I love you," I said. "But I can't help you if you won't let me in on it."

"I don't need any help."

There are times you watch your own kid go down the drain. It isn't pleasant, and the more you try, the faster they seem to slip. This was one of those times.

"Please, honey, I don't want you to be unhappy. I know it's rough on you with me here, but I'll be out in a few weeks and we'll be together again. Till then, can't you hang on? I know Aunt Kate doesn't know too much about taking care of a kid but . . ."

He turned around and I swear when I saw the look on his face I nearly gasped. It was filled with rage.

"Don't you say anything against Kate!"

"*What?*"

"If you were half as nice as she is . . ." he turned back to the fucking radiator without finishing.

"Charles, I wasn't attacking Kate . . ."

"See that you don't," he said and each word was a bullet.

Bob Randall

"What the hell," I stammered and then the anger hit. "Get over here, young man, and sit down!"

He froze by the window.

"I said, get over here!"

Not a word, not a move out of him.

"Charles!"

He obeyed. Slowly. For a moment neither of us spoke. He just sat there, beside the bed, looking at the floor with me staring at him.

"What the hell is with you?" I started. "I'm in this damn hospital with half my bones broken, Kate just buried her husband and you're hassling us! What's with you? What do you need, a shrink? For crying out loud, Charles, have a heart. I know this summer is shit on a stick, but you're making it worse! I'm telling you, you lay off Sissy and stop acting like a spoiled brat or when I get out of here, you're going to be sorry."

"I hope you never get out of here," he half said, half whispered.

"What?"

"I'd rather be with Kate than with you any day!"

That did it.

"You little bastard! You want to be with Kate so much? Then get downstairs and wait for her in the lobby. She ought to be back in a couple of hours!"

With that he ran out the door. Oh, Christ. I lay there, staring at the ceiling, trying to figure out what the hell had just happened and then the dam burst. I'm not a crier, but I could've won a trophy for tears shed in that next half hour. My own son hated me. And he was right to. I was a lousy mother. When he was little and needed me the most, I was too broken up to give him anything. You don't make a kid secure and happy by just giving him a roof over his head and

52

three meals a day. He needed more than that and, God forgive me, I didn't have it to give. Look, I don't believe in crying over spilled milk, but I'll go to my grave with this on my conscience. I let my own kid starve deep down.

KATE

I got back to the hospital a little after four to find Charles sitting forlornly in the downstairs waiting room.

"Honey, what are you doing here? I thought you'd be upstairs with mother."

"They said she had to sleep."

"How long have you been down here?"

"An hour."

"Oh, Christ. Why didn't you buy a magazine or something?"

"I didn't have any money."

"Why didn't you ask mother for some?"

"She had to sleep."

I put my arm around my brave little soldier and decided he was due something special, a treat to make up for sitting alone in a strange place without complaining. There was a country inn on the way back to the house; one of those grandiose colonial affairs with costumed waiters and hyped prices. Just the thing for a small boy with pretentions to adulthood. Charles leaped at it.

"And I can have anything I want?" he asked when we were in the car on our way.

"Anything you want."

"Oysters?"

"Not in July, dear."

"Can I have a drink?" he smirked.

"What'd you have in mind?"

"How about a martini straight up?"

"How about a Shirley Temple on the rocks?"

"God," he moaned.

We got to the restaurant shortly before eight with Charles roaring the last few miles about how hungry he was. The room was lovely, lit entirely by candlelight, romantic and charming. We were shown to a corner table by a waiter who bore a striking resemblance to Paul Revere and we settled down to study the voluminous menus.

"You look beautiful," Charles said to me across the candlelight.

"Thank you. You look pretty beautiful yourself."

And he did. His blue eyes were glowing with excitement and in the dim light he seemed, well, if not exactly grown up, on the way.

"Can I order for us?" he asked. "Please, Kate?"

Definitely on the way. "All right."

"How much can I spend?"

"How much have you got?" He looked embarrassed. "Just kidding, darling. I've got a charge card, so the sky's the limit."

As he studied the menu, his entire demeanor changed. He was so serious, so earnest, I had to turn away several times lest he see me laugh. When the waiter arrived, Charles dealt with him with amazing dispatch. We were to have roast duckling, a favorite of mine, asparagus vinaigrette, another favorite, and strawberry shortcake, my downfall. I smiled over at Charles, somewhat awed by his knowledge of my preferences, and he tried valiantly not to look pleased but failed.

"Will the lady have a drink?" the waiter asked me directly, no doubt offended at having to deal with a child.

"Yes," Charles said, also offended. "The lady will have scotch and water. The gentleman will have a Coke."

The waiter, thus dismissed, sauntered off, probably to commiserate with the chef about *city kids.*

"That was wonderful, Charles. You ordered everything I love."

"I know."

Again, his unwilling pleasure shone through. Who was it, I wondered briefly, that he reminded me of? Someone who thought it a slight to his manhood to openly express his boyish glee? Then I remembered. Of course, it was Alan.

Our meal was singularly quiet. Perhaps it was the drowsying effect of the candlelight, perhaps Charles's desire to appear adult, but we hardly spoke. We smiled across the table at each other, occasionally commenting on the excellence of the food, the quaintness of the restaurant, small talk. I was so pleased to have brought him there. He seemed, after a trying day, to be really enjoying himself. I regretted having to get down to business.

"How was your visit with mother?"

"Fine."

"Did you two talk about anything in particular?"

"If you mean about me, yes. I promised her I'd stay in line." He reached across the table and stroked my hand. "And I promise you, too, Kate."

I must say I was a bit floored. And embarrassed. There was something so oddly reasonable about him, which, as you well know, was not a word one used to describe Charles very often.

"Thank you, dear," I said.

"You're welcome, *darling*," he replied.

I stared at him for a moment, wondering exactly what was going on. Was he being his usual smart-ass self or had the romance of the atmosphere made him silly? I decided on the former.

"*Aunt* darling," I said, and he laughed.

When the waiter brought the check, he took his turn in the smart ass follies by pointedly handing it to Charles, thereby embarrassing him.

"I'll have that," I said icily. There was no need to humiliate the child.

After paying for our meal and a *ten* percent tip for his condescension, we left and continued the drive homeward. We reached the house after ten and a sleepy Charles gave no flack in going to bed promptly. All in all, he had been a dream the whole evening. There was hope for him, praised be Allah.

And then Molly called.

"It was horrible . . . horrible," she said.

"Molly, I just don't understand it. He didn't say a word to me. He told me everything went fine."

"Compared to *what*? The Third World War? Jesus, Kate, I don't know what to do. Do you think he needs a shrink?"

I personally thought we all needed shrinks. "It's not such a terrible thing if he does. It's a difficult summer for him . . ."

"Summer, my ass. He's always been off the wall."

"Well, then, maybe a psychiatrist is a good idea. Jackie's girl went for two years and it did wonders for her. You remember how shy and inhibited she used to be?"

"God, what I wouldn't give for Charles to be shy and inhibited," she said, and I felt much the same reaction to her as I had to the waiter when he brought the check.

"That's not fair, Molly, and you know it."

"Go ahead, defend him."

"Well, somebody has to. He's just a child and when his own mother turns on him . . ."

"Listen, will you get off the soapbox? I already got a problem kid, I don't need a problem sister."

I suddenly felt quite angry with Molly. Yes, I would certainly defend Charles against her if need be. He needed someone in his corner, after all.

"Look, we'll talk tomorrow," I said, knowing that an argument was moments away. "Right now I'm too tired from the trip back."

"Swell."

"I'm sorry, Molly, but I don't want to go into it right now."

"There's nothing to go into. He's my kid and I'll do what I please with him."

"Yes, that's what we're all afraid of," I said and hung up.

Five agitated minutes later I called Molly back, we made a temporary truce and I went quickly to bed.

It was sometime later, in the middle of the night, that Charles came into my room and woke me.

"What is it?" I said, still half asleep.

"My stomach feels funny."

"Oh no, you ate too much. Are you nauseated?"

"A little."

"You want bicarb?"

57

"No, it doesn't feel that bad. I just don't want to be alone, okay?"

"Okay, crawl in."

I lifted the covers and he climbed into bed next to me. His body warmth felt good on my side, familiar and comforting.

And then Alan stormed into the room.

"All right, what the hell is going on here?" he demanded.

"What?" I asked, drowsily.

"Who's that in bed with you?"

"It's Charles, who did you think it was?"

"Oh, the brat."

"Don't call him that, Alan. He's not a brat."

"Oh, please . . ."

"I mean it, Alan. I don't like when you attack him. He's a lonely child. He needs some loving, not the constant picking on he gets from you and Molly and Sissy. Why don't you all have a little compassion for a fatherless ten-year-old whose mother never had any use for him . . ."

"Get him the hell out of the bed. I don't like him sleeping with you. It's not healthy."

"Oh, for crying out loud . . ."

"Out!"

"Don't you dare touch him! What on earth is wrong with his sleeping here? He doesn't feel well. He just needs a little comforting. We *all* need a little comforting now and then, Alan, including me. I don't see you doing much comforting lately . . ."

"Jesus, Kate, what do you want me to do? Claw my way out of the grave just so you won't have to feel lonely?"

"Yes, that's what I want you to do! That's exactly what I want you to do!"

"Brother . . ."

"And since you won't or you can't, then go back to your damn inescapable grave and let me find comfort where I can!"

With that, he did and I fell fully asleep.

Several days later, Charles's eating started. By that I mean my dear little companion became the household locust, devouring everything in sight. It took a few days for me to realize what was happening, but late one afternoon I found him in the kitchen, half hidden behind a sandwich that would make Dagwood Bumstead blanch.

"Good Lord, Charles, what are you going to do with that thing? Move into it?"

"Eat it," he said, and stuffed one corner of the thing in his mouth.

"We're having dinner in an hour," I argued.

"I'll be ready."

"Come on, Charles, you're going to ruin your appetite."

"No I won't."

I hesitated for a moment, recalling an article I'd read in the Sunday *Times* that proposed children were the best judges of what they should eat, and gave in.

"All right, it's your stomach."

It was indeed and scarcely an hour later, it was empty again. He sat across the dinner table from me, eating like a whirlwind.

"Slow down, dear," I said. "Nobody's taking the food away."

"Uh-huh," and he shoveled another small mountain of mashed potatoes into the bottomless pit.

"Somebody's sure enjoyin' their dinner tonight,"

Sissy said, standing next to him, smiling, hoping for a moment of peace between them.

He looked up at her hostilely. "It's all right, I guess."

"Wait'll you see what I made you for dessert, honey," she tried again. "Rice puddin'. You like that?"

"Yeah, yeah," he begrudged.

"And I got some heavy cream. You want me to make you some whipped cream for on top, sweetie?"

"Just leave me alone, will you?" he growled, sending her out of the room.

I pushed my plate away from me. "That was so damned gratuitous, Charles," I said angrily.

"What's that mean?"

"It means unfair, uncalled for and unkind. You promised me you'd stop being mean to Sissy."

"Sue me," and he shoved a dinner roll into his mouth.

"That did it! Out!"

"What?" he asked, mouth full.

"Get out of the room. Out of the house. Go take a walk until you can behave decently."

"Kate . . ."

"Don't *Kate* me! I can't eat across the table from an ill-mannered, ill-tempered lout. Now move it!"

"But I'm not finished eating . . ."

"You are now. I'm not going to allow you to sit there enjoying Sissy's work when you're so rotten to her, so you can just move it!"

He went ashen. "But I've got to eat, Kate!"

"You've had enough, Charles. I'm not backing down. I want you to leave the table."

"But I've got to eat! *Now!*" And his voice was near panic.

"What on earth is the matter with you?"

THE NEXT

"You don't understand! *I've got to eat!*"

"Charles . . ."

"I'll apologize to her!" he said, holding the sides of his plate so that his knuckles went white.

"Charles, calm down," I said, suddenly frightened.

"I've got to eat!"

"Stop it!"

"You don't understand," he said, and I realized he was near tears.

"No, I don't."

"Please let me finish dinner! Then I'll apologize to Sissy. I'll never be mean to her again, I swear, if you'll just let me finish dinner!"

I felt cold and frightened, totally unable to deal with it.

"All right, then *I'll* leave the table," I said, getting up. He didn't reply but continued eating as fast as he could. I went into the kitchen, actually shaking, and closed the door behind me. It was as if something ugly was happening in the dining room I wanted to block out; but what on earth was it?

"What's the matter with that one?" Sissy asked, eating her own dinner.

"I don't know."

She must have seen how upset I was. "Listen, child," she said, "don't distress yourself so. He's just goin' through a phase. You went through plenty yourself, I remember. You recall the time I had gettin' you to eat meat the year you decided killin' animals was a sin?"

"No, this is different, Sissy. I just don't understand him. Sometimes he's so dear and then, suddenly, without warning . . . it's as if he has attacks of some kind."

"Maybe you oughta take him to Doc Shiff in town. He always knew how to take care of you and Molly."

"Maybe I should," I answered, and I heard the kitchen door open behind me. I turned and saw Charles standing there smiling.

"Sissy," he said, walking over to her and putting his hand on her shoulder, "I'm really sorry for what I said. It was rude and disrespectful."

Rude and *disrespectful?*

"I'm really going to try to see things from your point of view from now on and not be so headstrong."

Headstrong?

"That's okay, honey," Sissy beamed up at him, totally taken in.

"And now," he continued in a voice as smooth and unctuous as any I'd ever heard, "if I'm not disturbing you, I'm ready for dessert. May I help whip the cream?"

"Sure, darlin'." Sissy answered in seventh heaven.

I was so horrified by the scene before me I said nothing and left the room. As I passed through the dining room, I glanced at the table. Charles's plate was empty.

As was mine.

A few days later Charles and I were shopping in town when we passed the children's clothing store. I glanced down at his ankle-length pants.

"Let's get you some new pants, Stretch," I said.

"Okay, honey."

"And don't *honey* me."

We mutually agreed on two pair of jeans, or rather *I* agreed on them since Charles had his heart set on what he termed "grown-up clothes." As the clerk put them in a bag, he smiled at Charles.

"And how old are you, fella?"

"Ten."

"Really? You're big for ten, you know?"

"Yes, I know," Charles smiled proudly.

"At that age they grow like weeds," he said to me.

"And eat like horses," I added.

We were driving home when I realized why the food bills around our house were rivaling those for the New York Jets.

"You're in a growth period, kiddo," I said.

He beamed at me. "You bet, honey."

"Well, slow down. Those pants were twelve bucks each."

"Mom'll reimburse you."

I smiled at my little man. "My treat."

"Okay, then she'll reimburse you for my new sneakers."

"What new sneakers?"

"The ones I need. These are tight."

"Oh, Lord," I said, and turned the car around.

Beyond our pond is an acre of woods that backs on to the township's picnic area and lake. A small path cuts directly through it. As children I recall Molly and I lumbering along that path, laden down with jugs of overly sweetened lemonade and inevitably burned chocolate chip cookies to sell to the picnickers. Those who purchased our wares were entitled to an added benefit; a guided tour through the woods and a viewing of our house and pond, the latter of which had its own flotilla of makeshift cardboard galleons. Needless to say, mother was not overly thrilled with our enterprise. I remember her wading out in the pond, collecting our boats, putting them under her arm like some gigantic God cleaning up the Spanish armada. Some gigantic thoughtless God, for Molly and I stood on the lawn pleading with her to leave them alone. I swear that woman had a sixth sense about her; whenever we were having fun, her antennae would twitch and she'd sail in to ruin our good times, few though they were. But enough of sweet childhood reveries, back to my point. Beside the lake was a gazebo, a charming keepsake of another, as they say, more gracious time. Driving home after buying Charles an outrageously expensive and gaudy pair of sneakers, he asked if we might have dinner there.

"What do you mean, have a picnic in the gazebo?" I asked.

"Sure! It'll be neat!"

"Oh, Charles, that means we have to drag everything through the woods and the path is full of poison ivy and besides . . ."

"Please, Kate! I'll do everything! You just go there at seven o'clock and wait for me. I'll make dinner and pack it and . . ."

"You're aware that I don't care for peanut butter and jelly sandwiches?" I said, giving in.

"Listen, I didn't do so bad at the restaurant last week, did I?"

"Okay, kiddo. You've got yourself a date."

He was delighted. "And let's dress for dinner," he said.

"Dress? As in *up*?"

"Right. Wear your green dress and your white shoes and do something with your hair."

"*Do something with my hair?* Charlie, you sound like somebody's uncle instead of my nephew."

"Promise?"

"Okay, okay."

"And you'll fix up your hair?"

"And precisely what is wrong with my hair?" I asked, amused and insulted. "I've been told I have very nice hair."

"It sort of lays there."

"Well, what would you have it do? Spin around my head?"

He laughed. "Promise?"

"I promise, I promise, now stop talking about my hair before I develop a complex, you insensitive little creep."

After a moment's silence, he said, "Wear it up."

"Shut it up," I answered.

Three hours later, I sat at my dressing table, the dutiful aunt, pulling my once crowning glory and now total embarrassment into shape. I did as I was told and wore it up. I then put on my green dress as directed and white shoes. It was inexplicable to me that I was following the orders of a ten-year-old boy who had to be cajolled into washing his hands more than once a week, but I was enjoying it. It felt safe somehow to be directed, as Alan used to do. Safe and warm and familiar. I went to Charles's room, the door of which was closed. I knocked.

"Hey, kid, your date's here," I called out.

"Don't come in!"

"Okay, okay, I'll wait downstairs."

"No, you're supposed to wait for me in the gazebo!"

"Oh, for crying out loud, Charlie, let's at least go together."

"No way! Go! Go!"

"Yes, *mein führer*," I said, and went downstairs

to the kitchen where Sissy was doing battle with that week's tarnish on the silver.

"What'd you make us?" I asked.

"Nothin'. He wouldn't let me. Kicked me right outa my own kitchen, he did."

"What did he make?"

"Dunno. He made me promise not to peek and when he let me back in, everything was cleaned up and put away."

"Where's the basket?" I asked, having made no such promise.

"Upstairs in his room. He's guardin' it."

"Oh, well, good-bye pot roast, hello peanut butter and jelly," I said, leaving.

As I walked past the pond with the sun glowing red over the tops of the trees I felt a singular excitement, and then, realizing what it was, I laughed at how silly I was being. It was the excitement of a date, of something real and special to do, of being *expected*. And by whom? My own nephew. Ridiculous, but then, lonely pre-middle-aged women are frequently given to ridiculous emotions, I decided, and thought no more about it.

The woods were damp and cool. I'd forgotten how lovely the air in the woods felt on one's skin; Lord, how long had it been since I'd walked down that path? I was right about the poison ivy, it was everywhere. A beautiful double-trunked dogwood caught my eye and I went to it and found the faint traces of Molly's and my initials, put there centuries ago. Something moved in the undergrowth and I hurried back to the path. Snake? Squirrel? It made no difference, I had never developed much of a love for any animal, even if Sissy could remember my humane vegetarian year. I wondered about that.

I came out the other side of the woods and looked out over the lake, which was lovely. On the far side, a young couple were packing the remnants of their picnic, scraping the leftovers into a bowl from which an animated German shepherd was eating. He immediately reminded me of Charles, though his table manners were of course better. At least he wagged his tail. As the young man folded their blanket, his companion leaned over and kissed him. It wasn't a particularly passionate kiss but it nevertheless had the effect of depressing me slightly. And so I called on Alan to cheer me.

He was waiting in the gazebo when I got there.

"Hello, darling," he said.

"Hello, yourself."

He kissed me as the young woman had kissed her lover and we sat together on the railing of the gazebo and watched the couple walk arm in arm to their car and drive away.

"Why so dressed up?" Alan asked.

"Charles asked me to."

"You still giving in to him, Kate? Don't you think it would be better if you called the shots? After all, he's spoiled enough."

"Don't start," I said, and moved a few inches from him.

"Okay, okay, let's not get into a hassle about it," and he put his arm around me. "Give us a kiss."

I obeyed but clearly didn't enjoy it. I started to resent the demonstrative pair that had forced me to call Alan, for before their kiss my mood was gay and now the hint of an argument loomed. Why was it, I wondered, that I invented arguments between Alan and myself?

"What are you thinking about?" he asked, drawing me back into my fantasy.

"Nothing," I lied.

"Hey, Katie, I've got an idea. Let's go back to the house, sneak upstairs, smoke a joint and do the beast with two backs. What'd you say, sexy?"

"Not now, Alan. I'm having a picnic with Charles."

"Oh, for crying out loud, the brat again."

"Don't call him that," and I moved to the other side of the gazebo, briefly glancing over at the path to see if Charles was on his way.

"You'd rather eat with that kid than screw with me?" he said in that tone of voice of his that announced we were indeed to have an argument.

"They're not mutually exclusive, Alan. It's just that I promised him and he's already made dinner and . . ."

"Screw him and his dinner." And he started to sulk.

I came out of the fantasy for a moment, preferring the beauty of the setting to my own tedious script, but then, feeling disloyal to Alan, I slipped back into it.

"I'm sorry," I said.

"Sure, sure."

"Later. I'll meet you back at the house later."

"The hell with later. I've got a date with some worms later."

"Don't talk that way, Alan, please."

"Well, what do you think being dead is all about? Or maybe you haven't thought about it . . ."

"Of course I have . . ."

"No, you haven't. You've been too busy with your

goddamn nephew to give a thought to me. Hell, I might as well stay in the fucking grave."

I didn't answer.

"Is that what you want?" he asked.

I still didn't answer. He came to me and held my face in his hands, suddenly becoming tender.

"You want me really dead, Katie?"

"No, of course not . . ."

"You want me gone forever?"

"No . . ."

"Then get rid of the kid. Send him to a camp somewhere. Hell, send him back to his mother. It's her job to take care of him, not yours. Get rid of him, baby, so we can be together again."

"I can't."

"You won't," and the hard edge returned to his voice.

"I can't!"

"You're full of shit . . ."

"Alan . . ."

"No, don't give me that *I can't* crap. You dig the little bastard. You like sitting around waiting for the little shit, doing what he tells you, letting him rule the house like a fucking tyrant. You know what he needs, Kate? You know what he really needs? A swift kick in the ass, that's what he needs."

"That's what Molly said," and my anger with them both returned.

"Well, she's right and, goddamn it, I'm going to stay right here and give it to him."

"Leave him alone, Alan."

"The hell I'll leave him alone. When I'm through with him he'll do cartwheels to stay in line . . ."

"Go away, Alan. I want you to go away now."

He looked at me with genuine surprise. "You mean that?"

"Yes."

"You want me to leave?"

"Yes."

"You really are choosing him over me, aren't you?"

"It isn't a competition, Alan . . ."

"The hell it isn't!"

"All right, then, damn you! I choose Charles! I choose the living over the dead. I choose solace with a loving child over endless arguments with you. I was wrong to bring you back. You're dead. You're a hundred miles from me at this moment and you can't talk to me or hold me or tell me what to do! You're dead!"

And with that, Alan disappeared.

I left the gazebo and walked to the edge of the lake. There was a bullfrog half submerged a few feet from me. His enormous eyes blinked several times at me and he swam away, frightened. It amused me. A bird, possibly a mallard, passed by high overhead and I marveled at its effortless flight. It occurred to me that I, too, was in flight; from pain to pleasure, from loss to gain, from aloneness to companionship. I don't think it truly matters whom one loves as long as one loves. The loving of a friend, even a child, is enough. I blessed Charles at that moment.

"Hey! Kate!"

I turned to see my little savior coming out of the woods, staggering under a load of bundles.

"My God, what did you bring?" I called as I hurried to help him.

"Everything," he answered, refusing my assistance.

He entered the gazebo and started to unpack as

I leaned against the railing, smiling, happy, full. He was wearing a blue blazer, his new jeans and sneakers and the shirt of Alan's that I had given him. His hair was still damp from what must have been endless combing; all the cowlicks were neatly pasted down. He looked magnificent.

"You're one hell of a handsome guy," I said, and he smiled up at me. "My Lord, you really did bring everything, didn't you?"

Everything included two couch pillows, blanket, transistor radio and the large picnic hamper.

"You ain't seen nothing yet," he said, and opened the hamper to withdraw candles, two of father's best china plates, two complete services of sterling and last, but not least, one perfect rose in a bud vase. I laughed.

"Happy?" he asked.

"Blissful."

He came to me and hugged me and the joy welled up again. Then he turned on his radio, found a station with blessedly geriatric music and asked me to dance.

"Why, sir, I do believe I have this dance free and I can't think of any gentleman here I'd rather share it with than you."

We danced. He led me round the gazebo with surprising aplomb. He even dipped me.

"My God, where did you learn that?" I asked.

"On TV."

He dipped me again, showing off, but this time my balance was off and I landed as gracefully as I could flat on my backside.

"Well, there goes our chance for the Harvest Moon Ball," I laughed.

He helped me to my feet and we glided round

the gazebo again. It was charming; totally and gloriously charming, if a little tiring.

"Whoa, Mr. Astaire, I think I need a drink. Did you bring any libation in your steamer trunk?"

"What's that?"

"Something to drink."

"Oh. Sure!" And he opened the hamper, careful to turn it so that the lid would hide its contents from me, and withdrew two Waterford goblets and a bottle of extraordinarily cheap wine.

"Where did you get that?"

"In town. I went back."

"Oh, Charles, that's so sweet."

"No, it isn't. I asked the man for dry."

I laughed again, almost giddy. "I meant the sentiment, not the wine. Hey, how do you know wine is sweet or dry?"

"I know lots of things," he said, undoing the twist cap.

"Do you also know I'm not going to permit you to drink it?"

"I sort of figured that," and he withdrew a can of Pepsi from the secret hamper. "Wine for the lady, Pepsi for the gentleman."

He poured for us both, handed me a goblet and held his up.

"A toast," he said.

"By all means. What shall we toast to?"

"To us, of course."

"Very well," and we clinked glasses. "To Aunt Kate and her darling nephew."

"To Kate and Charles," he corrected me, offended.

"That's what I said."

"No, it isn't." He sipped his drink and then looked up at me as if he had something important to say.

"Kate . . ." he hesitated.

"Yes?"

"You've got to stop thinking of me as your nephew," he said in dead earnest.

"What?"

"I want you to think of me as just another man, not only Molly's son."

I almost laughed but he was so serious I couldn't. What exactly was happening? Was my ten-year-old nephew actually about to romance me?

In a moment I had my answer. He leaned across the hamper and kissed my lips. As his face left mine, I sat there speechless. Good God, how do I handle this?

"Say something," he said after a silence, staring into his soda.

I didn't know what to say. I knew children did develop crushes on adults, but when confronted with it, it seemed so bizarre, so ridiculous.

"This is silly," I blurted out, making a joke of it. Another silence.

"I won't always be a kid, you know."

"Talk to me in ten years," I said, still trying to make light of it and then, thinking better of what I had said, I added "No, don't talk to me in ten years."

His entire body seemed to cave in at that; he sat there, forlorn, crushed, as alone as I had been in my worst moments.

"Oh, honey," I said, trying to repair the damage, "I love you . . . I do love you, but this is silly. You see that, don't you?"

He nodded no gravely.

"I'm your aunt and I'm forty-one years old and

you're all mixed up because of all we've been through these past weeks . . ."

"I'm going to marry you someday," he said soberly, without looking up.

Well, that did it. I laughed. It seemed so dear and young and harmless that I realized I was taking this much too seriously. It fell into the same category as wanting to be a fireman when one grew up. It was suddenly amusing to me.

But not to Charles.

He looked at me with a mixture of anger and hurt and ran from the gazebo.

"Charles!" I called after him. "Charles!"

He ran toward the woods.

"Charles, please come back!"

And he disappeared into them.

I sat there on the pillow he had brought me, cursing my insensitivity and stupidity. A lonely child had offered me his most prized possession, his love, and I had laughed at him. I'd make it up to him, though. I'd give him a while to calm down and then I'd make it up to him. I opened the hamper to see what he had brought and was made twice as miserable. No, there were no peanut butter and jelly sandwiches. Far from it. He had roasted game hens. I felt simply awful.

I don't know how long I sat there staring out over the lake. I must have had two or three glasses of wine, for I felt slightly high and more than slightly weepy. I had been a cow in Charles's emotional china shop. Even the metaphor didn't help.

And then I felt his hand on my shoulder.

"Oh, Charles, I'm so glad you came back."

He smiled down at me calmly.

"There's no sense in arguing. When I'm bigger we'll discuss it again."

"Very well," I answered innocently, but the pact was made.

MOLLY

Remember me? While all this tender loving crap was going on, I was flat on my back as usual, counting the leaves in the friggin' tree in the friggin' print on the friggin' wall of the friggin' hospital room, going not so quietly out of my mind. Jesus, you'd think they'd give you something to do instead of letting you lie there listening to your fractures heal. Anyway, one thing did happen. I got a really snot-nosed letter from Charlie's school saying they were sorry I had decided to take him out of there and they wished I had given them more than a month's notice so that they could have filled his place. Well, given the fact that I had not taken Charlie out of the school, I was more than a little upset so I got one of the nurses to dial the school for me. After waiting around on the phone for a year and a half, they finally connected me with the principal. From the sound of her voice, I could just picture this beauty. She probably still wore a bun. Anyway, I told her that I had no intention of taking Charlie out of the school, she told me she had a letter from me saying so, I told her politely as I could that she was full of shit, she intimated that if I was changing my mind I should come out and say so, I told her not so politely that I never wrote the damn letter, moreover my writing hand was buried in a ton of plaster. A convivial conversation it wasn't. But we got it straightened out; Charlie would remain in the school at so much inconvenience to her it made the Thirty Years' War seem like a station break. When I finally hung up, I was steaming. Who the hell had written the letter? It took about a quarter of a second to figure that one out. I had nursey dial the house.

"Sissy? It's Molly. Put Charles on, will you?"

"Molly, honey," she started, "how are you feelin'?"

"To tell you the truth, a little tired," I answered, wanting to get on with it, "Is Charles around?"

"Just a second, honey, and I hope you'll be real well soon. You know, we can't wait to have you here. Your old room is . . ."

"Swell," I cut her off, "but I gotta get off the phone quick. It's time for my bath."

"I'll go get him," she answered, and put the phone down.

I waited. And waited. When I got up to seventy-two leaves on the tree, he finally picked up.

"Hi, mom," he said matter-of-factly.

"Hi, yourself. Listen, I just talked with your school."

"Yeah?"

"Yeah. You know what they told me?"

"Nope."

"They told me they got a letter saying you wouldn't be going back there next year."

"Yeah?" he said, bored.

"Yeah. Only I never wrote them a letter."

"No?"

"No."

"Oh."

"You got any idea who did?"

After a brief pause he answered, interested as ever, "Nope."

"It couldn't be you, could it?"

"Nope."

"You sure?"

"Yup."

"You positive?"

"Yup. Anything else?"

Terrific. First he takes forever to get on the phone, then he's too bored to stay on. What a kid.

"I just wonder who the hell is playing tricks, writing the school that you won't be back. I'd just love to know, that's all."

"Yeah, well, it's sure a mystery," and he lays a fat yawn on me.

"You being a smart ass?" I asked, losing patience with him.

"Nope."

Nope, his ass. Well, I figured I'm never going to get him to admit it over the phone and this call is starting to give me a swift pain so I decided to either change the subject or hang up.

"You wanna ask me how I'm feeling?" I opted for the first choice.

"Yeah," he says with the same cliff-hanging interest.

"Like shit."

"Oh."

That was it. So much for your filial devotion.

"But I'm healing fast. I'll be up there in a few weeks to look after you," I warned him. "I'm going to do a lot of looking after you when I get there, you can bet on that."

"Uh-huh," he answered. "Look, I gotta go, okay?"

"Yeah, you go," I said. "You go and I'll get well on the double and be there before you know it. I'm practically there now."

"Good," he said, and hung up on me.

The little bastard.

KATE

Several days later, Charles's cold appeared. There were no apparent symptoms other than the effect on his voice; it was suddenly husky and hoarse.

"What's with your voice?" I asked him when he came into breakfast.

"Dunno. I got a little cold, I guess."

"How's your throat feel? Sore?" I asked.

"Nope."

I leaned across the table and felt his cheek. Cool.

"Don't fuss over me, Kate. I'm not a child."

"Well, pardon me. I thought the age of consent was still twenty-one."

"I've got a cold, that's all. Let's not make a big deal over it, huh?"

"Fine with me, foghorn."

Sissy entered with his breakfast and hearing his raspy voice tried to talk him into tea and honey. In Charles's defense, I must say he did try to be reasonable for several minutes before the onslaught of her maternalism, but patience was of course not his forte and he soon was off and running.

"Will you two get off my back!" he shouted in that bullfrog baritone. "I don't want your damn tea and honey, I don't want your damn concern and I don't want your damn interference in my life!"

With that, his voice cracked and he ran out of the room. Sissy and I, long since used to his temperamental outbursts, merely cocked eyebrows at each other.

"He's been good for two days," I said. "I knew it couldn't last much longer."

"Business as usual," Sissy said, returning his breakfast to the kitchen.

I sat there lingering over coffee considering various ways of committing the perfect murder; of Charles, naturally. The best I could come up with was to tie him to a chair and play his taped tantrums back to him full blast.

Three days later, the cold was still there, his voice still thick and heavy. I was sitting beside the pond reading when he came out of the house in his bathing suit.

"And what do you think you're doing?" I asked.

"I'm going in for a swim," he croaked.

"Want to bet?"

"Why?"

"Charles, you've still got a cold. Now go inside and put some clothes on."

"Come on, Kate . . ."

"Come on, Charles," I imitated his wheezing voice, "behave."

"Let me have a swim, then I'll behave."

"No."

"Yes."

"No!"

"Yes!"

"*No!*"

He started to smile. "*Yes!*"

I found myself smiling, too. "*Absolutely not!*"

He laughed. "*Definitely yes!*" And he tossed his towel in my lap and ran for the water.

"Don't you dare," I started after him. "Charlie, I'm not kidding, you'll never get over that cold."

"So I'll get pneumonia," he called back over his shoulder. "They can cure that."

"I'll send you to military school, you little beast," I called, chasing him around the pond.

"Great! I like marching," he called back, out-distancing me.

"I'll send you to a reformatory!"

"Terrific, it's time I had some new friends."

Despite myself, I was laughing. "I'll tell your mother on you!"

"Aggghhh, you got me!" And he clutched his heart and fell face down into the pond.

"Oh, Charlie," I chastised him as he burst up through the water joyfully. "What am I going to do with you?"

"Buy me a cage," he answered.

"All right, enough. Get out of the water."

"Yes, Kate," he said, diving into it.

"Charlie, out!"

"Certainly, my dear," and he swam into the middle of the pond.

"*Charles!*"

"*Kathryn!*"

I did not, at that point, see the humor in his persistent disobedience any longer and I kicked off my shoes.

"All right, young man, I'll show you who's boss."

I waded into the water.

"You're going to get a long overdue smack where it'll do the most good."

"Child abuse! Child abuse!" he called, floating on his back gleefully.

"Get over here!"

"Come and get me!"

"You don't think I can?"

"Nope."

Happily for me at that moment, the two talents I had seriously cultivated in my youth included swimming, the other one being sex. I dove headfirst into the water and started toward him.

"Oh my God, *Jaws!*" he shouted and rolled over to swim away.

I was on him quickly, my former prowess very much intact, and I caught him around the neck, lifesaver style, and began swimming him to land.

"Kate, you're strangling me!"

"That'll do for a starter."

"Help!" he called out, giggling, "I'm being molested by a total stranger!"

I got us to the bank, Charles now in a fit of hysterical laughter, I still determined to redden his backside. He fell onto the grass and I grabbed for the top of his bathing suit. It would be a good old-fashioned smack, with nothing between my hand and his cheeks. I started to tug downward at the suit.

"No!" he laughed.

"Yes! Oh yes!"

He struggled but I pulled at his suit and in one swift yank had it down around his ankles. My hand went up into the air in preparation. He rolled over on his back to protect himself.

And we froze.

In a moment, he got up silently, pulled up his swimsuit and ran for the house. I was still on my knees, hand in the air, stunned by what I had seen.

Charles had pubic hair.

That evening, Charles was late for dinner and I sat in the dining room alone, deep in thought. I knew I should call Molly and tell her, but I also knew there was nothing she could do about it except to worry and possibly retard her own recuperation. Charles apparently had some kind of glandular imbalance, that was obvious. What he did not have was a cold. His voice was changing, as was his body. I recalled a boy from my own elementary school days who, if the girls were right, shaved at twelve. Such things were not impossible, I knew. Rare, but not impossible, and presumably not dangerous. There was no real reason for the peculiar dread that was settling over me. On the contrary, this explained his lightning changes of mood. He didn't need psychiatric help at all; his glands were merely wreaking havoc on him. Why then my feeling of impending disaster? Charles would mature early, there would be difficult emotional adjustments for him, but Molly and I could help him. God knows, we had handled worse problems together.

All of which was no help whatsoever when Charles entered the room. I was instantly unnerved, almost frightened. He took his place, Sissy brought his usual mountainous plate and he started to devour it in silence, like some powerful beast preparing its strength for the kill ahead. Ridiculous. I was being silly. I attempted conversation.

"How's your dinner?"

He glanced up at me briefly and then back down

to the business at hand. "Fine."

We said nothing more, but during the course of our desultory dinner I glanced at him. Was it my imagination or did he indeed look older than ten? Twelve, perhaps? Thirteen? His cheeks appeared smooth, but if I inspected them closely would I find a fine fuzz already on the way? I thought of other investigations of his body and flushed with sudden embarrassment. My God, he was still a child, no matter what his stage of development, and I was an hysteric.

"I'm sorry about this afternoon," I said.

"What about it?" he asked without looking up.

"At the pond," I almost stammered, still too embarrassed to deal directly with it.

"You mean making me leave the water? You were probably right. I do have a cold," and he sank his fangs into his meat.

"No, not about that."

"Then what?"

I had to face it directly now or risk making him feel that his maturation was unwholesome and something to be ashamed of.

"What I saw," I said, still evading.

"And what do you think you saw?"

Now he faced me directly and the look of mock innocence on his face chilled me. Whatever effect this sudden growth had on his body, it was reiterated in that look, for he was no child feigning innocence. He was at that moment a man lying, daring me to press on.

I accepted the dare.

"You know what I saw."

"Then why not say it?" and he smiled.

"Charles, don't do this."

"What am I doing?"

"You're trying to lie to me. Honey, this is Aunt Kate. I'm on your side, remember?"

"I honestly don't know what you're talking about," he answered, still smiling that I-dare-you smile.

"Very well," I snapped, angry at his refusal to accept my help. "We won't discuss it. You can talk to Doctor Shiff about it in the morning."

"What?" he said, and the smile vanished.

"I want you to see the local doctor. I think he can help you."

"See him about what?" he shouted. "What the hell are you babbling about?" And then, as quickly as the anger came, it was dispelled. "Kate, honey, I wish you'd just tell me. Why should I see a doctor? Just because of a cold? The cold'll go away . . ."

"It's not going away, Charles, and it's not a cold."

"Then what is it?"

"Your voice is changing. You're growing up, maybe too fast." And having said it, I felt suddenly calmer. "Darling, it's nothing to hide and nothing to be ashamed of. It's a natural part of growing up. You just got there a little faster than most, that's all. I'm sure Doctor Shiff has seen many boys with your . . ." I almost said *problem*, ". . . rate of development. I remember when I was in the fifth grade there was a boy who shaved every day. He was a nice, sweet boy and the only difference between him and the other children was . . ."

"I still don't know what you're talking about," he cut me off. "I think maybe you stayed in the sun too long."

"Charles . . ."

"All I have is a cold," his voice was ice. "Just a simple, ordinary cold."

"Charles, you and I know that's not all you have."

"No? What else do I have then?"

"Charles, you have pubic hair! You're only ten years old and you have pubic hair!"

"What's that?" he baited me.

"Oh, Christ. Honey . . ."

"You mean *down there?*" and he pointed between his legs. "You're crazy!"

"I saw it at the pond. You know I did, that's why you ran away. Because you were embarrassed, but there's nothing to be . . ."

"I don't have any hair down there, Kate. For crying out loud, I'm only ten!"

"Charles, don't you trust me?"

With that, he pushed his plate away from him and stood up. I assumed he was going to do the usual whenever faced with a confrontation: run. But he stood there, his face smug and unmoving and he started to unbuckle his belt. I flushed as he undid the top button of his jeans, unzipped the fly and lowered the pants to just above his penis. He silently displayed the white space for a moment before redressing himself.

"Can I finish eating now?" he asked.

"Yes," and my voice came out as raspy as his.

Charles had shaved himself.

MOLLY

They found something new wrong with me. The cartilage in my right knee was healing all wrong and I'd need another operation on it. Christ, just what I needed. They ought to put zippers in, just to make it easier on themselves.

Anyway, I was lying there the night I'd been given the news, in my usual foul mood, when the phone rang. It was Kate.

"How are you?" she made the mistake of asking.

So I told her. And told her. Listen, I've never been one to pass up a good chance to complain and, brother, I had plenty to complain about. But she didn't sound so hot herself.

"What's with you?" I asked. "You sound like hell."

"No, I'm fine," she said, but there was as much complaint in those three words as in my whole tirade.

"Come on, what's up? Charlie giving you a hard time?"

"He has a cold," she said after a pause.

"So?"

"Nothing."

But it was something, I could tell. "Hey, Kate, come on, is there something wrong?"

"Molly, you've got enough to worry about at

the moment without my giving you anything more. He's fine. We're all fine."

"That bad, huh?"

"No, honest. So, when's the new operation take place?"

"Friday," I started, and the symphony of complaints was in high gear again.

By the time I finished I had forgotten she had something on her mind, and only remembered it after we'd hung up. Hell, I thought, if it gets really bad she'll call back.

I wish to Christ she had.

KATE

Sleep wouldn't come. I lay there in the darkness, seeing Charles expose himself over and over again until the remembered sight of it made me physically ill. I came out of the bathroom and saw his open bedroom door. In the silence of the night I could hear his breathing; he was asleep. I went into his room and stood by the foot of his bed, studying him in the moonlight. He lay there bare-chested, a child once more. Whatever changes were upon him at that moment were gone.

His expression changed in his sleep. Was he dreaming and if so, of what? Harmless little boys' dreams or something else, something dark I didn't understand?

Nonsense. Utter nonsense. Molly's right about me, I have a need for the dramatic. No wonder Charles was taking puberty so badly. He had me as an example to live down to.

He rolled over on his back and raised an arm up beside his head.

Innocent and serene.

What he needed was what Molly could give him. Molly the rock, the realist, the sensible one. Not Kate with her flair, her flamboyance, her chaos.

In the dim light it took a moment to recognize what I had been staring at as I stood there thinking. It was a darkening under his arm: a small, barely noticeable tuft of hair.

"We'll get through it, darling," I whispered. "I promise you."

The next morning I called Dr. Shiff and made an appointment for Charles at four that afternoon. As I hung up the phone, I turned to see Charles standing just inside the living room doorway watching me.

"I won't go."

"Charles, darling, come in and sit down." He didn't move. "Please."

"Why? There's nothing to talk about. You want to make appointments with doctors? You go and see them."

"Please?"

He moved slowly into the room and sat down on the couch across from me. He folded his arms in resolution and stared at me.

"Honey, we both know you shaved yourself yesterday." I hesitated, waiting for him to deny it but he said nothing. "Last night, when you were asleep, I went into your room and I saw . . . other evidences . . . "

"What'd you do? Strip me?" he almost sneered.

"Of course not. Honey, we do love each other, don't we?"

"Yes," but his reply was without any sign of affection.

"Then we can come to each other with our problems, can't we?"

"I don't have a problem, Kate."

Damn my choice of words. "Of course you don't, but you do have a condition that's unusual. That's why I want to help you. I want the doctor to help you . . . "

"I don't need help, Kate."

"Oh, honey, please trust me . . . "

"You trust me. Really, Kate. Trust me. I don't have a problem and I don't need any help."

"But you're developing too quickly . . . "

"Yes, I know I am."

He had admitted it. I smiled at him, almost gratefully.

"I'm glad you're finally telling me," I said.

"I wanted to," he answered, and his face warmed. "I really did, but you worry so much. You're making such a big deal out of it, that's why I didn't want to say anything."

"But it is a big deal, sweetheart."

"No, it isn't," and he came to me and took my hand. "I promise you, Kate, it'll all work out. For both of us."

That same seductive tone was back; the one he had used in the gazebo. I withdrew my hand from his.

"Charles," I said in an almost businesslike voice,

"I am your aunt and I am in charge of you for the summer. Like it or not, I want you to see Doctor Shiff this afternoon."

He hesitated, looking down at me, the warmth disappearing from his face.

"You insist?"

"I insist."

"Very well," he said flatly. "May I be excused now?"

"Yes, if you like."

I watched him leave the room slowly in his oddly mature stride and I noticed that his new jeans were already too short for him.

I had handled the whole thing badly; how badly I had yet to find out.

Charles didn't come in for lunch. Given his ravenous appetite, it was shortsighted of me to think he was off sulking, but at three-thirty I began to worry. I checked his room, which was in its usual state of chaos. I walked through the woods to the lake, which was deserted. At quarter to four, I got in the car and honked the horn, uselessly, several times. Sissy looked out the kitchen window.

"He ain't back yet?" she called to me.

"Not yet."

"He will be by dinner. I got a roast in the oven," and she disappeared without a care.

I didn't agree. I was sure that he would avoid the house until Dr. Shiff's office hours were over.

I was wrong. By seven o'clock that evening, Charles was still not back.

"What do you want me to do with dinner?" Sissy asked, worrying not about him but about her roast.

"Put it in the refrigerator," I answered sharply.

"It's gonna be ruined. And what'd I do about the corn puddin'? I can't put that in the refrigerator . . ."

"Sissy, I don't care what you do about it. I'm not hungry and Charles isn't here."

"Sure, and the moment he comes back it's gonna be my fault if dinner's ruined," she muttered, going back to her kitchen.

I waited, sitting there at father's table, my empty plate in front of me. Was Charles punishing me? Was this his childish way of flaunting my authority over him or was it something else? Was he, as I had sensed, *afraid* to see a doctor?

I left the house and got into the car, deciding it would be better to cruise around the area looking for him than to remain, impotent, at home.

I returned to the house after eight and went directly to Sissy's room.

"Has he come back?"

"Nope," she answered, her eyes riveted to her television set, glad to be rid of him.

"You don't seem very concerned," I said.

"Oh, honey, he'll be back soon as he's hungry enough."

I sat outside by the pond waiting. The sun was setting; soon it would be dark and a ten-year-old boy would be out there somewhere alone.

I called the local police and reported him missing. Their attitude was similar to Sissy's; they'd be on the lookout for him but they expected him to return on his own shortly. Kids are kids, they informed me.

Kids are kids. But not Charles. Charles was no ordinary child, stuck as he was between two worlds. And I had been no help. Just when I should have been my most understanding, I had destroyed his trust in me, ordering him as I did to see the doctor. But wasn't that the right thing to do? Right thing, wrong way, I decided and paced the living room nervously.

At ten o'clock I heard Sissy's television set being turned off and I lay down on the couch and waited.

As I closed my eyes, my own internal set turned on and I saw Charles at the gazebo in Alan's shirt, dancing with Alan's wife. Charles swimming gleefully in the pond. Charles climbing into bed beside me. Charles, Charles, Charles.

I woke with a start sometime in the middle of the night, the echo of some unknown noise still in my ears. I got up and went into the hall, trying to sense the direction of the noise. I tried the kitchen first.

The refrigerator door stood open and I looked inside. The roast was gone, as was most of the other food.

I hurried upstairs to Charles's room, hoping to find him there in the midst of a petulant eating orgy, but his room hadn't been touched.

I realized the sound I had heard in my sleep and raced downstairs to the back door, hoping to catch up with him. There was no sign of him by the pond. The moonlight outlined the woods and the entrance to the path. Like it or not, and I certainly did not, he was probably on the path at that moment with his cache of food.

I walked swiftly to it.

Stepping into the woods, I was instantly chilled by the cold, damp air and by the imagined snakes that might lie unseen just ahead of me. As I walked, careful step by careful step, hand up in front of me to protect me from unseen branches, I heard only my own footsteps, the crackling of leaves and twigs, my own heavy breathing. I came out beside the lake, thanking God that half the trip at least was made without incident. I could see the outline of the gazebo but not whether anyone was in it. I walked up to it and found it empty.

Nearly.

On the floor was a fork. I held it up in the moonlight and recognized the pattern father had chosen a millennium before.

"Charles?" I called out into the thick silence. "Charles?"

I searched the edges of the woods; it was no use. Had he been standing there looking at me, I couldn't have seen him. Deciding that he was, I called impotently to him.

"Please don't do this, Charles. Please don't frighten me this way."

Silence in return.

"Come back and we'll talk. I won't make you do anything you don't want to do."

Still no answer.

"I'm just trying to help you. I love you!"

And then the throaty croak of a bullfrog in reply.

I made my way back to the path, shivering, and once through it, hurried back to the safety of the house and my room.

Where I saw that my closet door was open.

Charles had taken Alan's suitcase as well.

On waking the next morning and finding Charles still missing, I made two phone calls. The first was to the police, who now took me more seriously, asking me for a detailed description of Charles and what he was wearing. The second was to Molly. She

Bob Randall

was his mother and the time was past due for telling her.

I dialed the hospital and was told that she was in surgery. I had completely forgotten the impending knee operation. Again I had abused her trust.

And so, alone with my fears and guilt, I drove into town to speak with Dr. Shiff myself. His office was off the local highway in a small white house, divided neatly into two rooms. Having given my name to his receptionist, I sat down to wait. Across the room was a young mother and her child, a girl of about five or six. A normal child, I thought. Here for a checkup, an examination of her tonsils, something simple, explainable, ordinary. What would the doctor think when I started to tell him about Charles? Would he think me mad? Would he believe me at all, or would he note in his diary that Kate was showing signs of menopause, possibly brought on by the untimely death of her husband? Perhaps that was it, after all. Perhaps there was nothing wrong with Charles; it was all in the mind of a woman desperately trying to force a child into replacing a husband.

No. I am no child abuser. God help me, I am many things but not that.

Dr. Shiff came into the waiting room, eons older than I remembered him and tiny. This man who had terrified Molly and me as children with his needles and icy cold stethoscopes was hardly taller than a midget.

"Katie," he beamed at me. "You're a day late, young lady."

"Yes, I know. I'm sorry."

"You're looking fine, just fine; of course that's

not a diagnosis," he chuckled. "You sit tight, be with you in a jiffy," and he ushered the mother and child into his office.

I picked up a copy of *Time* magazine from his coffee table and flipped through it, stopping to look at any picture of a young boy, to see if there were any discernable differences between him and Charles. There were not.

I tried to imagine how I would begin telling Dr. Shiff about Charles; however I planned it, I ended sounding hysterical and overimaginative.

In a very few minutes the mother and child exited his office, both looking happy and relieved. Would I leave his office the same way?

"Come in, Katie," Dr. Shiff poked his head in the doorway. "Come on in and tell me all about yourself." He closed the door behind me. "I looked you up in my records. You know it's been eleven years since you were in here? Well, that's the way." He settled into an ancient leather chair behind his desk. "Young people grow up and move to the big city. Don't know why, but all young people think life's better there than out here. Hey, young lady, I saw you on a television commercial about a year ago. Some soap or something . . ."

He rambled on and finally, mercifully, ground to a halt.

"All right, Katie, now what seems to be the problem? It can't be too big or you would've gone to a specialist in the city, I know that. What can an old country GP do for you?"

"It's about Charles."

"Molly's boy? I haven't seen him since that summer Molly stayed up here after her husband passed on. How's the little boy?"

95

"Not so little."

And I told him everything. Slowly. Coherently, I hoped. Calmly. To my surprise, he believed me.

"Is it dangerous for him?" I asked, when the whole incredible tale was finished.

"Well, I can't say it is and I can't say it isn't," he answered solemnly. "The primary sex changes don't surprise me that much. The secondary ones are more unusual, the underarm hair, that kind of thing. They usually come later. And he sure as hell could use some shots to slow the whole thing down. Vitamins, too. Soon as he gets back, you get him right over to me, day or night. Meantime, I'll do some reading up and make some phone calls. It's about all a country GP can do."

"But what if he doesn't come back?"

"Well," he said, getting up, "we're not going to think about that, young lady. This isn't the summer of forty-four and don't you go thinking it is. Doctor's orders."

"Mother," I said, half to myself, for that was the summer she went away.

He looked regretful. "I'm sorry, Katie, I wasn't thinking of your mother. I was thinking of the Harley boy. It was stupid of me."

"That's all right. That was thirty years ago, I've had plenty of time to recover." I took his hand gratefully.

On the drive home, I remembered the Harley boy had disappeared that same summer. Molly and I had watched them drag the lake for him, uselessly.

Would Charles be the second boy lost forever in this one small town?

MOLLY

I want to tell you, when it came to handing out luck, I must've been off somewhere taking a crap, because I sure as hell didn't get any. A simple knee operation almost put me away. The schmuck anesthetist made a little boo-boo. It seems when he was checking the records for my weight, he noted down my weight upon entering the hospital. The asshole forgot that in the weeks I had been flat on my back with nothing but hospital junk to eat, I had lost twelve pounds. So when he put me under, he really put me under. For two whole days. Malpractice suit, here I come. Anyway, I just wanted you to know that Kate did try to reach me but where I was only God could get through.

KATE

Now there were two of them to worry about and my penchant for high melodrama was in full gear. Despite Molly's justifiable contempt for the medical profession, I blessed it that night for one of its great inventions: Valium. One and my fears calmed; two and they vanished; three and the whole thing became a play in which I had been cast unwillingly, playing a part that had little to do with my real life. I wondered, sitting there in the living room, when the curtain would finally come down and I could discard this bothersome role. I didn't much care for the character; she was so little in control of herself, so willing to be swayed and pulled by others.

"You all right?" Sissy poked her head in the doorway, catching me staggering across the room.

"Sure thing."

"I'm goin' to bed. You want anything?"

"Another role like *Gypsy*, please," I echoed Merman's supposed wisecrack.

"What, honey?"

"Nothing, nothing."

"You call the police again?"

"Twice. The police twice. The hospital three times. There's no one left to call except information."

"What?"

"Nothing, Sissy. Go to bed. You're excused. *Exeunt* already."

With that, she did, and I floated over to father's corner bar, wondering what a teeny-weeny vodka on the rocks would do when faced with three itsy-bitsy Valiums. *Valia?*

Ten minutes later, I found out, as I drifted off, like Molly, into a sleep far deeper than intended.

I had a dream.

Sitting there, slumped over in that wretched wing chair, still holding the empty vodka glass in my hand, I dreamed I heard a noise—a dull, round noise I didn't recognize. In the dream I tried to open my eyes, still sitting in that chair, and managed to part the lids slightly. There was a light in the hall, dim, so dim. And someone standing there, looking in. A man, a short man. It was Dr. Shiff, smiling in at me. I heard our conversation, filtering through the drugged fog.

"Why, Katie, dear, you've dropped your glass. And you mustn't sit with your head tilted that way. It's bad for your neck."

"I'm sorry ... "

"Young people, always too busy to take care of themselves. You'll have quite a crick in the morning. It was lucky I was passing this way."

He came into the room slowly.

"Why, Katie, you've been drinking, haven't you?"

"Just one."

"One too many if you ask me," and he gently lifted my head and rolled it to one side so that it rested on the side of the chair. "That's better. We don't want a crick, do we?"

"No."

"I remember when you were a child, always running off the way you did. Always disappearing. You were a great friend of the Harley boy, weren't you?"

"No."

"Yes, you were. You and the Harley boy were inseparable. Did you do dirty things together?"

"Doctor Shiff, I didn't ... "

"Now, now, never lie to your doctor," and he started to stroke my hair. "You ought to wear your hair up, you know. *Do something with it.* Young people never want to do something with it. And old people are too old to do anything with it." He chuckled and the sound of it was miles away. "You get my meaning, Katie?"

"No . . ."

"Don't kid a kidder; I know you actresses, always in somebody's bed," and his hand cupped my breast. "What kind of things do you do in bed, Katie? What did you and Alan do?" He squeezed me. "Did he die from satisfying you? A lot of men go that way. I ought to know, I'm a doctor."

And he lifted my face to his and kissed my lips, gently returning my cheek to the side of the chair.

"You sleep now, Katie. Get lots of bed rest, take two aspirins and call me in the morning."

I closed my eyes and heard the soft shuffle of his footsteps receding into the mist.

"Don't forget," he called to me from the next galaxy, "I expect to see you in my bed first thing in the morning."

The dream gone, I fell into a deeper sleep and didn't wake until the late morning, when Sissy found me.

Charles had been missing for two days and two nights and now, with the start of a third day, I was near hysteria. Molly still couldn't be told but the danger to her, at least, was over. She was still sleeping but would awaken, they assured me, within hours. The police came by the house and when I told them that Charles had been home briefly, they went away, presumably still on the case but with obviously dwindling concern. Sissy was of no help; I think she was happy to have a few days rest without the constant disagreements with Charles.

I was alone. Truly alone for the first time. After

Alan's death, there had been Charles, and now there was no one.

I went upstairs to Charles's room, which Sissy had neglected to clean, no doubt her own subtle battle in their war.

I sat on his bed and picked up a pair of socks that still lay on the floor from days ago. They were filthy. How long had he worn them without changing? My little boy. My dirty, rude, sweet little boy.

I wept.

The night of the third day. I was afraid to take any more pills; afraid that if Charles returned for food in the middle of the night, I wouldn't hear him. I was determined not to sleep. Surely the food he'd taken would be gone now. I shooed Sissy out of her kitchen and began preparing for him. If I could offer him his favorite meal, perhaps he'd linger with me long enough to eat it, long enough for me to win him back.

By midnight, the meal prepared, I set the dining room table with father's best dishes and silverware, as Charles had done for me. The crystal goblets. The linen napkins. I brought in the food, the covered platter of fried chicken, the bowls of sweet corn and cranberry-orange sauce. An apple pie sat on the kitchen table cooling.

And I waited.

"Please, God," I said half aloud, "make him come back. Make him come back tonight."

At two o'clock I saw someone.

I was standing at the back door, looking through its glass window when I saw a shadowy figure come from the path and stand, dark against the trees, looking across the back lawn at the house.

Bob Randall

I threw open the door. "Charles!"

The figure leaped back into the darkness of the woods.

"Charles! Please!" And I ran. I ran across the lawn past the pond, headlong into the woods, no hand up for protection this time.

"Charles! Oh, God, Charles!"

A branch slapped my face but I kept running.

"Charles, please! I love you!"

I came out by the lake in time to see the figure reach the gazebo and dash inside. Breathless, I rushed to it, but didn't enter fearing that he'd leap out the other side and be gone again.

"Charles, just let me talk to you," I said, gasping for breath. "Just let me talk to you and don't run away . . . I won't make you do anything you don't want to . . . I'm sorry, I was wrong . . . Please, don't go . . . Just let me talk to you . . ."

I tried to see him in the gazebo but managed only a shadow in the corner, pressed up against one of the pillars.

" . . . I know you're mad at me . . . But I love you . . . I was only trying to do what's best for you . . . but you can decide yourself, Charles . . . Just don't run away again . . . I can't bear it when you're gone . . ."

The figure moved but then fell into the shadow again.

" . . . I made you dinner. Everything you like. Fried chicken and corn and cranberry sauce . . . I even made an apple pie, Charles, and you know how hard that is for me . . . I'm not the best cook in the world, darling . . ."

The figure took a step forward.

" . . . but we'll smother it with ice cream, so if it's not too good you won't notice . . ."

And another, so that the moonlight outlined him. "Charles?"

But the figure was that of a young man. I was suddenly frightened.

"Who is it?"

"Help me." His voice was deep but familiar.

"Who are you?" and I stepped back, prepared to run from the stranger to the safety of the house.

"Help me."

He came toward me; I was about to run when he sat down on the steps of the gazebo.

"God, I'm so tired."

The voice. Whose voice was it? Why did I know it?

"What are you doing here? Why did you come to my house?"

Overhead, the clouds that had obscured the moon were parting. The moonlight crept across the lake toward us, like a spotlight.

"Kate, help me. Please." And he lowered his face into his hands. "I'm so tired."

The spotlight reached him. The first thing I recognized were his clothes. Alan's clothes.

And then he lifted his head and looked at me.

It was Charles.

But not ten-year-old Charles. This was Charles at eighteen. His round face elongated and painfully thin. His hair knotted and long. His eyes deep-set and rimmed in black.

"My God in heaven," I whispered. "My God in heaven."

"It's me," he said in that familiar unfamiliar voice.

I took a hesitant step forward. "Charles?"

"Yes." He smiled weakly. "Kate, I haven't eaten."

I became conscious of my own body; the heartbeat in my temples, the tightening inside me. He held out his hand to me and in the moonlight I could see the two-inch fingernails pointing at me, witchlike.

"Who are you?"

"Kate . . ."

"Who are you?"

His hand fell limply into his lap, his head bowed, I could hear him start to cry softly.

And I knew it was he.

"Oh my God, my God," and I started to cry, too. "Come, baby. Come home."

I helped him to his feet; he was taller than me. We started toward the path, my arm around his waist. I could feel how horribly thin he was; my fingers moved upward along the row of his ribs, each protruding. We stumbled through the blackened path; he was barely strong enough to walk.

"It's all right, baby, I've got you . . . It's all right . . ."

As he approached the house his body became rigid against entering.

"Sissy . . ." he said.

"She's asleep. Don't worry, darling."

I helped him inside and up the stairs, each one torture for him. My bedroom was closest to the top of the stairs and I put him into my bed. It was then I turned on the light and got my first good look at what had once been my nephew.

"My God . . ."

Except in photographs, I had never seen a starving person before. His cheekbones jutted out of his face as if they might split the skin; his sunken eyes were bloodshot and the blackness around them terrified me; his bare feet were filthy and the toenails inches long and caked in dirt.

"Food ... please," he whispered.

I hurried downstairs and grabbed the platter of chicken; halfway back upstairs I realized he wouldn't be able to hold it down and so I ran to the kitchen. There was soup. My hands trembling, I opened the can, and I rushed back to him without heating it.

I held him in my arms, this child-man, and spoon-fed him.

"It'll be all right, darling. It'll be all right."

He finished the soup with enormous difficulty, the mere act of swallowing being a strain for him.

"More," he whispered when the can was empty.

I hurried back downstairs and opened a second can.

Hours later the sky outside my bedroom window was lightening. Charles had eaten three cans of soup and the entire dinner I had prepared. Exhausted, he lay back on the pillow and smiled weakly up at me.

"I don't understand, Charles. I don't understand," I said, stroking his hair, gently trying to undo some of the knots.

"Promise ... " he whispered.

"Promise what, darling?"

"Don't let anyone see me ... don't tell Sissy ... " he pleaded.

"I promise," and he closed his eyes. "But I don't understand. How did this happen?"

"For us," he whispered, and then he was asleep.

I sat there watching the sky outside my window turn from dark blue to white. That was a miracle of sorts; but an everyday understandable miracle. This change in Charles was something else. But what?

I remembered the myth of the changeling, filled with its demons and devils.

No, I thought, looking at his face, peaceful and serene.

No, it was Charles; my Charles.

"Sleep, my darling. I'm here. No one will harm you."

And I swore to protect him.

From Satan, if need be.

MOLLY

Well, there I was, Lady R. Van Winkle, fresh from my three-day hiatus from consciousness, feeling like a cross between a dishrag and an overdone noodle. I didn't call Kate the first day, because to tell you the truth, I wasn't exactly in the mood for her holier-than-thou attitude concerning me and Charlie. We'd had several arguments along the way, with him always coming out a cross between Sir Lancelot and Lord Fauntleroy and me pure Wicked Witch of the West. So me and my headache spent the day alone.

She, of course, didn't call. I guess she didn't want to disturb the big sleep. Nice of her, huh?

Anyway, I called her the next day.

"Molly?"

"Yeah. Guess what? I'm alive."

"Oh, honey, I didn't call!"

"Yeah, well, what the hell. Sisters are a dime a dozen."

"I'm so sorry. It's just that . . ." and her voice trailed off.

"It's just what?" I asked. Hell, why let her off easy? I was the one on death's doorway.

"I'm terribly sorry."

"Swell."

"I really am. It's just that . . . I haven't been feeling well lately and . . ."

"*You* haven't? You should be inside my head at the moment."

"Please forgive me."

"All right, all right, let's not belabor the point. How's everything at Disneyland?"

A pause. Then, finally, "Everything's fine."

"You don't sound too convincing."

"Really, Molly, everything's fine."

You'd think an actress could lie better than that.

"All right, lay it on me, what's he done now?"

"Nothing."

"I'll bet. Put him on the phone, will you?"

Another pause.

"I can't. He's . . ."

And another.

"He's what? For crying out loud, Kate, talk!"

"He's at a Boy Scout meeting."

"He's where?!"

And then she tells me this cock-and-bull story about the Scouts' day camp and how Charlie loves it and all the time I'm lying there thinking one of us is definitely crazy. My kid a scout? In a pig's eye. But I can't get anything out of her. Finally, I give up. I mean, I had my hands full keeping myself alive in that nuthouse, so I guessed I could do without another problem.

"All right, when he comes in, have him call me."

"I will. And take care of yourself, Molly."

"I better. Nobody else will."

And she hung up. Well, by that time my headache was sprouting wings, so I rang for nursey, the keeper of the demerols. After a fifteen-minute battle with her, I got one.

And off to dreamland.

KATE

Charles slept soundly until three the next afternoon. I handled Sissy by telling her he was back, that he was ill and that she was not to go into my room for any reason until he was well.

"Why not?" she asked, her face darkening.

"Because I think it best."

"Because *he* wants it that way," she said. "I never did nothin' to make that child take such a hatred to me," and she turned on her heels.

I felt guilt about Sissy, but I had promised Charles and I had seen the results of disappointing him. I would never do it again.

I went back into my room and sat beside the bed. He was handsome. Even in that state, he was handsome. He had a little of father in him, a lot of Molly, her strong aquiline nose, but finer. Oh, Lord, if his eyes were still pale blue he would be an Adonis. His hands were marvelous; long, strong fingers, the hands of a surgeon or a pianist. His jawline was prominent and firm but that might be the emaciation. The stubble on his cheeks was dark. I wondered about that. Why had his hair grown so long and not his beard? I went into the bathroom. Of course, my razor was missing. My darling had thought of everything.

My darling.

At that moment, I pushed the horror of his growth out of my mind and felt only the grandeur of it.

Where would it lead? I didn't think of that, either. He was back, he was safe, he was beautiful. That's all I knew, sitting there looking down at him.

Hours passed and he woke.

"Good morning," he smiled up at me. His voice was deep and resonant and wonderful.

"Afternoon," I corrected him. "Hungry?"

"Of course."

"Bacon, eggs, toast, coffee?"

"Tons of it."

I kissed his forehead and went downstairs to Sissy, ordering his breakfast.

"All that?" she asked in surprise to my suggestion that she scramble half a dozen eggs.

"It's for both of us," I covered quickly. I would have to be careful. Though Sissy was used to Charles's ten-year-old appetite, gigantic though it was, this new hunger would surely arouse her suspicions.

"Knock on the door when the tray's ready," I said.

"Don't worry. I wouldn't set foot in that room for anything," she growled in answer.

Upstairs, Charles was sitting, propped up against my pillows, looking like a young prince.

"Look at you," I said once the door was safely closed. "You look awful."

"I'll bet."

"But a lot better than you did last night. You nearly scared the life out of me, young man."

He held out one of his marvelous hands to me and I took it in mine.

"Ouch! Those nails have got to come off," I said.

"I've got a lot of cleaning up to do. How do you like my hair this length?" he asked. "Will I bring back hippies?"

"Not when I'm through with you."

His eyes were pale blue, still.

"I'm going to fatten you up and clean you up and beat you up if you ever run away again, understood?"

"It won't be so easy to spank me anymore," he smiled at me, and his face shone. "I think I'm bigger than you are now."

I sat down on the edge of the bed, still holding his hand.

"How, Charles? How did it happen?"

"I don't know," he answered, and quickly changed the subject. "Where's my breakfast, woman? I'm hungry."

"On the way, sir. Do you feel strong enough to get up? I could help you shower."

"Still a little wobbly. Maybe after I eat."

He touched my cheek. "You look tired," he said. "Did you sleep at all?"

"No."

"My ministering angel."

We sat silently for a moment and I realized I was blushing.

"I'm not much of a barber," I covered, "but I'll have to do. Would the gentleman prefer the continental look or the much in fashion layered cut?"

"Whatever the lady would like to see me in."

I blushed again.

"Where did you sleep?"

"In the woods."

"The woods? Charles . . ."

"Now, now, don't scold me, Kate. I'm too old to be scolded."

I looked at him, puzzled. "How old *are* you?"

He looked back at me, his skylike eyes gleaming, and he laughed. "I haven't a clue. What's your guess?"

"Eighteen, nineteen?"

"Let's say twenty-one and be done with it. That way I get to vote."

"My God," I said, a tidal wave of questions occurring to me. "What about your education? You can't go back to the fifth grade, not the way you are now."

"I think I'd stick out a little," he smiled.

"I'm serious, Charles . . ."

"Don't be. There's loads of time to sort all that out later."

There was a knock at the door. Charles looked at me, troubled.

"Don't worry," I said, going to the door. I opened it quickly and stepped into the hallway.

"His Majesty's breakfast," Sissy scowled, handing me the tray which was set for two. And then she added, loud enough for him to hear, "I hope everything's to his Highness's likin'," and she went back downstairs.

"I've been cruel to her," Charles said as I closed the door behind me.

"You might say so," I agreed.

"I like Sissy, but we'll have to get rid of her soon."

"What?"

"I can't live in this room forever, Kate."

I didn't want to think about it. I didn't want to think of anything except nursing Charles back to health. I put the tray in his lap and he started to eat.

"Your table manners have improved," I said, noting that although ravenous, he had slowed his gorging to a low roar. "Who taught you that in the woods, the chipmunks?"

"Maybe it's genetic," he smiled.

"*Genetic*? Listen to the words coming out of the ten-year-old."

He pondered that for a moment. "True, that's funny. I do feel like I've grown intellectually as well, but I sure as hell don't know a lot of things. I've got some reading to do. Help me?"

Something happens when you're in the midst of the impossible. Channels in the brain that can't cope with the illogic of it shut down and you simply go about the business at hand. And so there we were, mutant and aunt, making out a reading list for Charles. Insane.

When he had finished his breakfast, I helped him out of bed and realized how tall he was. He towered over me.

"My Lord, you're a long drink of water," I said.

"Speaking of which, how about that shower now?"

"You steady enough?"

"Uh-huh."

I prepared the shower for him, checked that

Sissy was not upstairs and helped him into the bathroom. As he unbuttoned Alan's shirt, which he still had on from the night before, he looked at me oddly.

"You plan on staying here?"

I blushed for a third time that afternoon. "I beg your pardon, I forgot you're all grown up now."

"How could you?" he smirked, and I left the bathroom laughing at my own stupidity.

Downstairs, Sissy was busily polishing father's prized possession, an art nouveau cabinet that looked like nothing so much as the inside of a coiled snake, when I entered the room, still laughing at myself.

"Somethin' funny around here?" she asked. "I could sure use a laugh."

"Oh, Sissy," and I put my hand on her shoulder, "you're getting a raw deal around here, aren't you? I'm sorry."

She smiled at me, grateful as alway for the smallest favor.

"That's okay, honey. I expect everything'll work out fine."

"I expect so, too," I said happily.

"Soon Molly'll be here and the whole family will be together again, like the old days."

Molly! How on earth would I tell Molly? Another channel in my brain closed, and I heard the shower stop upstairs. I hurried back to the insanity of grooming Charles.

"Hold still," I said to the beautiful man sitting on my bed in my robe as I manicured his talons. "Shall we save these?" I asked, cutting off a two-inch tip.

"For science," he said.

"What would science make of you, Charles?"

"Mincemeat, probably. That's one of the reasons

nobody must know. I'm not turning myself into a freak for the *Daily News.*"

"And what about your mother?" I frowned. "Shouldn't we tell her, at least?"

"Absolutely not, Kate," and his voice was filled with authority. "Not now. Later, when it's over."

I looked at him. "What do you mean, when it's over? Isn't it over?"

He laughed at me the way I had at him eons before when he was an adorable, unknowing child.

"No. You'll be a manicurist for quite a few days yet."

"How long will it go on?"

He thought for a moment. "Until I stop it."

"And how will you do that?"

"I don't know. I just will," he said and held out his pinkie to me. "Shorter, please."

"I hope you're a good tipper," I said, and went back to work.

Around five Molly called and I started what would become a torrent of lies.

MOLLY

God knows, I wouldn't want to steal the spotlight from the little idyll that was going on in the woods, but I do feel I ought to put my two cents in, just so you'll remember I was alive. Sort of. While Kate was playing nurse to Charlie, without my knowing it, I was playing another game with another nurse, Mrs. Golden, the horse's ass keeper of the Demerols. I should mention at this point that I was getting more than a little fond of my Dems. They solved a multitude of problems. Got a pain somewhere? Take a Dem, it vanishes. Got a kid somewhere? Take a Dem, he vanishes. Here a Dem, there a Dem, everywhere a Dem Dem.

Addicted? Nah. But on the way, I gotta admit. And glad to be there.

So old Mrs. Golden and I had our differences.

"Do you realize how addictive Demerol is?" she asked me one day when I requested one.

"I'll look it up soon as you give me one," I answered.

"It's a synthetic derivative of morphine and highly addictive ..."

"Swell. Gimme."

"I'm sorry but I can't. Doctor Phillips told me ..."

"Screw Doctor Phillips, I'm in pain!"

"Will you please ..."

"Pain! You understand the word? P as in *putz*, A as in *asshole* ..."

"There's no need to be ..."

"*I* as in *idiot* and *N* as in *nuts* to you and Doctor Phillips!"

I'm cute, no? Nursey didn't think so. She wrenched the phone from its cradle and called the doctor to tell on me, the tattletale.

When she handed me the phone, it was another Molly who talked to the doctor. That one, the poor thing, was in terrible pain but would do whatever the doctor said because she was such a good, brave girl.

I got the pill.

KATE

Within a week Charles was twenty-five.

And I? I felt a hundred. It had been quite a week. First, there was Molly to contend with. The daily calls, the daily lies; I had run out of excuses for why Charles couldn't come to the phone and so I had sent him off on an imaginary camping trip with the Scouts.

"Kate," Molly said on one of those torturous calls, "look, I'm getting scared. What the hell is going on up there?"

"Nothing, Molly. Really."

"Don't give me that, I haven't spoken to my own kid in over a week!"

I felt wretched but what could I do?

"Molly, you trust me, don't you?"

"I don't know, you won't tell me what's wrong."

"Nothing, darling. *Nothing is wrong.* He's just away for a few days with the Scouts, that's all. You're upset because you're in that terrible place, taking all those drugs . . ."

"Those drugs are the only friends I've got," she said, and my heart broke for her.

"Molly, you're my sister and I love you. I wouldn't let anything happen to harm you . . ."

"We weren't talking about me. We were talking about Charles."

"You know I love Charles . . ." And on and on it went. When I finally hung up, I was sick with disgust at myself.

And then there was Sissy.

Charles's appetite had become gargantuan; he had at least six meals a day now. There was no way to hide it from Sissy and so I had taken to driving into town each morning and ordering several takeout meals from a luncheonette. Then I'd drive back and sneak them upstairs, a thief in my own house.

But even that didn't work. Sissy became daily more suspicious and one afternoon coming upstairs I found her listening at my bedroom door.

"What are you doing?"

"Nothin'," she said.

"You were listening at the door."

"I just thought if he was asleep I could get in there and do some dustin'. He wouldn't have known I was there."

I flew into a rage. "I told you not to go in there under any circumstances, Sissy!"

"A little dustin' couldn't hurt nothin',"

"That's not your decision. This is still my house!"

"All right, all right," she snapped back, heading for the stairs. "Have it your own way."

"Damn right I'll have it my own way in my own house."

"What's he doin' sleeping in your room anyway," she muttered, descending angrily. "Takin' over the whole place?"

"That's also none of your business!"

I watched her hurry downstairs to the safety of

117

her kitchen, knowing how unwarranted my attack had been.

And as if that weren't enough, there was also Dr. Shiff. He called two days after Charles returned; I told him it had all been a mistake, that Charles was unchanged, that I supposed it had been my own over-active imagination all the time.

"Maybe you ought to bring him in, anyway," he suggested.

"What on earth for? I've told you ..."

"Well, it'd put your mind at ease, for one thing." And he added gently, "Also, it might not be a bad idea for me to give *you* a checkup, young lady. I might come up with a good tonic for that imagination."

"I don't think that's necessary."

"Of course, you actresses make a living out of your imagination, I know that, but too much of even a good thing is still too much."

"I'll think about it," I said, and quickly hung up.

Perhaps Dr. Shiff was right; I certainly felt the need of a tonic for all my lies and deception.

But then, there was Charles to make up for it all.

Each night as I went to sleep in his room, I lay there wondering what glorious changes were taking place on the other side of that thin plaster wall; what new miracles the morning would bring. And oh, how the miracles showered down on us!

The second morning he was home, I rapped softly at the door. "Charles? It's me."

The door opened and there he stood, magnificent, smiling down at me, the previous day's gauntness replaced by an athletic wiriness, already shaved, manicured, wearing a towel wrapped around himself.

He took my hand and escorted me in, closing the door behind us.

"You look a lot better this morning," he said. "You've slept, finally," and he held his hand to my cheek until, seeing my embarrassment, he removed it.

"*I* look better! Charles, have you looked in the mirror yet?"

"Uh-huh." He sat on the bed and stretched his enormous legs out in front of him, very pleased with himself. "Not bad, but still too skinny."

"You're breathtaking," I said.

"Well, if you see anything that displeases you, just let us know. We aim to please."

I burned.

"Hungry?"

"Not too. I raided the refrigerator at five."

"Charles, that's too risky. If you were hungry, you should have wakened me. I could have . . ."

"You needed your sleep," he said in a wonderfully parental way. "Besides, I can take care of myself now."

"Says you, you're still a child."

"Oh, am I?" he smirked. "Well, listen to what the child did this morning while his grown-up aunt was snoring to beat the band . . ."

"I don't snore."

"The hell you don't. What do you think woke me at five?"

"Never mind that, what did you do?"

"I left Sissy a note from you and some money, you'll find you're missing forty dollars from your purse. About an hour ago off she went to Lumberville and won't be back till this afternoon. If you weren't snoring so loud, you would've heard her car pull out."

"I don't snore!"

"Nonetheless, we, my dear, have the morning to ourselves and you're taking me out to breakfast and to get me some new duds. I can't live in towels and the rest of Alan's stuff is still in the woods. The deer have probably eaten it by now."

"How did you get rid of her?" I asked in delighted amazement.

"Errands! Tons and tons of beautiful, time-consuming errands!" and he leaped from the bed. "Now hurry up and put on something beautiful, beautiful. You're also teaching me to drive this morning."

With that, he kissed the top of my head.

"Move your ass, shorty," he said, leaving the room.

Move? I flew.

Two ecstatic days later, I was in tears over the horror of it all.

It was late in the evening and we had been in the room together all day, hidden away from Sissy and the rest of the world.

"You'll go stir crazy if you don't get out of here," Charles said. "Go trot around the pond."

"I'm fine."

"You're bored."

"I am not. How could I be?" and I meant it. Just being with him was exhilarating.

"Well, I am. Shoo! I've got private things to do."

"What private things?"

He put his hands on my shoulders and pushed me gently toward the door. "If I told you, they wouldn't be private anymore. Now go take a walk, take a drive, take a powder." He turned me around to face him and smiled down at me. "But don't be gone too long." With that, he opened the door and nodded toward the hall. "Scram."

"A lot of thanks I get around here," I muttered, leaving.

As usual, I did as I was told and went out back to the pond. Charles was right; the night air felt marvelous. We had been cooped up too long. I'd have to figure a way to send Sissy off for a few days or else we might go. The latter appealed to me. A few days' drive through the countryside would be delightful, as long as I did the driving. The other morning Charles had displayed a somewhat daredevil attitude toward the car, simultaneously thrilling and terrifying me. I would definitely do the driving.

I sat down on the sloping lawn beside the pond and listened to the night noises. The katydids were in rare form, shrieking to each other in their lust; a lone bullfrog sounded like the thump of a bass fiddle; a bird somewhere in the woods vocalized. A little orchestra, I thought, and stretched out, my head cupped in my hands, to look at the stars.

I was so perfectly happy. Had I ever been as happy, I wondered, and without intending to, started to run my life through my mind, backwards. The summer, the spring and Alan's death, the years of our marriage, the years before it, my childhood . . . Yes, there were moments of perfect happiness in my childhood. Brief, but they were there. That first time Molly and I had pitched a tent in the woods and cowered in it all night against the sounds I now listened to with pleasure. What a funny, unforgettable night that was. And the boy in the third grade I had loved with all the passion only a child can feel and who, luckily,

loved me back for a while. I lay there on the moist
night grass smiling in remembrance of the joys of
growing up.

The joys Charles would never know.

It struck suddenly, that pathetic realization. Half
of life lay in one's childhood, while the world is new,
before the humdrumness hits. And Charles would
never know it.

For us.

I had been mad with selfishness; thinking only of
my own need for companionship, my own ancient
Greek loneliness. It hadn't occurred to me that while
Charles was growing, he was also dying, for so much
of his life was being carved away.

And I had been a willing accomplice to the
murder.

I started to cry, one of the few decent things I
had done in the past few weeks. I sat there, my face
in my hands and I mourned the death of half of
Charles's life.

I didn't hear him come up behind me, barefoot
on the soft grass.

"What is it?" he said, putting his arm around my
shoulder.

"Charles . . ." I startled, trying to hide that I was
crying. "But Sissy . . ."

"She's asleep. Kate, what's the matter?"

"Nothing."

"You're crying."

"No, I'm not."

"Of course you are. Is it something I've done?"
His voice was so gentle, the most beautiful of all the
night noises. "If it is, tell me so that I never do it
again. I'm still new at this business of being grown
up. Help me."

"Oh, Charles," and the tears came again, "stop this thing. Stop it now before any more of your life is gone . . ."

"My life *gone?*" And he held me. "Kate, darling Kate, my life is just beginning. Don't you know that?"

"No, it's disappearing. Day by day I see it disappear. You're robbing yourself of so much. . . ."

"Who's that out there!"

I spun around to see Sissy outlined in the back doorway, her fists defiantly on her hips.

"Lie down so she can't see you!" and Charles did. I got up, wiping the tears from my face and hurried to her.

"It's me, Sissy."

"Who's that out there with you?" she asked when I reached her.

"No one, just a friend."

"What friend?"

"Sissy, I don't think that's any of your business."

"Honey, what's goin' on around here?"

"Nothing. Will you please go back to bed now?"

"Somebody I know?" and she looked past me into the darkness around the pond. Charles was lying on the ground, pretending to look up at the night sky.

"Sissy, will you please go back to bed!"

"Somebody from around here?" she continued to peer at his outline.

"No, from the city. Now go to bed!"

"All right, all right," she relented, opening the door behind her, still trying to get a glimpse of him.

I closed the door when she was just inside and stood there until I heard the scuffling of her slippered feet in retreat.

We remained by the pond for an hour until I was sure she was asleep. Charles was right; Sissy would have to go.

The next morning I came down for the breakfast tray and received an additional third degree.

"From the city?" Sissy said as I got out the linen napkins.

"What?"

"Your friend, last night. You said he was from the city."

"That's right."

"How'd he get here? There was no car in the driveway 'cept yours and mine."

"I picked him up at the station."

"I didn't hear you drive out."

Another rage hit. "Sissy, don't you dare spy on me! It's none of your business who he was! You work here, do you understand that? You're an employee, not my mother!"

And of course, she started to cry.

"Oh, God, Sissy, I'm sorry."

Her massive body lurched back and forth as she wept; she might have been having a fit. I came up behind her and put my arms around her.

"I'm sorry," I said.

"I'm not your mother," she said, turning around and clinging to me, "but you was always my baby."

We stood that way for a while, holding on to each other, until I heard my bedroom door slam shut. Charles had been downstairs and had seen us.

By the time I got upstairs with the breakfast tray, he was already dressed and scowling out the window. I closed the door behind me.

"She has to go," was all that he said.

Silently, I put the tray on the bed and pulled up a chair.

"Did you hear me?"

"Yes, I heard you."

He turned from the window. "Kate, every time you leave this room, she's up here in a flash. I hear her outside. I even stuffed the keyhole because of her . . ."

"Charles, I don't know what to . . ."

"Darling, we've got to get rid of her," he said, and he took my hands in his and softened. "Do you realize what she could do? Molly's going to be well enough to leave the hospital soon. She could call her, tell her about me! Molly's still my legal guardian. Who the hell knows what she could do to me if she had a mind to! We've got to protect ourselves!"

"I know, I know . . ."

"I don't want to be separated from you," he said, and this time it was he who clung to me.

And I to him.

MOLLY

Physical therapy.

Let me tell you something about physical therapy. If Hitler had known the techniques, he'd still be around today. It's a wonder he didn't, because they must have been invented by his favorite author, the

Marquis de Sade. Honest, the car crash was a mosquito bite compared to the joys of physical therapy.

But boy, did I go at it. A gold star every day. And why? Because I knew I had to get out of that damn hospital and find out what was going on with Charlie.

A dope I'm not.

Was he sick? Was he dead? Did he run away? What the hell was going on? It was useless to ask Kate. I was sure she thought she was protecting me. I mean, what else could it be? She wasn't holding him for ransom, that was sure. But something was up.

I decided to do something about it, posthaste, before the old arms and legs were back in shape. My one ally, Sissy, was scared to talk. I had the feeling Kate was there each and every time she answered the phone, just waiting to snatch it from her. Who else, I wracked my brain, was there?

And then I remembered.

Dear, sweet old country bumpkin, Dr. Shit. Shill. Shoot. What the hell was his name?

The long distance operator was a doll and in a few minutes I was dialing Dr. *Shiff*.

"Doctor Shiff," he answered when his receptionist clicked him on.

I reintroduced myself and went through the social amenities with him, like a goddamn square dance. This one really liked to shoot the breeze. He finally shut up and I told him I was worried about Charlie, that he hadn't sounded too hot on the phone these past few days and I asked him if he'd take a run out there and give the kid the once-over.

Then he tells me about Kate's visit.

"Puberty?" I stared at the phone, wondering which of us was off his rocker. "Charlie is ten years old!"

And then he tells me about Kate's call where she just imagined the whole thing, and all the time I'm thinking I've got to get off the phone and back to my sacred physical therapy.

Anyway, the upshot of the call was this: The good doctor would pay Charlie an unannounced visit and report back to me on the double.

My spy ring was in motion.

Incidentally, I ought to mention that I had followed old Nurse Golden one night, thanks to physical therapy, and knew exactly where they kept the Demerols.

KATE

"Hirsute," I said, and Charles stared at me blankly. "Hirsute," I repeated.

"There's no such word."

"Oh, isn't there?" I looked down at the dictionary in my lap. "Come on, *hirsute*."

"An item of women's apparel," he answered, and I laughed.

"Did you or did you not study the H's?"

"I did, your honor, but I maintain there was no hirsute among them."

"It means 'hairy.' "

"Ah, so," and he touched his hair, which was in need of a trim. "As in, somebody around here is getting pretty *hirsute* so why doesn't somebody else put down the dictionary and get the scissors."

"Yes, *mein führer*," and I heard the front doorbell ring downstairs. "Who on earth could that be?" We never had visitors. "Stay in here," I said, leaving the room.

Molly? No, of course not. Still—

I hurried down the stairs and saw Sissy escort Dr. Shiff into the living room. Oh Lord, what did he want?

"Good morning, Doctor Shiff," I said, calmly as I could manage. "What brings you out to this neck of the woods?"

"I was visiting the Thompsons down the road. Their little one's got the flu . . ."

A lie.

". . . And I thought long as I was out this way, I might as well stop in and see how you're doing."

"Just fine," I said lightly, trying to hide my anger. How dare he come uninvited into my house to spy on me. "But I told you that on the phone."

"So you did, so you did. You're looking good," he went on with his unwanted examination. "Rested."

"Yes, I'm feeling perfectly well, Doctor Shiff," and I started toward the door, indicating that I wanted him to go.

"Long as I'm here," he said planting himself firmly, resolutely in the middle of the room, "maybe I ought to take a look at that nephew of yours, just to put things to rest."

"Things are perfectly at rest, doctor," I said from the doorway. "Besides, he's out playing."

Playing. The mental picture of Charles, the Charles who now existed, out *playing* made me smile. Unfortunately, the doctor took that to mean I would relent in my wanting him to leave and he sat down.

"Why don't you call him in? It'd just take a few minutes and then we could all relax."

"We are all relaxed, doctor. At least Charles and I are."

"Well, it never hurts to get a professional opinion," and he tried to appear casual and failed. "No charge, of course. I'm not one of those city specialists who charges you to say hello," he chuckled.

"I know you're not," and my chuckle came out a sneer. "But I really have no idea where he is. He's so big now he wanders all over the place." If you only knew how big, you interfering old man, wouldn't you be surprised? I'd like to see you pouring over your moldy medical books, trying to find a Latin name for what's happened to Charles.

"Well, why don't we give it a try?" he said, smiling.

"I'm afraid I'm much too busy at the moment . . ."

The phone in the hall rang. Just what I needed; another of Molly's inquisitions with Dr. Watson already here.

"Excuse me," and I answered it.

It was the good doctor's receptionist. I called him and he took it.

"I'm afraid I've got to go. Emergency," he said, heading toward the front door. "Another lawnmower's struck. People ought to be more careful; lawnmowers are dangerous."

He was halfway out the door when I stopped him.

"Doctor Shiff?"

"Yes?"

"How did she know you'd be here?"

He looked back at me and missed a beat. "I must have mentioned that I might drop by."

"I see," I said, smiling, and closed the door.

"*Indigent,*" Charles read aloud as I entered the room.

"Lazy."

"Wrong, teach. It means 'poor.' Who was that?"

"Doctor Shiff, who just *happened* to be out this way and wanted to get a look at you."

"Why?" Charles asked, looking suddenly worried.

"Oh, darling, I did something I shouldn't have . . ."

And I told him about my stupid visit with the doctor, promising once again that no one would see him as long as I was there to protect him.

It was hardly a day later that my promise was broken.

I had to drive to town for vitamins, Charles devoured them by the handful, and when I pulled up in front of the house, the first thing I saw was Sissy, sitting on the steps. I got out of the car, thinking nothing of it until I drew near her and saw the look on her face.

The look I had had at the gazebo.

"Sissy? What is it?"

She glanced at me momentarily and then off again, into the distance. "God help us," she said.

I raced into the house and upstairs. Charles was sitting on the bed. He looked like a caged animal.

"What happened?" I asked.

"She saw me."

MOLLY

Left, right, left, right, see little Molly walk down the hospital hallway. See Molly's crutches. Hear Molly's curses. Left, shit, right, crap.

But I'm getting there. *Every day in every way*, to quote whatever-it-is. It's just a matter of time and I'd be giving the finger to all those wonderful people in white.

And the whole hand to Charlie's backside, once I found out what the hell he was up to.

I was halfway down the hall when one of the nurses told me I had a call. I left-righted back to my room and, almost exhausted, answered it.

It was Dr. Shiff with the worst excuse for a detective's report I ever heard. Charlie was out playing, Kate seemed fine, there didn't seem to be anything to worry about. Well, why argue with the nitwit? I thanked him for his trouble, asked him to keep trying to see Charlie and hung up.

Putz.

KATE

"I told you not to go out," Charles said accusingly. "I knew she'd try to get in here . . ."

"Charles, calm down and tell me what happened."

"What happened? Just what I said would happen! You were gone no more than five minutes when the door flew open and there she was, standing there, staring at me!" He paced back and forth, wringing his hands in front of him, shivering with fear. "Kate, what are we going to do?"

"Calm down, baby. I'll take care of it."

"How?" In his eyes I could see the old Charles, the child who needed me.

"I don't know yet. What did she say?"

"Nothing! She just stared at me like I was some kind of monster and then ran off." He sat down on the bed and held his face in his hands.

I went to him and held him. My poor baby. My poor frightened beautiful baby.

"It'll be all right. I'll take care of everything."

Sissy was in her room. I knocked several times without response.

"Sissy? It's Kate. Open the door."

"You alone?"

"Oh, for pity's sake! Yes, I'm alone. Open the damn door."

She did, slowly, and I saw she was holding her Bible, no doubt for protection from Charles.

"What's going on?" I asked.

"I seen him," she said, clutching that book as if it were a shield.

"You saw who?"

"You know who. Charles."

That was it then; she knew. It would be useless to argue the point, that would alienate her; no, I had to win her over, to make her a willing member of our conspiracy.

The book was my clue.

"You believe in God, don't you, Sissy?"

"Yes," she answered warily, studying me.

"Then you believe God can create miracles, don't you?"

She hesitated, no doubt wondering whether she needed protection from me as well, and then she said, "Yes."

"That's what you saw, Sissy. A miracle. Charles has been touched by God. I don't know for what purpose, he doesn't either, but I do know that it's up to us, to you and to me, to help him. To help this miracle."

She stood in the corner of her small room, back against the wall and it occurred to me that she was afraid of me. Perhaps she was right to be, for as I spoke I realized there wasn't anything I wouldn't do to protect Charles. Anything.

"I know it's hard to understand," I continued my heretic sermon. "I'm not sure that we can understand it or that we ought to. All I know is that I've been given an opportunity. An opportunity to serve some higher purpose than my own life and I'm committed to it. I want you to become committed to it, too, Sissy. He needs you . . ."

And all the while I spoke she stared at me without emotion, still clutching that book.

"Talk to him, Sissy. You'll see what I see. The greatness that shines out of him. Believe in him, Sissy. Trust him and believe in him."

It occurred to me that I was going too far; had she been more sophisticated she might have laughed. But then, she was Sissy, born to a heritage of slaves and voodoo. She didn't laugh.

She simply said, "The devil also makes miracles."

"She promised she wouldn't say anything to anyone," I told Charles.

"And you believe her?" he asked, that same panic in his eyes.

Now there were two of them to look after; two frightened children. Perhaps the best thing for both would be to face each other.

"I want you to come downstairs and talk to her, Charles."

"What? I can't!"

"Of course you can," I took his trembling hand. "Just talk to her. Right now she thinks you're some kind of demon. Let her see what you really are. How sweet and . . ."

He pulled away from me sharply. "Maybe she's right. Maybe I am a demon."

"Oh, darling, don't," and I held out my hands to him. "You're no demon. I know that. Let Sissy see it, too. Then we can leave this room. We can be free."

He came toward me reluctantly, put his hands in mine and suddenly held me in his arms. "I love you," he said.

"I love you, too," I answered, not sure of how either of us meant it.

"I'll come down to dinner," he said, and finally smiled.

"Good."

"Who knows," he added, "I can always keep her quiet by threatening to turn her into a frog."

"I'm sure it won't come to that," I said, not sure at all.

Dinner was . . . how shall I put it? A very quiet, restrained Armageddon, which had exactly the reverse effect I hoped for. Sissy said nothing throughout the serving of the meal. No, I don't mean she said virtually nothing or next to nothing. *Nothing*. Not one word. Not even one of her characteristic grunts. In comparison to her, Charles was positively chatty. He, at least, thanked her as she placed his meal before him. Once, I think, he even complimented her cooking, to which she looked quickly at him and then instantly away, as if the sight of him might turn her into a pillar of salt. I started the meal intent on trying to make the mood casual, but I soon gave that up and joined in the grand silence.

After Sissy had served coffee and broken some speed record getting back to the safety of her room, I turned to Charles.

"We'll have to try again," I said.

"I still think the frog idea was best," he said, and our mood lightened.

It was wonderfully liberating to be having the meal in the dining room. That, at least, was something to be grateful for.

"Now that we're not prisoners anymore, how about a walk down to the lake?" I suggested.

"Done," and he got up. "Or better still, how about a swim?"

"In the pond?"

"No, in the lake. I recall the last swim I had in the pond. I don't want to get whacked again."

The picture returned. Me on top of Charles, when he was little, the downward pull of the swim-suit—I think I may have blushed at that moment.

"Very well, last one in his swimsuit is a rotten egg."

"Swimsuit?" Charles stopped at the foot of the stairs. "Guess who doesn't own one?"

"Oh, dear, we forgot."

"That's okay," he said. "You get in yours."

"What will you do?"

"I'll skinny-dip." And he must have seen the look of embarrassment flash across my face. "You can keep your eyes closed, chicken."

I obeyed and in a few minutes we were stumbling through the woods, laughing, drunk on our new freedom.

We came out on the lake, a huge silvered mirror lying there, waiting to be hung. Yes, I was more than a little poetic that evening, what with Sissy apparently assuaged to some degree, and the cell door closed behind Charles and me.

"In we go!" he shouted, running toward the embankment.

I followed slowly, dreamily. The setting was perfect, the night warm, the stars everywhere. As I took off my robe, standing several yards from Charles, I smiled over at him and watched.

I watched as he took his shirt off and tossed it in the air with a whoop, still the excitable child. I watched as he stepped out of his shoes and threat-ened, laughingly, to throw them into the water.

And I watched as he slipped out of his pants and stood there, a grown man in the moonlight, naked.

I finally averted my eyes, but too late. I had seen what I didn't wish to see and had felt the flush I didn't wish to feel. *Blasphemy*.

I hurried into the cold water as Charles did and quickly forgot the guilty moment. I swam it away, going far out into the lake.

"Hey, Florence Chadwick, remember me?" Charles was calling to me.

I swam back and stopped a few feet from him, a few *safe* feet.

"Teach me how to swim," he said.

"You know how."

"Not the way you do," and he pushed his palm into the water, splashing me.

"If you don't stop that, I'll teach you how to drown," I sputtered.

"Says who?" and he splashed me again.

Instinctively, I dove under the water toward him. I grabbed both his ankles and pulled hard, toppling him. When we came up, we were both laughing.

"That's war!" he said, grabbing my wrist.

I flipped over on my back and kicked my feet, dousing him. "Give up?"

"Never!" and he pulled me toward him. My feet went down to the bottom and I was standing, pulling away. He was stronger.

"Now you'll pay!" he said and pulled me easily into his arms.

I felt his body on mine and we froze. Then, real-izing what we were doing, I said in a voice far colder than I intended, "Let me go."

He released me quickly.

"I'm going in," I said. "I'm cold."

"I'll go with you."

I left the water and went to my robe, putting it on while facing away from him. I started toward the woods. He caught up with me as I entered the path and we went through the woods in silence. Once out, in view of the pond, Charles spoke.

"I always seem to get in Dutch when I go swimming, don't I?"

"Maybe you ought to take up golf," I said. "Come on, let's not sulk. I'll go through the L's with you."

"Loggerhead, lithic, libertine," he chanted.

Things got steadily worse with Sissy. The next day, she claimed she was sick and spent the day sequestered in her room.

The day after that, she emerged, none the worse for wear, and went about her chores mutely. If Charles entered a room, she left it immediately. When I tried to talk to her, I was met with stony silence.

On the third day, we had it out.

In all the years I'd known her, I'd never seen Sissy's full anger before, but I saw it that day. We stood in the living room like prizefighters, circling each other, at first arguing, then screaming. She had decided, resolutely in her gospel-voodoo-jungle-Bible-thumping way, that Charles was evil; that his growth was ungodly; that he and I were possessed.

"What do you have, a direct line to God?" I asked, furious.

"Baby, think! It don't take no college degree to know that *thing* upstairs is the work of the devil!"

"How dare you!" I sputtered. "How dare you

judge him or me! You're exactly what he was afraid of, narrow-minded, bigotted . . ."

"He got you believin' him. Child, wake up before it's too late. Get him outa here!"

"What are you going to do about it?" I asked very quietly, for the shouting was accomplishing nothing.

She didn't answer.

"What are you going to do about it?" I repeated.

She looked at me and once again I saw the hidden fear.

"I don't know," she finally spoke.

It was then I decided to let her go.

It took several days to arrange for Sissy's money. In that time I avoided open conflict with her. That part was simple enough, for she had fallen into a brooding muteness.

The morning her check arrived, I determined to wait until evening to tell her. She would have to leave the next day. I spent the afternoon by the pond with Charles, reading, helping him study, trying to numb myself to the guilt I felt over Sissy.

Forty-two years she had been with us. She had been my mother, my safety, my source of love.

That night Sissy and I sat across the kitchen table from each other for the last time.

And she told me about my mother.

MOLLY

I had had it. Sister or no sister, I was going to call the cops and get them out there. One way or another, they'd get my kid on the phone or haul him back to town. He could sit in a corner of my hospital room for as long as it took, I didn't care. Anything would be better than the fantasies I was having.

Jesus, the fantasies!

She thought he reached puberty? How the hell would she know, anyway?

Oh boy, the fantasies.

But, sap that I am, I decided to call her first and lay it on the line.

Which is just what I would've done, but for the grace of AT&T. The phones all over the area were out. Honest to God, talk about your narrow escapes.

One more day, I decided. I'll give Kate one more day and then, phone or no phone, I'll get my kid.

In the meantime, however, I'd pop another Demerol; part of the little cache I stole when Golden wasn't watching.

Might as well have some fun while I waited, no?

KATE

"There's things you don't know about your mama," Sissy started, and I felt myself tighten to the onslaught. "After your daddy died, she kinda went to pieces. Maybe you don't remember, but she spent most of her time upstairs, locked up in her room . . ."

"I remember," I said. Indeed I did. I remembered a hundred times when I wanted her, needed her, and she wasn't there.

"Losin' somebody you love is hard on some people, mighty hard," she said, as if I didn't already know. As if I hadn't lost Alan mere months before. "Your mama didn't have nothin' to hold onto after he died. She wasn't a religious woman and somehow instead of turnin' to you and Molly, she turned inside herself. I seen it before. That's why it's so important to keep God alive in yourself, honey," and she took my hand as if willing Him through herself into me. "Instead, your mama took to drinkin'." She avoided my eyes at that, again as if she were telling me something I didn't already know. Has she forgotten, I wondered, the many times Molly and I took mother's empty liquor bottles, put SOS notes in them and hurled them into the middle of the pond, only to wait, uselessly, to be rescued?

"And at night," she went on, frowning with remembered pain, "after you and Molly was asleep, she'd take out the car and drive along the back roads, sometimes when she was drunk. Child, I begged her not to! I begged and begged but she wouldn't listen to me!"

I suddenly knew where the story was going.

"I don't want to hear anymore," I said, getting up. "It has nothing to do with me and Charles."

"Baby, you gotta know. To save yourself. You got some of your mama in you and you gotta fight it. You gotta believe in God and not do this awful thing!"

I sat down.

"One night, real late, I heard your mama's car pull up." Sissy went on and as she did she hung her head down as if ashamed. "She come to my room, all drunk and cryin'. There was an accident. She hit somebody on one of the back roads. I asked her if they was all right but she didn't know. She drove back home without stoppin'. I got up and dressed myself. I told her we had to go back there to see if they was all right. But when we got out to the car, God help us . . ." Her hands were over her mouth, trying to prevent the ancient truth from coming out, "God help us, Katie, there was . . . there was . . ."

"What?"

"Blood and . . . things . . . all over the front of the car. He must've got caught up in the grill on the car . . . She must've dragged him . . ."

I was so cold. So terribly cold.

"But we drove back out anyways . . . Till we found him . . . A little boy, Katie! It was a little boy!"

The Harley boy. I didn't feel the cold anymore; I was numb.

"Your mama, she got hysterical when she seen him. She started in cryin' they was gonna lock her up; they was gonna put her with terrible women in prison or maybe tie her up in the electric chair. And she started in beggin' me and prayin' to me to help her, that I was the only one she could turn to, that she didn't mean to do it and I had to help her so they wouldn't tie her up in the electric chair!"

Sissy stopped for a moment, exhausted, and I felt myself floating on a lake of glandular secretions, almost calm, wanting desperately to sleep.

"Go on," I called to her from the middle of the lake.

"We buried him in the woods, your mama and me and then we came back home and she went to sleep. I washed the car all night long. I scrubbed and scrubbed till there was nothin' left on the front for nobody to see. Then I went into my room and read The Good Book till I fell asleep. The next thing I knew, you and Molly was shakin' me, wantin' your breakfast. So I got up and fed you and prayed to God that nobody would ever know."

Silence again.

"And they never did," I said, coming closer to shore.

"Not till this minute," she answered. "But your mama knew. She knew all right. She stopped sleepin' that night. And when she'd try, she'd wake up, dreamin' she was drivin' down that road and hittin' him all over again. Then she'd get up and drive out there, to the woods where we buried him. Every night she'd drive out there, to check nobody found him, to ask forgiveness beside his grave. Two, three times a night she went there till she nearly went crazy from worry and lack of sleep. She didn't mean to do it, Katie. Your mama wasn't a bad woman, just troubled, terrible troubled."

Mother and the Harley boy. Me and Charles.

"Then, finally, she couldn't take it no more and

she told me to watch over you and Molly, that she had to go away. To go away for good . . ."

She with a car. Me with silence.

"She didn't want to leave you, Katie, but she had to go. If she stayed here, she'd have gone crazy . . ."

One life ended. One cut in half.

"She went down South somewhere last I heard. She wrote me to take care of her little girls, to tell them only good things about her . . ."

The curse of our family, still potent, still taking the lives of children.

"Then the letters stopped. I never heard nothin' about her no more. I guess somethin' bad happened, otherwise she would've come back one day to see her girls . . ."

I got up and went toward the door. My hand on the knob, I turned to Sissy.

"I want you to go," I said. "I want you to go tomorrow."

"But where will I go?" she asked.

"Go down South. Go and find my mother," I answered, leaving the room.

Thus I chose; villainy over decency, evil over good, Charles over Sissy.

For that was my heritage.

I was on my way upstairs to Charles when Alan, almost forgotten, appeared at the top of the stairs.

"Hello, stranger," he said, unsmiling.

"Go away, Alan. I don't want to see you now."

"Why not? Too guilty to face me?" and he sat down on the top stair, blocking my way.

"Charles is waiting for me."

"Let him wait. Proud of yourself?" he asked.

"No."

"Why not? You haven't done anything any red-blooded vampire wouldn't have done. Kicked an old lady out so you can be alone with Charles for your little incestuous relationship . . ."

"There's no question of incest," I snapped.

"Oh, really? Then what happened down at the lake?" and this time he did smile, derisively.

"Nothing happened. Nothing's going to happen."

"You're a fool, Kate. You've called me back from the grave to con both of us. I was there, you know, at the lake. I saw you look at him. Tell me, how does he compare to me? It isn't fair to make a comparison. After all, he wasn't aroused, but it's just a matter of time. . . ."

"Stop it, Alan!"

". . . now that you've gotten rid of Sissy, you two can . . ."

"Please!"

I tried to push past him but he stood up and held me tight by the shoulders.

". . . or aren't you going to wait until Sissy leaves? Are you going up there now to . . ."

And before he could finish his vile accusation, Alan was gone. I looked down at my hand and saw why. I had tightened my fist so hard I had driven a fingernail into my palm.

Upstairs, my room was empty; there was a note on the bed in Charles's still childlike handwriting:
Kate, look in the backseat of the car.

I hurried out of the house, down the stairs where Alan had accused me, past the kitchen from which I heard Sissy's muffled sobs in testimony to my guilt, past the phone I had used to torture my own sister.

Doomed, I thought as I rushed out into the black night. I'm doomed.

The backseat of the car was dimly lit, as if by a flashlight.

Eternal damnation. Yes, that's what Sissy would say. Eternal damnation.

I came upon the car and saw Charles sitting in the backseat, to one side.

"Your coach awaits, Cinderella," he called to me.

I opened the door.

Next to him, on the seat, was father's silver tray and on it a bottle of champagne and two goblets.

"You won't stop me from drinking with you this time, will you?" he asked.

I would never stop Charles from doing anything again. As I slid into the car I thought I heard the distant sound of a gavel being struck and a sentence given.

The next afternoon Charles carried Sissy's suitcases out to her car and put them in the trunk. I watched as he did, growing more and more depressed. So few suitcases after a lifetime in this house. So little to show for giving her heart to a family of—what had Alan called me?—vampires. That's what we were. Father had sucked the blood from us all, placing this house and his possessions ahead of us. Mother had drained the life from the Harley boy, as I was doing to Charles, for now I realized why Charles had changed.

For us? No, it hadn't been for us. It had been for me.

Sissy came out of the house, wearing her one good dress, now ancient. I remembered a thousand Sunday mornings when Molly and I would watch her come out of the house in that dress to go to church. And a thousand Sunday afternoons when she returned, changed into one of her work dresses and prepared the Sabbath meal. We had laughed when she called it that. I could almost hear the laughter of those two lost children, and it sounded maniacal in retrospect.

I went up to Sissy who stood in front of her car, looking back at the house in farewell.

"Sissy . . ." I started but couldn't continue.

She put her arms around me and I smelled her hair for the last time.

"Don't worry 'bout me, honey," she said. "I just pray you'll come to your senses."

"Forgive me, Sissy," I said. "My life is so empty without him."

We held to each other for a moment and then I broke away. "Where will you go?"

"I got a cousin in Mississippi. I'll go see her."

"If you ever need anything . . ."

"Honey, you already gave me more money than I ever saw before," and she smiled tenderly.

"If you need more . . ."

"I won't," and she got into the car. She rolled the front window down before she drove away from the house she had lived in for four decades and the child who had turned on her.

"I love you, baby," she said.

"I love you, Sissy," I answered.

I napped later that afternoon and dreamed.

I was walking somewhere in the city, watching the people in their gaudy costumes; it was some kind of Mardi Gras, I think. A man passed me dressed as a dog and I remembered I had a dog at home, a puppy. How long had it been since I'd been home? Had I left food for it? I became concerned and hurried through

147

the crowds to my apartment house. Running up the stairs, I heard no whimpering, no sign that it was waiting for me. I opened my apartment door and saw it sitting there in the middle of the hall, its head hung low, starving, too weak to come to me, its coat matted with its own excrement; it was dying.

Charles shook me out of the dream.

"The telephone's ringing," he said.

I got up slowly.

"It's been ringing for a while," he said. "It must be Molly."

I went downstairs; the phone must have rung six or seven times that I had heard. I picked up the receiver.

"Well, it's about time," Molly said angrily. "Where were you?"

"I'm sorry, I was asleep."

"Terrific. Where's Sissy?"

"Out," I answered.

"I suppose Charlie's out, too?"

"Yes."

"It figures. Okay, Kate, here goes. You better hold on to something," and she started.

She would call the police unless I put Charles on the phone, or explained fully why I hadn't before. I was still half asleep and groped for an explanation.

I recalled what Charles had told me about his last visit with his mother; that terrible fight in the hospital.

"Molly, he is here but he refuses to talk to you."

"What do you mean, he refuses to talk to me? You tell him to get his ass on this phone or . . ."

"I've tried a hundred times, Molly. It's no use," and I quickly conjured up the picture of Charles as he had been, to make the lying easier. "I've sent him to bed without his dinner, I've spanked him, nothing works. I didn't want to tell you because I thought you would be too hurt . . ."

"Hurt? Wait'll I get there, then you'll see who's hurt. That little bastard!"

She believed me. Thank God she believed me.

"You should've told me, Kate."

"I know, but how do you tell a mother her own child refuses to talk to her?"

"Listen, that's a lot easier to take than some of the things I've been thinking."

"What have you been thinking?" I asked, almost afraid to hear her reply.

"Never mind, you'll think I flipped out. Who knows, maybe I did."

Then she did suspect something after all. I had to put an end to those suspicions. And what better way than to join her in complaining about an unruly child? A normal, ten-year-old unruly child.

"It's been no picnic here without you," I said. "Charles gets ruder by the day. I suppose he's going through some phase or other . . ." Make it sound normal. Don't alarm her. ". . . sometimes he's sweet as a lamb and other times he's a little devil . . ." A little devil, like all normal ten-year-olds. Now blame yourself. ". . . I don't suppose I'm the best disciplinarian who ever walked the earth . . ." Give an example. A nice normal example. ". . . the other day he brought home a jar of tadpoles . . ." A bad choice. A silly choice. ". . . I finally gave in and let him keep them . . ." On and on I went, inventing complaints that sounded more like a TV sitcom than reality, but luckily that was what Molly wanted to hear, for she calmed and eventually even laughed.

"Listen," she said, "I owe you one. Hey, I've got

some good news. They're letting me out of here in a week. So you can put the little monster in the car and come get me. At least the rest of your summer'll be saved . . ."

One week! That was all the time we had!

I looked up the stairs in panic; Charles was standing there. He saw my expression and hurried to me, taking me in his arms.

"That'll be wonderful, Molly," I said, resting my head on his chest. "Look, I'd better go do the shopping or they'll be nothing to eat tonight and I promised my nephew franks and beans if he's good."

Charles ran a finger across the frown lines in my forehead and I smiled up weakly at him.

"Just don't put any rat poison in it," Molly said. "At least not until I get there."

As I hung up, Charles cupped my face in his enormous hand and said, "I heard it all. You'll make a great counterspy someday."

"Molly's getting out in a week."

"Then we'll have to make some plans," he said calmly, and kissed my forehead.

MOLLY

Talk about your fool's paradise. This fool spent the rest of the day happy as a goddamn lark. Nothing was up at the old homestead; nothing except the usual, but that I could handle. I pictured myself at the house, sprawled out on a chaise beside the pond, Sissy waiting on me hand and foot, barking orders at Charlie, getting him in line, popping Demerols . . . ah, that was the life.

Like I said, a fool's paradise.

KATE

The next morning I awoke to find the house empty. On the kitchen table was a note from Charles:

Get the griddle going, Katie, my girl. I'm driving into town, God help us all. Will be back shortly, if I don't mistake the gas peddle for the brake. Chuck.

I didn't find his last statement amusing; we had driven together several times in the last few days and Charles was not precisely dependable behind the wheel. He drove the car as he had his bicycle a few weeks before; daredevil tricks, showing off, the whole gamut of childishness. As I prepared breakfast, an ordinary breakfast, for Charles's appetite had diminished dramatically as his growth slowed, I wondered about this strange mixture of adult and child in him. In so many ways he was more than grown; he was sensitive, intuitive, wonderfully bright and caring. But then, just as I supposed he was completely mature, some sign of his true age would show itself.

Like the night before.

It had been a horrendous day what with sending Sissy off and dealing with Molly. All I wanted after dinner was to soak in a hot tub and go directly to bed, but Charles would have none of it.

"I've got an idea," he announced over dessert. "Let's drive over to the roadhouse and go dancing. You can teach me."

"Oh, God, not tonight, Charles. I'm exhausted."

"No, you're not . . ."

"Charles, believe me. I'm the one inside this body and I'm telling you, it's just about ready to pass out."

"Don't be an old lady."

"I am an old lady, kiddo. I'm forty-one, going on a hundred."

"Big deal. For all we know, I'm older than you now."

I studied his face, wondering about that. He had filled out completely by now but he still looked boyish to me.

"Late twenties," I said.

"Early thirties is more like it."

"Early thirties, my foot. You still don't have a wrinkle on your face."

"I've got lots," and he squinted at me, causing laugh lines. "Let's go dancing."

"No."

"Yes."

"Charles . . ."

"Yes, yes, yes . . ."

"Please don't . . ."

"Charles wanna go dancing!" he pouted. "Charles is ten and will throw a tantrum unless Aunty Kate takes him dancing!"

"Don't," I said, suddenly terribly upset.

"Wanna go! Wanna go!" and he pounded his fists on the table.

Inexplicably, I burst into tears.

"Jesus, Kate, what's the matter?" He pulled his chair next to me.

"I don't know," I looked away. "I don't know."

"Honey, I was just kidding around."

"I know . . ."

"You're still frightened by all this, aren't you?"

I didn't answer.

"What did you think, that I had reverted? That you'd have a six-foot ten-year-old on your hands?"

I smiled slightly to show him how silly the idea was, but had it indeed been what went through my mind?

"I was just kidding," he reassured me.

"I know. I'm being silly," I said, sniffling.

"So, how about it? Do we go dancing?"

"Charles . . ."

Eventually, I won and went upstairs to bed but not before I recognized the problems that would lie ahead in dealing with both sides of Charles.

Breakfast was nearly ready when I heard the car pull up and screech to a gear-stripping stop. He bounded into the house, calling to me.

"Kate? Up and at 'em!"

"In the kitchen," I called back.

He entered, beaming with triumph. "Four minutes flat from the gas station to the front door. Move over, Mario Andretti."

"It isn't funny, Charles. We already have one member of the family in the hospital from a car accident, we don't need another."

"Okay, okay, lecture me over breakfast. I'm starved."

"You're always starved," I answered, sulking.

"What're you up in arms about?" he asked, trying to kiss my cheek but missing as I moved my face away.

"Just cranky," I answered, thinking about his selfishness the night before.

"Well, knock it off," and he pulled my face toward him and kissed my cheek against my will.

"Don't do that," I said.

"You are cranky, aren't you? Well, I've got news to decrank you. Look at these," and he fanned out a stack of road maps. "We're going on a trip."

"What?"

"We're leaving Friday morning for the open road..."

"Friday?" I stammered. "When did all this happen?"

"This morning while you were snoring. We really have to do something about your adenoids, old girl. Anyway, I decided, since Molly's coming here, the best thing for us to do is hit the road. We'll go through New England, see Mystic, maybe up to Provincetown..."

"But . . ." I said, nonplussed.

"But what, pussycat?" he asked, seriously.

"We'd be running away," I said, thinking of Molly arriving to find an empty house, that is, if she could find a way to get here.

"That's right. On the lam. Can you think of anything better to do?"

Of course, I couldn't. Charles was right; better to be two fugitives for a precious while than to face Molly and the inevitable.

Time. Time to earn my damnation.

MOLLY

My pardon was set for Monday morning when, sporting a cast to the knee and a back brace, I would finally rejoin the world of the living. I had already made two more middle-of-the-night sojourns to the drug shrine and come away with a nice little collection of Dems. A couple more trips and I could open up my own happy shop. By the way, if anybody ever tells you crime doesn't pay, laugh in his face.

So, early Friday morning I called Kate to give her the good news.

No answer.

No answer in the afternoon, either.

Or the evening.

Or two o'clock in the A.M.

Where the hell was everybody?

KATE

Off the road we were driving on, to the left, was one of those calendar farms: white stone buildings, a silo, white picket fence, cows, MGM couldn't have planned it better. I slowed down so we could get a better look at it; yes, after some extensive discussion I had ended up behind the wheel.

"Shall we buy a farm someday?" Charles asked. "I'd like to see you in a gingham dress collecting eggs . . ."

"Stepping in cow manure," I added.

"Come on, you're not one of those city girls who's afraid of a little cow flop, are you?"

"Not afraid, but it's never made my list of all-time favorites," and I stepped on the gas.

"All right, then," Charles stretched and leaned his head back on the seat, thoroughly enjoying himself, "we'll live in the city and hang out in smoky nightclubs and get terribly pale and sardonic . . ." and he went on and on painting his pictures.

Planning our future. What future, I wondered? We had been driving the better part of the day. Half of one day gone. How many more days would we have before it was all over? Before we went back to face Molly and whatever punishment was waiting?

What could they do to us? Was this a crime? It felt like one, surely, but who was the victim? Charles, who rambled on, happier than I'd ever seen him? Molly, who had yet to discover she'd lost a child?

Yes, of course, it was Molly.

"Hey, if you're going to think so much, do it out loud," Charles said.

"I'm hungry," I said, avoiding the truth.

"Well, for once I'm not. Let's not stop yet. I want to get to . . ." and he consulted his map, "Pinksville. I want to see if all the buildings are pink and the people. Maybe we'll see a pink cow. You ever see a pink cow, Katie?"

"Nope. The most I ever saw was a pink lady."

"What's that?"

"A drink."

"God, I'm so ignorant," he said, and leaned over to kiss my cheek. "But you'll teach me, won't you?"

"Uh-huh," and the gentleness of the kiss drove Molly from my mind.

We had a late lunch in a roadside stand whose signs boasted homemade everything from chili to apple pie, but if they were homemade, it was in a home I didn't care to be invited back to. As we drove away, I felt tired and bloated. I suggested we look around for a motel in which to spend the rest of the afternoon and night.

"Not yet," Charles said. "I want to see the world. We've hardly started."

"Charles, I'm tired of driving."

"Then I'll drive."

"I didn't say I was tired of living, just driving."

"Come on, Kate, look at those green hills, just over the next one is a vista that'll knock your eyes out. Don't give up yet."

"All right," I said, but my tone was obviously annoyed.

After a moment Charles said, "I'm sorry. Let's stop at the next motel we see."

"It's all right, we can drive for a while."

"No, you want to stop, we stop."

"I'm not falling asleep, Charles, it's all right . . ."

"No way. Kate's tired, Kate must rest. We'll see the vista tomorrow. Right now we're going to find you a nice motel with a pool and a TV set and a bar that serves pink ladies. I'm going to take care of you, kiddo. That's my job."

"Is it?" I asked, wanting to believe that more than anything.

"You'll see," he answered.

Ten minutes later we passed a sign pointing off the road to a local flea market and Charles insisted we go.

We reached the Motel in the Woods around five. It was an assortment of half a dozen small wooden bungalows, each slightly different, all boringly the same. They faced the highway with their backs up against a small grove of trees, presumably the woods they were named after. There was a space carved out of the woods and in it had been placed a pool, which looked as if it had been dropped there by mistake. Next to the pool, a soft-drink machine and a pay phone, around it a group of chaises the same plastic blue color as the pool's water. We entered the central bungalow, which had a handwritten sign "Office" on the door. Behind a desk there sat a woman staring at a portable television set, intent on a *Marcus Welby* rerun.

"We'd like a room," Charles said with an air of self-importance that surprised me.

"How long?" the woman asked, her eyes still on the set.

"Just for the night," he answered offhandedly.

"Number six. Twelve dollars," she said, turning the register around toward us. She looked at us then and an eyebrow raised imperceptibly. "Cash or charge?"

Charles glanced at me surreptitiously.

"Charge," I said.

"Sign the register," and she smiled to herself.

Of course. An older woman with a younger man,

the woman paying. I went to the window and stared out, too embarrassed to stand by the desk.

"Here's your key. Checkout's at eleven," I heard her say behind my back.

Charles opened the door to cabin six and we went inside. Now I was not only tired but depressed as well. The room had a history of transience about it: the cigarette burns on its Formica-mahogany-look-alike furniture, the garish bedspreads on its twin beds that matched the ill-made curtains, the stained carpeting. Everything in the room bespoke a quiet squalor. I sat on one of the beds as Charles went for our suitcases, thoroughly wretched and humiliated.

But then, wasn't this exactly what I should have expected? A hideout rather than a hideaway. A room off a road with none of the pretentions to decency that I struggled to keep. The punishment was beginning.

"Be it ever so humble," Charles said, closing the door behind him. "Hey, what's the matter?"

"I'm just tired," I lied.

"Why don't you stretch out for a while? I'll go scout the area for somewhere to have dinner."

"All right," I answered. "But please, Charles, drive carefully. If a policeman stops you, you don't have a license. We could get in an awful lot of trouble."

"Worrywart," he said, kissing the top of my head, which irritated me. "Sack out. I'll be back later, God willing."

"Don't joke with me, Charles. I am worried about your driving."

"No more than thirty miles an hour, I promise," he said, blowing me a kiss. "Beddy-bye."

As I heard him drive off, I wondered why so

many things annoyed me about him that day. I was getting as irritable as he had been weeks before. Perhaps, I thought, stretching out, I would also change for the better. Too much to ask for, I decided, and closed my eyes.

"Hey, sleepyhead, it's after seven," I heard Charles call to me from far away. I had been pushing Molly's wheelchair around the pond to her. She was sitting dangling her feet in the water, fully grown but dressed in a pinafore she had worn when we were children.

"Katie, my love, time to wake up," Charles called.

"Don't go, Kate," Molly said. "I need you to help me into the chair."

"But I have to go," I answered.

"Oh sure, His Majesty is calling," Molly pouted. "I'm just a sister. They're a dime a dozen," and then she added, smiling, "How many cents is that for each of us?"

"No sense," I replied. "None of it makes any sense."

I woke to Charles's face, close to mine.

"Boo," he said. "I made it back in one piece."

"How long have I been asleep?"

"Almost two hours. Hungry?"

"I guess so."

"Good, because I found us a duck farm."

"A what?"

"Honest to God," he said, getting up and opening his suitcase. "A duck farm. They raise ducks and there's a little restaurant attached to the place where, for the *poultry* sum of four ninety-five you can get a complete duck dinner. Hey, that wasn't bad, was it?"

"What?" I asked, still groggy.

"*Poultry sum.*"

"Oh."

"Hey, give a guy with a vestigial wit a break, huh? I'm dancing as fast as I can."

"I'm sorry," I said, sitting up. "I usually require a few minutes of being awake before I can decipher a pun."

"Okay, I'll repeat it later when you're receptive."

He took off his shirt and went into the bathroom. I watched as he turned on the tap and bent over the sink to wash his face. His back was beautiful, I noticed for the first time. He had those marvelous back shoulder muscles that athletes have. I smiled to myself in appreciation. I felt so much better now; perhaps a few hours sleep was all I needed to regain a normal disposition.

"How do you like our little palace?" I asked, looking around the room that now amused rather than depressed me.

"Some swell digs, huh?" he said, coming out of the bathroom and rubbing himself with a towel. "Hey, get dressed. I spotted a duck with our names on it and they already sent for a priest."

"What for?" I got up and went into the bathroom.

"To give it the last rites, dummy."

"Ah, yes, I've heard of that," I said just before closing the door. "A duck's bill of rights."

"Yuk, yuk," Charles called through the closed door.

Dinner was gay with both Charles and myself in holiday moods. And it was a holiday; our first day of complete freedom. I was finally kind to myself and didn't give Molly or Sissy a thought. This time at least belonged to no one but the two of us.

The two of us. What a glorious phrase!

"What are you thinking about?" Charles interrupted my reverie.

"Nothing. Everything."

"That makes a lot of sense."

"I'm not going to be sensible tonight," I said. "Tonight is for extravagance. I'm going to be gay and outrageous and peculiar."

"I'll drink to that," Charles replied, finishing his second glass of wine in one gulp.

"Go easy," I said. "You're not used to drinking."

"I thought you weren't going to be sensible."

"Right you are," and I finished my second glass, too. "More, please."

We finished our carafe, ordered another and by the time our check arrived, we were both giddy and lighthearted. We stumbled out to the car, arm in arm, arguing as always over who would drive.

"No, no, no, no," I said.

"Yes, yes, yes, yes," and he took hold of the car keys that were in my hand.

"Help, police," I whispered, holding on to the keys. "There's a mad chauffeur after me!"

Finally I gave in and sat beside the driver's seat, chanting, "Our Father, which art in Heaven . . . "

Charles drove with surprising caution, which pleased me tremendously. He was growing up in all ways. Praised be. If only Molly could . . . but of course she couldn't, I thought, and quickly forgot about her.

It was shortly before eleven when we got back to the motel and entered cabin six.

"Tackerama," I said looking around, and then, imitating Bette Davis, "What a dump!"

I sprawled out on one of the beds, suddenly feeling quite dizzy, while Charles fiddled with the TV set, looking for an old movie.

"Guess who at this moment is drunk?" I asked.

"Johnny Carson."

"Johnny Carson is drunk?"

"No, we're going to watch Johnny Carson. There's no movie on."

"Oh," I smiled, closing my eyes. "How nice. How very nice. Heeeere's Johnny!" and I was sound asleep.

It was after two when something woke me. I half opened my eyes and saw Charles sitting next to me on my bed, naked. I closed my eyes quickly, instinctively.

"Kate?" he whispered, and I felt suddenly out of breath, as if I'd been running. "Kate?"

I moaned slightly, pretending unconsciousness and rolled over to face away from him. I hoped he didn't notice the heaviness of my breathing.

"Kate? Wake up."

He said I snored. I forced a low soft growl and lay perfectly still.

In a few minutes, he got up and lay down on his own bed, and I remained frozen for what seemed like hours before I dared turn the other way.

MOLLY

The forgotten woman spent Saturday on the phone, trying to reach her loving sister. Only, where the hell was the loving sister and adoring son? Where the hell was the faithful old retainer? Where the hell was anybody?

I was getting mad, which you know is not at all like me, but for crying out loud, couldn't they check in at least?

I decided to call Kate's best friend and see if she knew anything.

"Oh, God, Molly, if you knew how many times I've meant to come by the hospital and visit you," Creepy Jennie started in when she heard it was me. "If you only knew but you know, things keep coming up and I keep meaning to get over there but you know . . ."

"I know, I know," I said, trying to get her off the fake guilt trip.

" . . .if it's not one thing it's another and Lennie's become a nut on sailing so everytime I turn around he's dragging me off to Westport otherwise . . . "

"Gotcha," I interrupted. "Listen, Jennie, have you heard from Kate lately?"

"Not a word. Why?"

"I was just wondering where she was. She's supposed to come get me Monday but I can't get her on the phone."

"You're leaving the hospital?"

"So they tell me."

"Oh, God, that means you'll have been and gone and I never once visited you! I feel awful, Molly, really awful."

"Listen, Jennie, don't give it another thought because to tell you the truth, I'm glad you didn't come over."

"Why, dear?" Creepy Jennie asked.

"Well, to be frank, *dear*, I never cared for you," I said and hung up.

Goddamn, that felt good.

KATE

A siren had gone off somewhere; its howl distant and subdued though it came from within me. It persisted the entire next day; wherever we were, whatever we were doing, I heard its warning. By late afternoon, I could no longer tolerate the tension. Charles and I were at a country fair we had read about in one of the local papers. Standing on the lawn of a high school, examining patchwork quilt rugs, I finally spoke about it.

"Charles," I started with enormous difficulty, "last night . . ."

"Yes?" he asked after an interminable pause.

"I wasn't asleep," I answered, hoping he would understand and save me the embarrassment of speaking about it directly.

"I know," he smiled gently. "Look at this one, it's a beauty, isn't it?"

"You knew?"

"Of course. Shall we buy it?"

"Charles, I don't want to talk about rugs. This is important!"

He took me by the hand and led me to a large weeping willow tree sufficiently far from the booths and crowds for privacy. We sat beside it and though I had broached the subject, I remained silent. He finally faced it for me.

"Nothing is going to happen between us, Kate, that you don't want to happen. Nothing. I swear it."

"Do you mean that?"

"Of course I do. I love you."

His look was so gentle, so sincere that I felt ashamed.

"Try to understand," I said. "You're so strong. You defied a law of nature and won, but I don't have that kind of strength. I don't even have the courage to defy a law of man."

I was looking at him expectantly, hoping for his forgiveness. He gave it beautifully, leaning over to kiss me and then say—

"You're perfect as you are. Come on, I want to buy you something."

We went to a booth that sold antique costume jewelry and Charles selected a string of Venetian glass beads.

"For my lady," he said, fastening them around my neck. "For my most beautiful lady."

The woman behind the booth heard him and smiled at me, almost, I thought, enviously.

And well she might have.

The Canal House, our stopover that night, was everything the motel hadn't been. It dated from the 1860s and was filled with wicker and rattan; wonderful old pieces with matching chintz cushions in green and white. The walls in the lounge were filled with deer horns and antique clocks. The tables, hundred-year-old oak and mahogany, shone like mirrors. Even the carpeting on the stairs was in perfect condition, held in place by recently polished brass rods.

"This is more like it," Charles said as he entered our room, breathless from the stairs and suitcases.

It was done in cool blues and white wicker and shone as if it had just been scrubbed, top to bottom.

"Give me Victoriana or give me death," I said, stretching out on one of the beds whose mattress seemed to billow up around me. "Oh, this bed feels good. Try yours."

He flopped down heavily on his bed, groaning.

"Good?" I asked.

He snored in response.

"All right, lazy," he said in a moment. "Who gets to sack out and who gets to hang up the clothes?"

This time I snored.

"Tell you what," he went on, "I'll think of a number from one to ten. You've got five guesses. You win, I hang up the clothes. You lose, you do."

"You'll cheat," I said.

"The hell. Come on, guess."

"Six."

"Just my luck," he said, bounding out of bed and attacking the suitcases.

I lay there smiling at him. "I told you you'd cheat."

"Shut up and enjoy it," and he took a blue linen dress from my suitcase.

"Wear this one tonight, okay?"

"Uh-huh."

"Did you notice the restaurant downstairs?" he asked.

"Uh-huh."

"Shall we give it a try?"

"Uh-huh."

"Going to say anything besides 'uh-huh'?"

"Uh-uh," and I rolled over and closed my eyes, leaving my protector to see to the clothes.

MOLLY

All right, so I got a little crazy by Saturday night and called the police, just to check if there had been an accident or something. There hadn't been. Then, not knowing what the hell else to do, I called Dr. Shiff and asked him if he'd drive out to the house. He agreed, reluctantly.

Oh, I also called the telephone company to check the line, which was working, and an old boyfriend of mine, just to cry on his shoulder, which, surprisingly, was also working.

Then, bored with the telephone, I reached under my mattress for a hidden Dem and screwed 'em all.

KATE

I lay there late that night, a few feet from Charles, unable to sleep, listening to the even sounds of his breathing, the crickets outside, the infrequent cars on the distant highway.

I loved him.

God forgive me, I loved him.

Mother had left me, Alan had left me, only Charles remained; remained, changed, sacrificed. All for me.

The Harley boy had sacrificed . . . no, he had *been* sacrificed. That was different. That was an act of horror, this an act of love.

He loved me.

How else could he have done it?

It was permitted. The words came to me and I thought of Sissy, holding desperately to her Bible.

It is permitted. No, it is not permitted. Oedipus. Electra. It is not permitted.

I thought of Sissy in the South, homeless, wandering the last years of her life.

And mother. Wretched, old, crazy. Walking down some street in some hot, ugly town. Talking to herself. "I didn't mean to do it . . ."

It is not permitted.

Alan, opened, dead, decaying. Molly, alone and harmed.

I started to cry.

"What is it, darling?" Charles asked softly.

"Nothing."

A pause and I cried again.

"Hold my hand," he said.

I reached out between our beds and put my hand in his. He held to me firmly.

It is not permitted!

Father, mother, Sissy, Alan, Molly.

It is not permitted!

"I love you, Kate."

"I love you, Charles."

Death. Mutilation all around me. Always.

"I'd never do anything to hurt you, darling . . ."

And one pinpoint of light, one drop of love amid the chaos.

" . . . trust me, Kate . . ."

I had always lived in hell. And now, one voice called to me from outside.

" . . . trust me, darling . . ."

One person fought the flames to save me.

" . . . I love you . . ."

"Hold me," I pleaded. "Oh, God, please hold me!"

He did and one more crime was added to the list that night.

MOLLY

By Sunday night I was a basket case.

I had narrowed the field down to several possibilities: They had all drowned in the pond, they had all been kidnapped, a UFO had taken them all for a nice intergalactic jaunt. All right, first possibility was out. Kate was Jaws III. Kidnapping? Where was the note? A UFO definitely seemed the most probable.

But seriously, folks, a basket case.

If I ever got my hands on that sister of mine—but never mind, I had things to do. First, I had to arrange to get myself the hell out of that asylum and up to the house first thing in the morning. Then, I had to secure a carload of Dems that night, for although I had turned into a great cat burglar, I doubted whether the country hospital would be as easy.

I called a limousine service and arranged for a car and driver. So far, so good.

Then I waited. And waited. Around midnight I hobbled out of my room and to the treasure trove. Open sesame. Wham, bam, thank you, ma'am. I now had enough pills to invite Andy Warhol and all his buddies in for a week. Yum.

There was nothing left to do but lie there and

watch the dawn come up like thunder, which it did with me still watching.

Several hours later I was sitting in the backseat of a black Caddy being driven at gargantuan expense to Tara. Quite the *grande dame*, I, sitting there in my Dior back brace and St. Laurent cast. Eat your heart out, Jackie O.

We got to the house around two and the driver deposited me and my two little suitcases in the hall and then beat it back to civilization, griping about the size of his tip.

"Anybody here as if I didn't know?" I called upstairs, just to hear the sound of my voice.

Of course, the place was empty. And messy, I noted, hobbling into the living room. There were glasses on the coffee table, a half-filled ashtray and, interestingly enough, a pair of men's socks on the floor in front of the couch. I picked them up and looked at them. So, Kate had a friend in, huh? Curiouser and curiouser.

I went into the kitchen and saw the sink half filled with dirty dishes.

"You on vacation, Sissy?" I said. Incidently, when there's nobody better to listen to, I don't mind talking to myself.

Then I went into Sissy's room. Cleaned out. Wherever she was, she wasn't coming back. Not only were all her clothes gone, but a couple of clean squares on the wallpaper told me she had also removed her pictures.

How am I doin', Agatha Christie?

I don't want to bore you with a lot of self-pity, but at that moment I didn't feel so hot. The house was deserted, all right. No, not the kind of deserted when people are out for the afternoon. The kind when they've left. Moved out. Escaped.

And what in blue blazes was I going to do there all by myself? Listen, if you want to shed a tear for poor old Molly, hold on. It gets worse.

I hadn't eaten since the breakfast slop at the hospital, so I limped back to the kitchen and the refrigerator. Okay, so here's what the poor lonely crippled lady had to choose from: half a dead grapefruit, a fossilized English muffin and a jar of Grey Poupon *moutarde*. Whoopee. This was one hell of a homecoming.

"Thanks a load, gang," I said, going to the hall phone, "but I never eat on an empty stomach."

I looked up the local supermarket in the book and dialed it. Somebody half alive answered and I asked for a delivery.

"We don't accept phone orders," she said.

"You don't understand, I'm all alone here and I can't drive even if I had car which I don't . . . " I went on, trying for a little sympathy from the moron.

"We don't accept phone orders," she said like it was a whole new thought.

"Look, I'm stuck out here with nothing to eat but mustard, and even though it's French, I thought it might be nice to have something to put it on, other than my fingers . . . "

"We don't accept phone orders."

"Listen, am I talking to a person or a recording?"

"I'm just telling you our policy, madam."

"Oh, it is a person. Well, person, would you please put the store manager on? I just want to tell him what a swell job you're doing."

"Just a moment, madam," and she slammed the receiver down on something hard.

It beats me sometimes how my incredible charm evades some people. Anyway, I decided to attack the manager in a totally different way. I got in the mood by getting this terrifically innocent look on my face and upping my voice a few registers. By the time he got on the phone there was this little waif ready for him. I spilled my tale of woe all over him, apologized a dozen times for bothering such a busy man and ended up by giving him a shopping list a mile long.

Sometimes I think I should've been the actress, not Kate. Which reminded me, were her pictures also gone?

I sidestepped upstairs and went into her room. Nope, half her clothes were still there. Well, at least she was planning on coming back before the millennium.

Then I went into my room and found the dresser filled with Charlie's clothes. I checked the closet. His sneakers, good shoes and loafers were all there.

I sat on my old bed and reconnoitered.

Sissy gone, presumably for good. Kate gone, presumably coming back. Charlie gone, but all his clothes here. And a strange man left his socks in the living room.

Doo-dah.

I was still sitting there trying to make sense of it when the phone downstairs rang.

"Why the hell didn't we have another phone put in here?" I called to nobody as I hobbled downstairs fast as my plaster-of-paris appendage would permit.

It was the supermarket manager, calling to tell me they were out of some stuff. Terrific.

My suitcases were still in the hall, and after I hung up from the local yokel I dragged them upstairs and stopped midway between Kate's room and mine. Hers was bigger. She had the big bed. She had the nicer view. Even her wallpaper was newer. So I moved into her room for spite, 'cause I really didn't care about those things. I'm nothing if not easy to please, God knows. A regular egg, that's me.

After unpacking, I felt tired so I stretched out and stared at the ceiling. Lying there, listening to the damn silence, an old feeling from my hospital days came back. I was scared. Really scared. This wasn't kosher, this mass disappearance.

And whose socks were downstairs?

The idea of kidnapping returned but a kidnapper would hardly let Sissy take her pictures.

Goddamn.

I must've dozed off because the next thing I remember was hearing the back doorbell ringing like crazy.

"I'm coming," I called out and started the mile-long limp downstairs.

It was only the delivery boy with my groceries. I gave him a check, which he looked at as if he'd never seen one before, and he left. I unpacked, decided to celebrate all the good news with a tuna on white and spent the rest of the afternoon so low I would've had to stand on tiptoes to touch bottom.

Something happens when you're alone in the country at night with nothing but the sound of those damn screaming bugs to keep you company. You get edgy. It's why everybody in the country owns a dog. You get really paranoid. Somewhere in the bushes you're sure you hear the Manson gang. The creature from the black lagoon somehow got in your pond. Killer bees are massing on your rooftop. All of the above were happening to me, I was sure, as I sat there after dinner, alone in that haunted house. I mean I was really out of it.

"So, Molly, my dear, how'd you enjoy your dinner?" I asked myself out loud.

"Listen, you're one hell of a cook. I never had such a scrumptuous TV dinner before," I answered, wretched.

I carried my empty tinfoil tray into the kitchen and made myself a cup of coffee. Real coffee this time, no instant crap for the high-liver. I sat down at the kitchen table and pulled out another chair to rest my feet on. No sense in being uncomfortable as well as miserable. And then I saw something on the other chair, something I hadn't seen before.

Road maps. Aha, evidence!

I perused. Connecticut. Massachusetts. Maine.

I opened Connecticut first, being the thorough detective I am. Somebody had traced a line through various highways. Mystic, Clarksburg, up and across the map. I opened Massachusetts. Another route traced. One in Maine, too.

Somebody planning a trip? Was that all it was? A nice little family excursion?

Bull. Kate knew I was getting out of the hospital today. Besides, Sissy wouldn't have taken those damn pictures.

Oh boy, what the hell was going on?

"Don't lose your nerve, Molly, old girl," I said to myself out loud. "Just keep talking to yourself till the little men in white come and cart you away. At least then you'll have company. Jesus H. Christ!" and I gave in and cried.

Later that night, lying in Kate's bed listening

to the bees and the gang and the creature splashing around in the pond, I had this lovely little fantasy. I heard the front door close downstairs and Charles say, "Boy, that was sure one swell trip, Aunt Kate!" In my head I left the room and went to the top of the stairs.

"I'm glad you liked it, Charles," Kate said. "And wasn't the Mystic museum educational!"

"Fascinating, too!" he answered.

"I'm glad I brought my pictures," Sissy said, holding them proudly in front of her. "They sure kept me entertained."

"Hello, everyone," I said from the imagined staircase. "Better late than never."

"Mommy! Sweet mommy!" Charles shrieked and ran to me, planting one on my cheek.

"But, Molly, you weren't supposed to get out of the hospital until next Monday!" Kate said.

"*This* Monday," I said as Charles covered my face with kisses.

"Oh, no! How could I have made such a terrible mistake!" Kate said, running up the stairs to me.

"I'll make corn fritters and banana bread this minute," Sissy beamed up at me. "We'll have us a real homecoming party!"

Somehow the little scene made me feel even worse and I reached for not one but two Demerols. Hell, I'd have my own little homecoming party.

What I had the next morning was my own little hangover. During the night, Johnson & Johnson had made a delivery of cotton balls and stuffed them right in my head. Oh boy.

I crawled downstairs to the kitchen.

"Thanks a lot, Sissy, for the coffee," I said as I put up the water. "Thanks for the eggs and brioche, but I'm not sure I can find my mouth this morning."

And so me and my whimsical sense of humor had instant coffee together.

Now, what to do.

Call Dr. Shiff. What for? Why not, I had nothing else to do.

Call the police. What for? See above.

Call . . .I was running out of places to call and then it hit me. The one place I hadn't called, the logical place, was Kate's apartment in town. Suppose, just suppose they all went there? Suppose, just suppose, Kate got to the hospital right after I left? Suppose all this mystery crap was just in my head?

I almost shouted hurrah as I hippity-hopped to the hall phone.

"Idiot! Molly, you're an idiot!" I laughed as I dialed.

And then Kate's voice answered and, for a brief moment, I was in seventh heaven. Till I heard what she was saying.

"Hello, this is Kate, being brought to you through the courtesy of modern technology. At the sound of the beep tone you may leave a message, but please, nothing obscene. I'd rather hear that directly. Or, if you prefer, you may reach me at area code . . ."

"I'll leave you a message all right," I shouted into the phone. "This is your sister! Remember you got one? I'm here all alone and I'm going not-so-slowly crazy! Where's my kid?" and I slammed down the receiver.

"Damn, damn, damn!"

Back to the kitchen for more imitation coffee. The road maps were still lying on the table and I studied them. Routes in Connecticut, Massachusetts and Maine. Maybe they were on the road. But where? Not to mention why?

"Screw it, you're not going to cry again. Kate's the crier, not you. You're the brick, remember?"

Some brick. Scared of every noise, imagining everything under the sun, talking to myself.

Time to get hold of myself and do something. Anything except stare at those damn walls. Therein, like the man said, lies madness.

So I called Dr. Shiff and we had a nice chat. He hadn't been back to the house like I asked him but, more importantly, he had never seen Charlie at all. Kate's excuses to him sounded pretty trumped up to me, and what about that visit to his office?

"You're sure she said he had pubic hair?"

"Positive. I did some reading on the subject in the next few days just to acquaint myself with the most recent findings. Werner's syndrome . . . "

Get on with it, Doc.

". . . but she never called back. Then, when she did, she said it had all been her imagination . . ."

Nothing new here so I cut him short and hung up. I stood by the phone wondering who to call next. The police. I did and they promised they'd send somebody out to the house to talk to me.

Talk. That's about all I was getting. Lot's of talk and no action. She-it.

I spent the rest of the morning next to the pond on a chaise I had dragged out of the house. Not quite like I pictured it, with Sissy waiting on me hand and foot, but the sun felt great at least.

And I daydreamed.

I watched me and Kate swimming in the pond as kids, her the fish, me the rock.

"Kick your feet harder, dummy!" she yelled at me.

"I am!"

"You're not! God, Molly, you're so awkward!"

"I am not."

"Yes, you are. You're awkward and you're funny-looking. I'm the beauty in this family."

I watched myself storm out of the pond and go in search of Sissy to tell.

"If you tell Sissy, I'll deny it!" Kate called after me. "Besides, she won't believe you. She'll think you made it up, like everything."

"Go tell her, baby," I said from the chaise, but she didn't. She stopped and returned to the pond's edge, sitting down. Kate went up to her.

"I'm sorry," she said.

The then Molly pouted in response.

"I said I was sorry."

"I don't care."

"You're not awkward and you're pretty."

"No, I'm not."

"You are, too. I ought to know."

"Why should you know?"

"Because I know about such things. You're very pretty. Practically as pretty as me."

I watched myself smile up at my big sister.

"Really?"

"I swear. Now get in the water and kick harder!"

After a couple of hours and a couple of hundred reminiscences, the cop arrived. He came around the back of the house to find me, since I hadn't heard his car drive up.

"Can I get you anything?" I asked, determined not to be my usual smart-ass self with the law, just in case I really needed them. He glanced at my cast and said no. And then we talked and this time, thank God, it was more than talk. A lot more.

He told me that Kate had reported Charles's running away a few weeks before but that he had returned, according to a subsequent call from her.

"He ran away?" I stammered.

"That's what she said."

Of course. That's why I hadn't been allowed to talk to him. Simple. He wasn't there. But why the hell hadn't she told me? And then I remembered her saying she didn't want to worry me.

"He was back in a couple of days, though," the cop went on.

Or was he? Jesus, my mind was racing. I needed some time to figure it all out.

"Well, hold tight," I said, "because this time I've got a whole household of missing persons for you."

I filled him in on everything. He even took notes on a little pad, just like in the movies. And then he went away to do whatever it is cops do and I sat there, thinking. The big eureka came about two that afternoon.

Here's how I had it figured. Something had happened between Kate and Charles or Sissy and Charles that made him run away. Something Kate was ashamed to tell me or afraid to tell me. Somebody did something to my kid that made him bolt. And not in my direction. He was off. A real runaway. He hadn't come back like Kate told the police. That's why I hadn't spoken to him. He was still off somewhere. And Kate was chasing him. That's why the road maps.

But why hadn't she told the police? What could she have done to him that made her that afraid?

It took the rest of the afternoon for me to decide that I'd better calm down or else. I attempted that impossible feat by preparing a huge dinner, as if everybody was there. Crazy, I know, but it kept the old hands busy and I could always freeze the leftovers. So a little after eight I sat at the kitchen table, staring at a capon with all the trimmings, only to realize I wasn't in the least hungry.

"You're pathetic, Molly, old girl," I said, pretending it was the chicken doing the talking. "I mean, I am one hell of a good-looking bird and you're not even interested."

Listen, I know what to do when chickens talk to me. I poured myself a nice medicinal gin martini. And then another. And then I had my first really good idea.

If Kate was gallivanting around the countryside, she'd have to sleep somewhere. That meant, unless she'd taken a purse full of cash, she'd be using her credit cards. And God willing, that was the way to trace her.

First thing in the morning, I'd call American Express, but in the meantime, hit me again, bartender.

Drugs and booze, booze and drugs. Nice goings-on for a mother, huh? But what the hell, it beat feeling.

The next morning, our resident Miss Marple awoke around eleven to find a roast chicken dinner still sitting on the kitchen table, attracting flies. I salvaged what I could and threw the rest away.

Then on to my customary repast of instant coffee and to the business at hand.

I was on the phone with American Express for the better part of an hour. My tale of woe was that there had been a death in the family, that Kate was off on a vacation, that I had to reach her, et cetera, et cetera. It wasn't hard to act the bereaved role, 'cause to tell you the truth, that's just about how I felt.

The man at the main office of American Express was a doll and helped all he could but after he had clicked off to check the records, he came back with nothing. If Kate was using her card, nothing had come in yet. He promised to call me if anything did.

I did the same routine with BankAmericard, Master Charge and Visa.

Then, my detecting concluded for the day, I settled back to my real job: Going crazy.

KATE

I awoke in Charles's arms on the third day of my new life. We had made love until it was almost dawn and the warmth of him was still around me, protecting me from any guilt or doubt. We were lovers as we were intended to be, destined to be. Perhaps we had lived other lives together, if such things are possible. Perhaps we had loved each other throughout time, reunited century after century.

I looked at his sleeping face and tried to picture him as a knight, a Roman, an Aztec.

His sky eyes opened and saw me.

"Who're you looking at, funny face?"

"You. You look like a Babylonian prince this morning."

"And what are you?"

"Your slave," I whispered as he drew me closer.

MOLLY

It was the night of my sixth day in the house and I'd been drinking. I was sitting in the living room, the radio was on, I was staring at a vase on the mantel. It occurred to me that our father bought it when we were kids, before he ran out on us. I went over and picked it up. A nice little vase. Birch trees painted on it. Some kind of bird, too. Nice.

I let it fall to the floor, kerplop. I kicked the pieces into the fireplace. I looked upward.

"Sorry about that, dad, but you know how it is with us kids. We're always wrecking things."

There was an old clock on the mantel, too. Christ, I was drunk. Kerplop.

"Sorry again, dad. Miss Butterfingers, that's me, but you see, I've been drinking. A lot. I got a lot on my mind, you see. My kid disappeared, or did you know that already? They keep you informed up there?"

I could hear my voice echo out into the hall and that amused the hell out of me.

"I don't blame him, though, dad," I called out. "I'm not much of a mother. Pretty good sculptor, though. That counts for something, huh? Tell me, is Rodin up there? Give him a message if you run into him. Tell him I think he's swell, just swell. Give Da Vinci a hug from me, too."

I boogied to the music and spilled some of my drink.

"Oh, wow, daddy, I'm real sorry, I messed on your rug. Jeez, what a pity. What a goddamn pity. Oh well, what can you expect from a woman who'd screw in front of her own kid? You hear about that one up there? Yeah, it happened all right. Guilty, your honor. And that's just the start. You wanna hear what a terrific mother your kid turned out? You wanna hear how I ran out on little Charlie every chance I got after George died? You wanna know what my baby-sitter bill was? Could you see him from up there, that poor little kid in his little Dr. Denton's waiting to see which stranger was going to stay with him while his mother was out? Guilty as sin, your honor!"

Rather than cry, I opted to laugh and boy, did I. Like a lunatic.

"Oh boy, dad, you should have seen him standing there in the hall screaming at me 'You stay with me!' Can you believe the nerve? He expected his own mother to stay with him. Christ. And he had just lost his father. Can you believe the nerve?"

I went to the bar for a refill.

"I put him in his place, though. I really did a

185

job on him, like ma did on me. Oh, for crying out loud, is she up there, too? Hi ya, ma, how's tricks? You gettin' any?"

I was pouring the damn gin all over the bar.

"Look at that, just look at that, will you? Slobbo strikes again. Who else is up there? You ever see Toulouse-Lautrec? He's the little guy. Looks like Jose Ferrer on his knees . . . "

That really tickled me. I could barely drink from laughing, but I managed.

"Listen, if God's around would you give him a message from me? Would you tell him enough's enough already? I mean, talk about your being punished! Doesn't the guy have a sense of humor? I mean if mothers were all terrific where would analysts be? Oh wow, I just thought, is Freud up there? Does he look like what's-his-face . . . Clift . . . Montgomery Clift? Boy, I'm having a good time. Whoopee."

I chugalugged and almost gagged. But what the hell, I poured another.

"Hey, put George on, will you? Hi, George. How's it goin'? You shouldn't have left, baby. You shouldn't have checked out. I didn't do such a hot job on my own. But what the hell, I got him all his shots, at least. That's somethin', right George? Listen, baby, just in case I die tonight from acute alcoholism and don't get to see you again, you know I'm not comin' up there, I'm goin' downstairs, I want you to know it was fun while it lasted . . . it was fun . . . goddamn fun . . . whoopee . . . "

I stumbled and would have finally fallen flat on my ass if I hadn't caught the edge of the wing chair.

"Look at the klutz, will you? Kate was right . . . I'm a klutz . . . funny-lookin' klutz . . . Oh well, we can't all be beauties, can we, folks? You were beautiful, ma, you know? At least the little I can remember of you . . . "

I sank to my good knee and that really made me howl.

"Oh wow . . . drunken old klutz . . . Why the hell does everybody keep leaving? Why the hell won't anybody ever stay with me? *Stay with me!*"

I was shouting now. A real nut.

"No . . . shit . . . don't stay. I wouldn't stay with Charlie . . . Why should you stay with me? . . . It's only fair . . . No, that happened before . . . You left me before . . . You shouldn't have punished me before I earned it . . . Damn it! What the hell do you think you're doin'? . . . Get down here! . . ."

I stumbled toward the hall, completely out of my head.

". . . bastards! You're all bastards! You leave a cripple alone . . . standing in the hall in his Dr. Denton's . . ."

I made it to the stairs.

". . . Stay with me . . . sure, kid, sure . . . I'll stay with you like they all stayed with me . . ."

I started to drag myself upstairs.

". . . wise up, Charlie . . . nobody ever stays . . . that's the way it is, baby . . . beautiful baby . . . you were a beautiful baby, Charlie . . ."

Now I was crying, too. Christ.

". . . you had the palest blue eyes I ever saw . . . goddamn beautiful eyes . . ."

I got to the top stair and pulled myself up. The whole upstairs of the house was stretching upward, like it was made of rubber and God was pulling on it. I knew I had less than a minute to make it to the john before I vomited.

". . . such a beautiful little face . . . oh, Charlie . . . I'm sorry, Charlie . . ."

I crashed into the wall and felt my way along it toward the bathroom.

". . . forgive me, Charlie . . . forgive me . . ."

I never made it. I was out like a light.

The next afternoon I got my first break.

The guy from American Express called. A week ago Kate spent the night in the Motel in the Woods in Carversville, Connecticut. I thanked him like crazy and made him promise to call if any more charges came in. Then I hotfooted it to the kitchen and the Connecticut road map. Carversville was smack in the middle of the penned route. At least now I had some idea of where she was heading, but given a week, she could be almost anywhere on the route. Or off it, for all I knew.

The next logical thing to do was to have a talk with someone at the motel. Maybe, just maybe, they knew something.

I struck gold. The old biddy who answered the phone must have been sitting there in the woods champing at the bit to do a little down-home gossiping. After I asked her about Kate and she found her in the register, we got down to the nitty-gritty.

"Oh yes, seems like I do remember that one," she said, bloating her voice with innuendo.

"Was she alone?"

"Hardly. Had a young man with her," and I could just picture this one leaning into the phone, spittle forming on her Yankee pursed lips.

"Yeah?" and I let my own voice get real interested, just to give the old gal a thrill. "Who was he?"

"Her husband, according to the register," she almost chuckled. Boy, we were having a good time.

"She doesn't have one," I said to egg her on.

"Doesn't surprise me. He was a good ten years her junior," and I thought I heard her eyebrow raise. So, Mister Socks was along for the ride, huh?

"What'd he look like?" I asked.

"Oh, good-looking enough, I suppose. A little slick for my liking, though . . ." Judge Hardy would be too slick for this one, I thought. "A little too sure of himself, if you get my meaning."

"I get you," I said, ever the willing ear. "Did they have a kid with them?"

"Nope, just the two."

"You wouldn't have any idea where they went after your place, would you?" and I crossed my fingers.

"No, and I don't care, long as they don't come back here."

"Why?"

"Rowdy. They come in about eleven at night making all kinds of noise. Laughing, carrying on. Not the kind of people we like to have as guests, if you get my meaning."

"I get you," I answered, and then, deciding I had gotten all the information I was likely to from her, it was my turn to have a little good-natured fun. "Listen, I think it's only fair that I tell you something," I said, letting my voice go real serious.

"What's that?"

"The woman was a plague carrier."

A pause from Ma Kettle and then, "Beg pardon?"

"The plague. You know, the Black Death? If I were you, I'd start scrubbing that cabin right away. Or better still, burn it."

I hung up, happy for the first time in a week.

KATE

Even in paradise, one has doubts.

Charles and I had been arguing over where we would eat dinner. He had checked our guide and found a four-star French pretension that was outrageously expensive, and since my little angel was developing wickedly extravagant tastes of late, I thought it best to curtail him, just this once. That had led instantly to a pout, the pout to a sulk, and, as we drove along, the sulk to a gloomy silence.

"Charles, it's ridiculous to spend fifty dollars on dinner," I said, ending the silence.

"It wouldn't be that much."

"Of course it would. The guide said dinners from eighteen dollars . . ."

"That's thirty-six for both of us," he snapped.

"Darling, your arithmetic is accurate but your knowledge of restaurants isn't. That's *from* eighteen dollars. That's probably for the cheese sandwich. And it doesn't include wine, of which you drink a great deal."

"All right, I'll switch to bread and water."

"Oh, Lord," I said, wishing I hadn't interrupted that restful quiet.

"You know what your trouble is, Kate?" he asked, turning around in his seat to face me.

"Let me guess," I answered, holding tight to the wheel.

"You're grounded. You're wingless. You live a safe little life and that's the way you want it. If adventure came up and bit you on the nose . . ."

I admit to a certain loss of temper at that. "What on earth are you talking about?" I decided to get my own licks in. "Do you realize what you and I are having might just possibly be described as an *adventure*? An adventure my foot, it's an odyssey! Do you realize there's not a state in the union that wouldn't put me behind bars for what I'm doing? You call that a safe little life?"

"All right, don't blow your stack."

"Honestly, Charles, you just don't listen to what you say half the time."

"Yeah? And what about you?" he said defiantly.

"What about me?"

He hesitated and, then, "I don't know."

Against my will I laughed and that seemed to break the mood.

"Come on, honey, one more good restaurant and from then on it's McDonald's all the way, okay?"

I glanced over at him and saw the boyish hope in those beautiful eyes.

"All right, one more." I gave in.

"That's my girl. And to celebrate our return to frugality, we'll have champagne with dinner," he chirped.

"Oh, Lord."

It was while toasting with that champagne that I saw Charles's first gray hair.

"To our odyssey," he was saying. "To our wonderful . . ."

"Charles!"

"What is it?"

I stared at it as if it were a harbinger of doom.

"Kate, what is it?" he repeated.

"There," I pointed at it. "You have a gray hair!"

He laughed. "Is that all? Why the big deal?"

"Charles, how old are you now?"

"I don't know. Thirty, maybe."

"You have to stop it now, Charles. Please stop it now before it's too late!"

I was shivering. Suppose he couldn't stop it? Suppose he went on aging permanently? Would he be forty by next month, seventy the month after? Would his life be over in one short summer? He seemed to read my thoughts and he took my hand.

"Calm down, baby. Everything's under control."

"You don't understand, it isn't under control! You have to stop it now!" and the people at the next table turned to look at me.

"Kate, I promise you . . ."

"No! I want you to stop it!"

And the table next to theirs turned.

"Kate, calm down," and his hand closed firmly over mine.

"Charles, please . . ."

"Calm down and we'll talk about it."

I tried but it was impossible. The panic was exploding inside me. I left the table and went quickly to the restaurant's terrace, all eyes on me. In a moment Charles was beside me, his arms around me, trying to comfort me.

"Honey, listen to me," he said. "Stop crying and listen to me. I can control it. I always have. I slowed it down when I saw that it frightened you . . ."

"You did?"

"Yes. And I can stop it completely whenever I want to . . ."

"Then stop it *now!*"

"Soon. I promise you, darling. It'll all be over soon. Believe me, I'm not going to turn into an old man in front of your eyes. At least not for a long time," he smiled down at me reassuringly.

"Are you sure?"

"I'm sure."

"Are you positive?"

He laughed at me. "Yes, my sweet little dope, I'm positive. Just as positive as I am that our dinner is getting cold."

I pressed into him and began to feel myself calming. He was so strong, so certain. He had to be right.

"Oh, Lord, I can't go back in there!" I said. "I made such a fool of myself! Everyone was staring."

"Good. We'll let them stare."

"Oh, Charles . . ."

"Come on, head up," and he raised my chin with his finger. "Shoulders back," he took my arm. "Their Highnesses are ready for dinner now."

We strode back into the room with me staring straight ahead, not daring to meet any of the glances of the other guests. Once at the table, Charles lifted his champagne glass.

"As I was saying, To our odyssey. To our calm, uneventful little odyssey."

"And to it remaining that way," I said, thoroughly ashamed of myself.

It wasn't until dessert that the fear came back, but this time I kept it to myself.

MOLLY

Sherlock Holmes, you've met your match.

Three days after my friend at American Express called me, he called again, bless his corporate heart. A second charge, this time from the Freemont Inn, Freemont, Connecticut. I got out the road map and a ruler. From the Motel in the Woods to the Freemont Inn was three inches and a bit. Or about a hundred twenty miles, according to the map's scale. The charges were three days apart, which meant Kate was traveling approximately forty miles a day, which would put them somewhere around New Britain at that moment.

Molly, you're a genius.

Now, what to do with this stunning piece of detective work?

The cops?

No. Not until I knew what was up. I mean, whatever she did, Kate was still my sister. Also, it didn't escape me that maybe it was Charles who had done something. Oh maybe nobody.

Round and round it goes, where it stops, nobody knows.

So I sat there, looking at those two points on the pen line, then up to New Britain, still on the route, up to Hartford and points north.

And I decided.

I would rent a car and start after them.

"Jesus, Molly, you're crazy," I said aloud. "How the hell are you going to drive a car with a bum back and a leg in a cast?"

"Shut up," I answered. "He's my kid. Besides, I owe it to him."

And that was that. Crazy? You bet, but at least it meant doing something, not sitting there falling apart. Besides, wasn't there some mythological guy the gods forgave his sins after he went on a pilgrimage? Maybe it'd happen twice.

Two days later, after five hours in a rented car, I checked into a motel outside Willimantic.

I now know what hell must be like: It's sitting behind the wheel of a goddamn Pinto, trying to find a comfortable position when you're in a back brace and using your left foot on the pedals. I walked into that motel doing a great imitation of a human pretzel.

First things first. A long hot bath to see if my back muscles and I could get back on speaking terms. I got to my room and went straight to the tub. One thing about motels; no matter how tacky they are, they have these great bathtubs. Long enough to stretch out in, accessorized to the teeth. Mine had a hand shower, four different squirts if you please, three bars of the cutest soap you ever saw, a nice long brush for your back and a washcloth you could eat off. Oh, I was in heaven all right, stretched out in the hot water with my plaster leg hanging out over the side.

"God bless you, Gerberman and Sons," I said, reading the little blue letters that were stamped on the white porcelain side of the tub. "May you all work together in peace and harmony. May Mister Gerberman love his daughters-in-law and may they call him dad."

Heaven.

An hour later, it was now about six-thirty, I went over to the motel's cocktail lounge for my customary nip or two. Or three. Or maybe even four, what the hell.

As I crossed the courtyard, the summer sun was still blazing away, still trying hard as it could to burn up everything in sight before the moon took over. And then into the cold, dank, dark bar. I was feeling a lot better by now, but even if I hadn't been, the sight of that place would have made everything all right. Those rows and rows of gin bottles behind the bar: Gilbey's, Beefeater's, Gordon's, it was Santa's workshop come true.

I slid into a booth, ordered a martini and a bowl of peanuts, and looked around the place.

At the bar there were three people: a couple who looked like they were on their way to visit their kid in camp; you know, bored, tired of driving, tired of each other. Down the bar a single man. A salesman, I decided. Of machine parts. A real yuk-yuk kind of guy with a little potbelly and one hell of a sense of humor. Lord save me from him, I thought, as my drink arrived and I dove in.

If there are any hard-core alkys out there, you know how it feels to take that first icy sip of the day. It's like getting out of a sauna and jumping into a lake somewhere in the Canadian Rockies. You can almost see the steam coming off your body and you know all your troubles are on a ramp going into a 747 heading in the opposite direction. It's second only to a multiple orgasm. Maybe first.

Tomorrow I would reach the area I figured Kate

would be in and the work would start, so why not tie one on tonight, just to celebrate?

Listen, any excuse in a storm.

I was halfway through my second martini when yuk-yuk sauntered over, hitching up his pants on the way to cover the pot.

"You alone?" he started.

No, there were seven other guys in the booth with me; what was he, blind?

"I'm waiting for my husband," I answered and gave him a pleasant enough mini-smile. I mean, why be hostile when you're beginning to float upward in a pool of deliciously chilled gin?

"Me, too," he said, "for my wife."

Now there were two bull-throwers.

"My name's Sam Kane," he said, helping himself to a seat opposite me. "From Willimantic. I'm in concrete blocks."

Close, but no cigar, I thought as I did the breast-stroke in that gin pool. I introduced myself and added, "I'm in sculpture."

"No kidding, you're an artist?"

"Uh-huh."

"No kidding?"

"I wouldn't kid you, Sam, I swear."

"What d'you know, we're in related fields. We both deal with stone," and he laughs as if he just said something funny.

Despite myself I laughed, too.

"Let me buy you another, fellow mason," and he laughs again, signaling the bartender.

I, too, dickens that I am, laughed. What the hell. Any guy who's in concrete blocks can't be all bad, am I right?

"What happened to you?" he asked real sympatheticlike and for a moment I thought he was talking about Charlie. "You fall off one of your statues?"

"Oh, the brace. No, I was kidding around with Rudolph Nureyev and he dropped me."

"No kidding?"

I've impressed him. I can tell because his head pokes forward like a turtle.

"No."

"So what happened?"

"I got in a fight with Anne Bancroft. She's got a wicked left."

This time he laughed. "You're quite a kidder, aren't you?"

"You bet."

"So what happened?" Mister Persistence asked again.

"Car accident."

"Ah," he nods yes like he finally got the truth.

"That you believe, huh?"

"Yeah. Isn't it true?"

"No."

And he howls. Boy, is he having a good time. Then he stops laughing and suddenly gives me this incredibly dirty look. Honest, I wouldn't have been surprised if he stood up and exposed himself after that look.

"It must be . . . inconvenient to wear one of those things, huh?"

Oh my. I think I've just been handed a telegram.

"Yeah," I answered, and gave him an innocent look as if I hadn't a clue to what he was referring.

"I'll bet, you poor little thing," and he reaches across the table and gives my hand a pat.

And all the while Valentino is strutting his stuff

across the table from me, I'm wondering whether or not to kid him along or drop him.

"It would take a real gentle man to know how to deal with a woman in a brace, you know?" he says in a purple voice, half closing his eyes.

I laughed.

"No, I mean it," he says and again his eyes go half mast.

This one is just begging for it and so I decide to give it to him.

"I'll bet you do," I say, putting a little Mae West on it. "Are you a gentle man?"

"Never had any complaints," and he's practically foaming at the mouth.

Well, then our friendly neighborhood bartender arrived with the drinks, I chugalugged the rest of my second martini, I hate having more than one glass in front of me at a time, people might think I'm a drinker, and I started on my third.

"Slow down, honey," he says. "You don't want to get too drunk."

"Too drunk for what?" I asked, little Miss Butter-Would-Melt.

"For anything," eyelids drooping.

"Why, Sam," I cooed, "are you suggesting something off-color?" Off-color, my foot. This is a charter member of the Degenerate of the Month Club I'm sitting with. I wonder if they give out points for making it with a cripple.

"I'm up for anything you're up for," he answered.

"I'm up for armed robbery," and he howled again.

"I love your sense of humor, Molly. I really do. I think a sense of humor makes a woman sexy." And again he pats my hand, like it's a guard dog he's trying to win over.

"Yeah? You ever make it with Phyllis Diller?"

And he yuk-yuks, real loud, so the camper's folks at the bar glance over.

"Shhh, I'm known here," I say.

Suddenly he stops laughing. "Then let's go somewhere else."

"Oh yeah? Where'd you have in mind?"

"A friend of mine has some model apartments about a mile from here. I got the key to one of them."

My God, he wants to make it with a cripple in a model apartment. I mean, talk about your peculiar tastes!

"Yeah?" I coo. "How's it done?"

"How's what done?" he asks as if I'm the one who's talking dirty.

"The apartment. French Provincial, Early American . . ." and he yuk-yuks again. "I'm serious. What style is the apartment in?"

"I don't know . . . contemporary, I guess."

"Contemporary? Nah. I can't relate in a contemporary setting."

"You kidding?" he asks for the hundredth time.

"Nope. Honest, Sam, my first experience was with an interior designer in his contemporary apartment. It was a lousy experience and ever since I can't make it if the furniture around me has clean lines. Now, if your friend's apartment was Renaissance or even Jacobean, that'd be a whole different story. Hell, I can even function in *moderne* . . ."

"You putting me on?" he asks all serious.

"Not in any contemporary setting, I'm not," I answer, straight as I can, which is getting pretty hard to do.

Now he just stares at me for a moment, trying to figure out what's going on. I can't resist.

"You wouldn't know anybody with a Rococo place, would you? You know, a lot of gilt ormolu, cut crystal . . ." and he stands up. "I'm crazy about Rococo. It's like an aphrodisiac to me . . ."

He starts to walk away and I holler after him, "Listen, I can even make do in Louis Quinze or Swedish Modern . . ."

Shucks. Lost another one. Oh well, nothing to do but a slow backstroke to the edge of my glass, drinking all the way.

Our modern-day Solomon, David Susskind, once had a TV show about alcoholism and one of the guests was giving the danger signals of the disease, one of which was the big blackout, which is my roundabout way of saying I don't remember anything after that. For all I know, Sammy boy came back and got his points.

KATE

I could see Charles's body clearly in the moonlight as he slept. The changes were subtle, but real. The thickening of his waistline, the almost imperceptible growing heaviness around his jawline, the coarseness of his beard. He was approaching mid-thirties.

I studied him with an almost clinical interest,

determined not to cry myself to sleep again that night. I was terrified by it. The more he assured me it would stop, the more I disbelieved him. This, then, would be my punishment: To murder rather than love and to be left more alone than before. I was not surprised; I had always known the circle would be completed. I would end my life the way it began, alone.

No, not really alone, for there had been Molly.

Molly. Where was she? Who had helped her to leave the hospital? Who was there to tend her?

One crime begets another, like a chain reaction of madnesses. Murder, incest, abandonment, all leading to . . . what?

Where was my sister? What was she thinking, alone, her child gone . . .

I turned away from Charles and despite myself the tears came.

Molly, oh Molly, please don't suffer . . . please don't suffer . . .

I had to call her. The next morning I told Charles.

"Are you crazy? What the hell do you want to call her for?"

"Charles, she's my sister. Your mother. Think what she must be going through . . ."

He said nothing at first, just stared ahead petulantly. Then he spoke and his voice was filled with resentment.

"Sure, you call her and she'll put on the poor, hurt mother act and wrap you around her little finger. First thing I know, we'll be on our way back and that'll be the end of us. Is that what you want?"

"Of course not, but I can't . . ."

"That's what'll happen, though. Kate, I swear to

you, she won't understand. She'll put the police on me if she has to . . ."

"Charles, she wouldn't do that. She's your mother. She loves you."

"Yeah, sure."

I took his hand. "Baby . . ."

"Don't call me baby," and he withdrew it sharply. "I haven't been a baby in quite awhile, in case you haven't noticed."

"Can't we talk about this without arguing?" I pleaded.

"What's there to talk about? You're going to do what you want to do, like always," and he walked away, leaving me frustrated and confused.

Perhaps he was right. Perhaps we needed to wait awhile longer before calling Molly. I didn't know. At that moment I only knew I couldn't bear it when Charles was angry with me. I caught up to him and promised not to call.

"That's my girl," he said, putting his arm around me. "You let me take care of things and everything'll be fine."

MOLLY

I rolled out of bed around ten, all excited. I was about fifteen minutes from Greenville, the town I would try first. In some perverse way, the idea of coming across Kate and Mister Socks really got to me.

I had no idea what would happen when I did, but there'd be fireworks sure as hell—and that I was looking forward to. Fireworks your ass. There'd be a whole A-bomb blast.

I paid the motel bill and headed for a luncheonette next door. What I needed was a little fortification. And a roll of dimes.

The fortification was terrific; I treated myself to waffles and bacon. The roll of dimes wasn't so easy. The gal behind the cash register had grown very fond of them, but after she got a load of my incredible charm she parted with a couple bucks worth. Very big of her, the little twit. As she handed them over, I threw in a little dig.

"Listen, honey, from one gal to another, I'd do something about that mustache if I were you."

And she scowled at me as I limped out of the place. Like I said, some people have no sense of humor.

Twenty-five pretzel-bending minutes later, I pulled up in front of a drugstore in Greenville, got another couple of bucks worth of dimes and settled back into the phone booth to do a little light reading.

There were only fourteen motels in and around Greeenville, according to the phone book. Dime number one was spent on the local Holiday Inn. Nothing. Likewise nothing from the Regency House, the River Edge Motel and the you-should-excuse-the-expression Dew Drop Inn. Eleven dimes later I bid a sad farewell to Greenville, land of the scorching midday sun, and headed back to the highway.

God bless air-conditioned cars.

A sign ahead said Danieltown was the next exit, so I took it. Danieltown. Nice vibes. Daniel in the lion's den. I was in a kind of lion's den, wasn't I? Nice and prophetic.

Phooey. Danieltown turned out to be literally Daniel's town, 'cause the whole thing could have been owned by one man. Motels? They had two guest-houses, so twenty cents later, I was back on the high-way following my nose.

Beverly, next exit. Hiya, Bev. Heard from Kate? She hadn't.

Riverton, next. Nothing. Nothing in Beaverdam either, except for a truly rotten hero sandwich and a mild case of the runs.

Oh boy, was I having fun.

And then, around three o'clock, I hit pay dirt. It was in Schuylerville, God bless it and keep it. The Motel on the Mount. Kate and Mister Kate had been there the night before.

The night before!

I almost hit my head on the roof of the phone booth from jumping for joy. I was one day behind them, they were still on the same route, I was a genius.

I decided to push myself as much as I could to make up the day's difference, so I headed back to the highway, got pointed in the right direction, put on the radio and settled back.

You want to hear coincidence? On the radio the first song I heard was "Sentimental Journey."

Somebody's trying to tell me something, am I right?

KATE

The next night I dreamed of Molly. I can't remember the dream; only that I awakened from it around seven in the morning filled with a sadness so deep that I knew I had to speak to her, no matter what the consequences.

Charles was sleeping soundly next to me. I got up and dressed quietly and tiptoed out of the room. Downstairs, the hotel staff was already busying themselves for the day ahead. I found a pay phone in the deserted bar and dialed the operator. I would charge the call to my home phone so no charges would be on the hotel bill for Charles to see. I was risking his fury, but I couldn't help myself. There are limits, even to my selfishness.

As I heard the phone ringing in Molly's apartment in town I realized I had no idea of what to say to her. I would simply assure her that everything was all right. I would try. It would be useless.

The ringing stopped.

"Hi, whoever," Molly's voice said, and I could feel the adrenalin pumping into my blood. "This is one of those rotten machines so . . ."

I stood there listening to the recorded message she had made a century ago. Before the accident. Before Alan's death. Before I took Charles. God, had only a few months gone by? I realized I experienced time, not by any clock, but by the changes in Charles, and decades had slipped by since I had last seen Molly. Years had passed since I had spoken to her. Her voice, distant and mechanical, was almost unrecognizable.

She had been alone for years.

I hung up and dialed the country house, certain I would find her there.

Forgive me, Molly. I can't tell you what's happened. Not yet. But I swear we'll come back for you. I swear you won't be alone much longer.

The ringing started.

It's a miracle, Molly. A miracle. You must accept it. It's God's will, this change. Please, please try to accept it. Be a part of it, Molly. Be a part of our lives.

Still ringing.

I didn't cause it. I swear to you I didn't cause it. I didn't. I didn't.

The ringing went on and on. She wasn't there, either. I hung up and sat there in the darkened bar for a few moments before going back upstairs to our room. Charles was still sleeping. I undressed and slipped into bed next to him.

"Good morning, kiddo," he said, opening his sleep-filled eyes. "Come here."

In his arms, I tried to forget Molly and failed.

MOLLY

The next day I got up and realized I had nothing to do. If my calculations were right, I was about five miles behind them. There was no sense in calling motels yet; they wouldn't be checking into one for hours.

So, a little time off. I made a mental list of the ways I'd like to spend it. A dip in the pool? Not unless they had a resident Sister Kenny to hold my cast above water. A little nip? Nope. Not if I intended to catch up with them that day. Should I go search out another Sammy? Please.

I ended up in the car, whittling that five miles down to nothing.

The sign ahead on the highway said Thompsonville. It sounded good to me, so I pulled off. It was good. One of those picture postcard, little seventeenth-century-colonial-square-type places. You know, very big on manicured lawns and quilts for the tourist. Not a dog dropping in sight. Which reminds me, where do the doggys go poo-poo in the suburbs, or do they just mail it all into town? If so, I wish to hell they'd pick a zip code other than mine. Honest to God, there's one monster on my block who drops a Volkswagen every morning, despite the law.

So, utterly charmed by the scenic splendor, I

parked the car and went for a little hobble around town.

Jesus, I never saw so many brass plaques in one place in my life. Evidently, the entire Revolutionary War took place in this one town. Concord and Lexington? Feh.

I was fleeing from a little souvenir shop, having developed a sudden allergy to bald eagles, when I saw this really cute movie theater across the street playing, of all things, *Grease*. Listen, the combination of air conditioning and John Travolta is more than any red-blooded woman can resist, so I dragged the old body over and went inside. I had the time to kill and, besides, a little middle-aged lust couldn't hurt.

It was swell. I even treated myself to buttered popcorn, the small size, which turned out to be this huge tub that cost about a year's college tuition. Boy, it sure ain't like in the old days when for twenty-five cents you could keep yourself in acne for a week.

Well, after two hours of glorious Technicolor and ear-splitting rock and roll, I emerged into the blinding glare of midafternoon and started toward the car. To work. I'd drive to the next town and get cozy behind a pay phone. Maybe, just maybe, they decided to call it a day already and had checked in somewhere.

Incidentally, I've never considered myself a looker but maybe I'm wrong, 'cause on the way to the car this guy across the street started a stare campaign at me.

You think maybe John Travolta's a cripple freak, too? Please, God.

KATE

I was picking out a surprise present for Charles, who had tired of shopping and was off somewhere, when he burst into the store looking for me.

"Come on, let's go," he said.

"Oh, Charles, go away. I'll meet you outside in a few minutes."

"Come on, Kate, let's go back to the car."

"I'll meet you there," I answered, spotting a marvelous wallet in the case before me.

"No," and he took my hand and practically pulled me out of the store.

"Charles, what on earth is the matter with you?" I asked as he hustled me along the street toward the car. "Why are we racing?"

"I'm just tired of poking around, that's all. I want to get back on the road."

My darling was definitely getting cranky. Too much sun, I supposed. We got back in the car and headed toward the highway.

"You hungry?" I asked.

"Nope."

"Thirsty?"

"Nope."

"Sulky?" I added, knowing full well that he was.

"I'm fine, just fine. Stop third-degreeing me."

Did I say sulky? I meant downright cantankerous.

"Next stop, Winsted," I said, remembering checking the map earlier.

"Let's not," Charles said firmly.

"Why not?"

"I'm bored with this route. Swing over there and let's take the next road to the west."

It was hardly worth arguing over, so I didn't. One town would be pretty much like the next. But I was surprised at Charles. I thought Thompsonville was charming.

MOLLY

Come evening I was really in a foul mood.

Winsted? Nothing. Pelham Landing? Nothing. Adams? Ditto. North Adams? Ibid. Screw all the Adamses and all the New England towns along with them.

Definitely a foul mood.

I was soaking in a hot tub in some stinking roadside motel, listening to the trucks groan by, deciding that this whole trip was a stupid idea, wanting nothing more than to pull the plug and disappear with the bathwater. I mean, what a crapped-up life. What a rotten, miserable crapped-up life.

I got out of the tub without bothering to dry myself and went to my purse. I popped two Demerols and went back to the bath to wait for a little peace to descend. Thirty-nine years old and where the hell was I? Up the creek. Nowhere. Nothing, with no prospects. I was kidding myself that I'd find Charles. I'd probably never see him again. Like my old lady. And George.

What a stinking, smelly, stupid crapped-up life.

Finally, mercifully, pharmacology took over and my mood brightened a bit. So, now that I had a nice cozy buzz on, what to do with it? I decided to dress my buzz up and take it out to dinner. A nice dinner, no counter food for me and my buzz tonight. A few glasses of wine, a little food, an after-dinner nip, a blackout, what more could anyone ask?

An hour later I was seated at a table in The French Way, a cute little restaurant in the metropolis of Wahconah Falls. On the banquette to my right was a young couple busily reading the menus, the guy sweating a little at the prices. To my left were two guys I was pretty sure were gay, I don't know why, maybe because they were a little too well dressed for the hub of chic, Wahconah Falls. Anyway, I ordered a glass of red wine, deciding that maybe martinis on top of double Dems was baiting the fates a little too much, and I settled in. To eavesdrop.

". . . so Joanie and Bernie and Harriet were standing in the middle of the pond naked, holding up sparklers," one of the guys was telling the other, "and Suzy and Sandy turned on the floodlights. You never saw three people dive underwater so fast. It was the greatest weekend . . ."

I toasted silently to great weekends. I recalled a few myself. Listen, life wasn't always a dungheap.

". . . Jane and Paul got back," the girl on my right was telling the guy. "They stopped over in Portugal . . ."

Great weekends, traveling, hell, life could be nice. I wondered if it would ever be nice for me again. Come on, Molly, I started in on myself, you know it will. Seven good years, seven bad, that's in the Bible, kiddo and if it was good enough for Jesus and Moses, it's good enough for you. Just hold on. Keep that chin up. There's a great day coming tomorrow. Happy days are here again. Every cloud has a silver lining.

Crud.

". . . and Jeffry, who is easily the biggest lunatic I know . . ." the happiness boy was going on.

I tuned out. I wasn't exactly jealous of his terrific weekend, but I wasn't exactly thrilled either. When you're up to your neck in feces you can get a little begrudging. Just wait, I said to him without making a sound, just wait till your turn on the rack. You'll see what a dumping ground this little planet is.

"Just wait," and it came out aloud.

I guess the wine was getting to me. He looked over at me, the weekend reveler.

"Sorry," I said. "Just thinking out loud."

Then he smiled, a really beautiful smile. Kind. Nice.

Boy, what a rat you are, Molly, wishing bad stuff on a nice guy like that and I took another half-glass sip. The wine was definitely getting to me.

A second glass of wine and I was raring for a little conversation that included me. The straight couple didn't appeal to me. They chomped their food. Screw 'em. But the guys ate nice and neat and their stories were friendly. Not a bitchy word, so I opted for them and zeroed in.

". . . but who can afford a beta max?" one of them was saying.

"I can," I said, which I thought was a neat way of entering the conversation.

They both looked over at me, paused for a second and then smiled.

"Congratulations," the weekender said.

"Listen, that's nothing," I went on happily. "Last year I bought one of those electronic TV games for Charlie . . ." I blathered on for a good five minutes before I caught the looks that passed between them. They didn't want to talk to me. Hell, they probably had a lot to talk over themselves. I was acting like a creep.

"Look, I'm really sorry. I didn't mean to interrupt," I said, scrounging around for my wallet.

"That's all right," one of them answered, but it wasn't all right.

I pulled a five-dollar bill out of my wallet and plunked it on the table. I would've run out in a flash but my table was jammed up against theirs.

"If you could just help me move the table," I said, "then I'll get out of here and leave you alone and you can go on with your nice dinner. I'm really sorry . . ."

"That's perfectly all right," one of them said again, moving the table out.

"I'm really sorry. Really," and I got up. "It's just that I . . . I seem to have a little curse on me at the moment, but it'll go away one of these days. One of these days everything'll be fine again. You go on with your dinner. Enjoy yourselves. I'm really sorry," and I stumbled out of the place.

God knows how I got back to the motel without wrapping the car around a pole. I guess He protects children, stray dogs and drunks.

KATE

Charles's sulkiness continued into the next day. I had no idea what was bothering him, but thought it best not to inquire. This I decided after the hundredth time I tried, and the hundredth time he snapped my head off.

So, whatever the cause, I would try to be a cheery counterbalance.

"Hey, grump," I said in my cheeriest way as we sped along the highway to nowhere, "if we keep going in this direction we're going to miss the Barrington Caverns."

"So?" he grouched.

"So we planned on seeing them, remember? The book said they were one of Nature's Great Marvels. Wouldn't you like to see another of nature's great marvels, besides yourself?"

"We can't go to Barrington," he said as if that was that.

"Why not? We don't need a passport."

"Kate, I left the road maps back at the house."

"We have another one. What's the difference?"

"Don't you see?" and he was annoyed with me once again. "I drew our route on the maps. If Molly goes to the house and finds them, she can trace us. She could put the police on our trail . . ."

"Good God, that is the most baroque thinking. . ."

"There's nothing baroque about it, Kate. We have to stay off that route. The risk is too great."

He sounded so much like a character out of a *Kojak* episode that I became annoyed.

"I was looking forward to seeing them." I started a little sulk of my own.

"We'll see them another time."

"Charles, even if she did tell the police, they'd be looking for a woman and a child. Not a woman and a grouch."

A moment's silence in which I regretted what I had said.

"Sorry."

"Okay," he answered, but his voice was still down.

What a charming afternoon this is going to be, I thought and pressed down on the accelerator.

By evening, Charles had worked himself into a symphony of dejection. In an attempt to turn his mood around, I suggested we dine extravagantly, but even that didn't work. He ate his eleven-dollar lobster indifferently, merely toying with his two-dollar-ninety-five-cent chocolate mousse. I, on the other hand, was determined to enjoy myself at those prices. My ten-dollar duck with cherry sauce was superb. As we lingered over coffee and after-dinner drinks, I had had it with his gloom.

"All right, Mister Raskolnikoff, out with it. What is the matter?"

"Nothing."

"In a pig's eye, nothing. You've been one grand charmer all day and I want to know what's happening. Have I done something?"

"No."

"Are you getting tired of me?"

"Don't be silly."

"Because if you are, may I remind you that you're quickly advancing in age yourself. You've even sprouted a little potbelly in the last few days, so if you think you're too young for me, if that's what the matter is . . ."

Suddenly I stopped chattering. I knew what it was. My worst fear, stilled for a while, was back, fully realized. Charles had grown an almost middle-aged stomach. He was also graying at the temples.

He couldn't stop it!

I must have gone white, for he looked at me with concern.

"What is it?" he said.

"I know, oh my darling, I know," and I was trembling.

"What do you know? Kate, what do you know?"

"You can't stop it!" and I thought, I will not cry, I will not bolt from the table, I will not burden him with my hysterics. I will be calm for both of us.

"No, that's not it," he said.

"Charles, you don't have to worry about me. I'm all right. You can tell me."

"Sweetheart, I swear to you, that's not it. The change is almost over. I've been thinking seriously about stopping it anyway. No, I'm upset over something else. Please don't ask me what it is . . ."

"You're lying. Oh, darling, please don't worry about me. It's you we have to worry about. We'll go to New York. To Mount Sinai. I know there's something they can do . . ."

"Kate," he took my hands in his, "I saw Molly."

I stared at him, wondering what those words meant.

"What?"

"I saw her. In Thompsonville the other day. She's following us."

I don't know how long it was before I spoke, but I was aware of the waiter passing our table and looking at me, sitting there stunned.

"You saw her?"

"Yes. She was walking down the street . . ."

"But it couldn't be . . ."

"It was her. She had a cast on her leg and she looked back at me. It was her, all right."

I must have still looked ashen, for the waiter came over.

"May I get you something else?" he said, studying my face.

"No, thank you," Charles answered, but the waiter stood fast, looking at me, as if trying to tell me he would rescue me from Charles if that were the trouble.

"No," I said, and he walked away. "Did she recognize you?"

"Of course not."

"Was she . . . all right?"

"She seemed to be."

"Really?"

"She was limping but she seemed fine. She's lost some weight."

"Too much?"

"No, no, she's okay."

I was overwhelmed and suddenly felt almost faint. The picture of Molly, crippled and desiccated, in a strange town flashed before me. And Charles as he had been in the gazebo. And Alan, in the hospital. I handed Charles my wallet and got up.

"You pay the bill, dear. I think I'd better lie down for a while."

I went upstairs to our room. By the time Charles returned, I was asleep.

MOLLY

The next day was the pits, as usual. I spent the morning, one hand on my throbbing head, the other holding the phone getting nowhere.

Nothing. Plenty of nothing. It was as if Kate had vanished. I even called the local police and asked them about road accidents. That would occur to me, wouldn't it?

Again, a big fat nothing.

So, in the early afternoon I sat in a luncheonette on the outskirts of nowhere, reconnoitering.

Had Kate gone home? Had she decided to skip the rest of Connecticut and hotfoot it to Massachusetts? Or were she and the Socks Kid on a plane to Dresden? Listen, anything was possible, it was occurring to me. Including the fact that my little trip was the wildest of goose chases. Triple damn.

God, I'm tired of complaining. I've done nothing but rail at you all day, but take heart, I'm almost railed out. I just think at this point, to get the whole gist of our story, you ought to know I was getting pretty low on the emotional totem pole. And the thought of chucking it all was getting pretty attractive. No, I don't mean chucking the trip. I mean chucking the whole thing. El-suicido. The final bow. The big Demerol-gin stew.

All right, so I'll knock off the melodrama.

In the midst of my happy thoughts, I had been staring at a mother and her kid down at the other end of the place. He must have been about five and what he was doing to a bowl of ice cream was something; he had it all over his face, the table, the floor; listen, for all I know, passing cars got some, too. And all the while his mother just sat there, beaming down at him, occasionally giving his face a gratuitous wipe. Charlie had been like that only a few years ago. My little slobbo. But where this woman was enjoying her kid, I would have driven mine crazy. I would've nagged and browbeat him until the ice cream stuck in his craw. Some mother, huh?

Well, like the man says, we reap what we sow.

I got up and passed the kid's table. I tussled his hair.

"How old?" I asked the proud mother.

"Three and a half."

"He's big."

"Yes."

"Big and beautiful." I leaned down nose-to-nose with the little guy. "You're a big boy, you know?"

"Yup," he said, just as pleased as punch.

I pulled a dollar bill out of my purse and handed it to his mother.

"Listen, do me a favor, will you? Let me buy him his ice cream."

She looked at me like I was crazy.

Which I was.

KATE

It was over. Everything joyous and carefree had gone out of us and the specter of Molly wandering alone loomed over us like the threat of a sudden storm. We tried not speaking of it, but that made us unable to speak of anything. And so, Charles and I glumly continued our odyssey, wrapped in our private thoughts and guilts, sharing none of it with each other.

It was after a full day of despair, that night in our sullen bed, that Charles spoke of her.

"Do you think she's suffering?" he asked, as much to himself as to me.

"Of course."

That was all we said, lying there next to each other.

There are moments, forks in the road, corners to be turned, when one holds one's destiny in one's hand. We were at such a moment, Charles and I. Driving silently through the countryside the next day, I prayed that Charles would make the right choice.

If not, I would.

I would leave him for Molly. I would find her somehow and take her home.

But first, I had to make sure that he could indeed stop the change. If not, I'd be sacrificing one for the other. That would be a fit punishment for my part in what we'd done. To pull one love from the water and leave the other to drown.

A fit punishment.

It never came to that.

That evening, sitting in the car, pretending to watch a dazzling sunset, Charles turned that corner.

"Let's go find Molly," he said, and I thanked God.

MOLLY

Suicide attempt number one.

All right, not exactly a full-fledged attempt. A flirtation, okay? A who-the-hell-cares-what-happens-I-leave-it-in-the-hands-of-the-gods flirtation.

It was about two in the morning in another one of those depersonalized rooms off the road. I was studying the mar-proof plastic top of the night table, honest, it had come to that, sipping my second or third lukewarm gin, wondering how many people had slept in that bed before me and what their stories were.

Had anybody ever died there? Maybe some fat salesman had picked up a trick and had a heart attack right there.

One good thing about dying in a motel room; they find your body at checkout time. No need to lie around rotting till the neighbors complain about the stench.

What would they do if they found me, sprawled out on that bed, the empty Demerol bottle on that mar-proof table?

Hell, they wouldn't even find that. I kept my pills in a perfume bottle.

"Poor thing stank herself to death," they'd say.

"Help me lift her, would you? We got a guest waiting for the room."

Where would they put me? Out back with the rest of the rubbish?

"Hey, cart this away, will you? The guests are complaining about it, now that the wind's changed."

Would they send the body home? Who to? I decided to count my pills, a recent hobby. I lined them up nice and neat on the room's desk. One little piggy, two, three, et cetera. I had sixteen of them left. I wondered if Golden ever found out I had skipped with her precious pills. They keep count of that kind of thing, don't they? I hoped she knew.

I picked up one little piggy and downed it with a slug of gin. Then, little piggy number two joined little piggy number one.

A note. I ought to leave a note, just in case, right? I opened the desk drawer and took out a sheet of stationery. But where was a pen? Gone. Stolen, no doubt, by the salesman before he had his heart attack.

I searched my purse for a pen. Piggy three, meet piggies one and two. Damn, it was getting hard to hold my hands still. I was getting the shakes. Must've been from the warm gin, since the three little piggies hadn't a chance to digest yet. But give 'em time.

Something felt like a pen, but it turned out to be a lipstick. I put some on. What the hell, why not look my best?

I overturned my purse onto the bed and went through the contents scrupulously. Here pen, here pen.

A notebook, compact, hairpins, comb, crap, crap, crap. And my wallet, lying there open.

A picture looking up at me.

A man, a woman and a kid.

Who the hell were they?

It was George! Hiya, George.

And me. Hiya, me.

And little Charlie makes three.

I leaned down real close to it and planted a kiss on little Charlie.

"I'll never see you again, kiddo," I said out loud. "Best of luck in your future endeavors."

And then I changed my mind.

Supposing, just supposing I lucked in? Supposing Charlie did come back? I couldn't do him much good in the rubbish heap, could I?

"All right, kiddo, I'll give you one more day," I said, and I went into the bathroom, or rather, stumbled into it.

By now I was getting pretty professional at reverse peristalsis.

KATE

I awoke to find Charles looking at me, smiling like the cat that ate the canary.

"What's the matter?" I asked.

"Nothing."

"Then what are you smiling at?"

"At you. Can't I smile at the woman I love?"

"That's not an I-love-you smile. That's an I've-got-a-secret smile."

"Egad, the woman is bright," he said, and rolled over on top of me.

"Hey, get off. You weigh a ton."

"That's right. I start my diet today," and he smiled the secret smile again. "From now on I'll have to watch what I eat carefully. *Like any normal forty-year-old.*"

"Could you please lie on the bed and not me, like a normal forty-year-old?" I grunted.

"Well," he huffed, rolling off, "If that's all the congratulations I get, the next time I have good news I'll keep it to myself."

"What good news?"

He was nose-to-nose with me now, beaming.

"God, you're dense this morning," he said. "What do you need, a telegram?"

"Evidently."

"All right, if that's what it takes. Kate—stop—good news—stop—you thought I couldn't stop?—stop—I stopped—stop."

"What?" and then I understood. "Charles, is it true?"

"Yes, darling."

"But how do you know?"

"I just do. Believe me, Katie, it's over. From now on, we'll age together nice and slow, complaining all the way."

"Sweetheart," and I buried my face in his chest, "I'll never complain. I swear."

And I never would.

Hours later, we sat in the car, Charles behind the wheel studying the road map.

"If she continued on our route, she ought to be somewhere around Otis, Mass. by now. You navigate, okay?"

"Aye, aye, captain," I said gaily.

Charles pulled back on the highway and we were off.

"Your driving's improved," I said, grateful to be sitting there with unclenched teeth.

"Thank you, first mate," he answered, and slowed down just a hair.

We were ten miles from Otis when I asked him about Molly.

"How will we find her?"

"Well, the first thing we do is to call the local police. If she's looking for us, she might have called them for help."

"What if she didn't?"

"Then it becomes a problem," he said. "We'll check the hotels, the tourist bureaus, whatever. Don't worry, we'll find her."

He sounded so much in charge, so sure of himself.

"What will you say to her?" I asked.

"I don't know. But I do know one thing. I'm not afraid of her anymore."

It had finally happened. My lover was a man at last.

MOLLY

I once heard that before a person freezes to death, there's this moment when everything's okay. You're warm, everything's hunky-dory and you're real cozy in your bed of ice and snow.

Well, I had me a moment like that.

It was in Lee, Massachusets, in one of the lesser palaces on my itinerary. I mean, even the roaches in this place were on strike for better conditions. I spent an hour or so in my room, inhaling Lysol and calling ahead. Nothing, as usual, so I decided to go out and find myself a little action. Hell, maybe another Sam was just what the doctor ordered. At least it couldn't hurt.

I stopped by the desk to ask the fat guy on duty to direct me to the local hot spot. Behind Mr. Fat was Mrs. Lean, in a little office, and as he's directing me to a place he assures me is more fun than a barrel of monkeys, she's giving me the once-over. Then she slithers out of the office like a little garter snake and leans over the desk, real buddy-buddy.

"You're not thinking of leaving us already, are you?" she hisses.

"Whatever gave you that idea?"

"Well, you've been calling all those hotels," she says and her pointy little tongue zips out and back in.

What do you know, an eavesdropper in such a swell place.

"Nope, just trying to locate some people," I said.

"Who?" the fat guy asked.

What the hell, might as well tell all.

As I described Kate and her sockless wonder, the fat guy and his reptile wife started to throw each other little looks, like they knew something I didn't.

"They have a kid with them?" she asked.

"Maybe."

"Boy? Around eight, nine?" he asked.

"Yes! Have you seen them?"

"About an hour ago. They went up to their room. Three fourteen. I thought there was something funny about them . . ."

I didn't hear the rest. I was hobbling fast as my damn leg would let me to the stairs.

Three fourteen!

God, please, God, oh please please please please . . .

Two stairs at a time, pulling myself up by the banister.

Oh, God, God, God, God . . .

Then, in front of the door to room three fourteen—

"I'll do anything, God! Please!"

I knocked and silently promised a thousand changes, a million penances, an eternity of subservience.

And then the woman opened the door and I could see the boy behind her.

One little discrepancy, though.

They were both black.

"Yes?" she said.

"No," I answered.

I laughed all the way down the stairs.

Next stop, depravity.

I should have figured that any place the folks at the Roach Palace recommended would be one rung down from Studio 54, but it didn't occur to me till I got there, not that it would have made any difference anyway.

Louis' Place, I swear that was the name, turned out to be a seedy bar on the outskirts of town, and where as my hotel had smelled of insecticide, this dump smelled of an exotic mixture of beer and urine. Maybe because the johns were right next to the bar. As I entered and looked around at the collection of tramps and trollops draped around the place, I knew I had finally hit rock bottom.

I hoisted the old body onto a bar stool and ordered a martini from a guy behind the bar who looked like the son of Typhoid Mary. Please, God, I thought, don't let him mix the drink with his finger.

He didn't and I figured it was all right to drink it. So, as I sipped it in my most ladylike way, I tuned in on some of the repartee around me.

And for no reason whatsoever I thought of my mother. We never heard officially that she was dead; maybe she was alive and at that moment was sitting in another chic spot like her second daughter.

"To you, ma," I toasted aloud.

"What'd you say?" a guy on the next stool asked.

The gentleman was what is politely called burly, or to be more exact, a pig. Doubtless a cousin of my hotel proprietor. His dress was remarkable in that nothing matched. The flowered blue shirt, the stained brown pants, the really swell work boots.

"Nothing," I said, burying my nose in my drink.

"You said something." A real truth seeker, this one.

"I coughed."

"No, you said something."

I almost crawled into my glass to get away from the lummox.

"What'd you say?" he asked like it was a threat.

Uh-oh, Molly old girl. You don't kid around with this one. This one is probably in the cement shoe business.

"I said 'To you, ma,' " I answered obediently.

"Yuma? In Arizona?"

If I wasn't so scared, I would have laughed.

"No, to my mother."

He looked around me.

"She ain't here," said my little brain surgeon.

"I know. She's dead."

"Yeah?" and I thought he softened at that. "So's mine. She lived to eighty-three. How old was yours?"

Just keep answering, Molly old thing, unless you want instant surgery.

"Sixty-two," I answered. It was as good a number as any.

"What'd she die from?"

What was he, taking a census? A hundred jokes came to mind, but I resisted them.

"Heart attack," I said meekly.

"Mine dropped dead from old age. In her sleep. She lived with me. Now I live by myself. You live by yourself?"

Yes, your honor. Any more questions?

"Yes."

"I don't like it. Do you?"

None of your fucking business, fatso.

"No."

"Yeah, me neither," and he turns back to his beer, but not for long. "It's lonely, you know?"

"Yeah, I know."

"My name's Hank Ryan," and he wipes his hand on his shirt and extends it to me. "What's your name?"

"Judy Forest," I answer. It was as good a name as any.

I took his paw in my hand and was surprised to find that he didn't intend to break my fingers. He pumped my hand nice and gentle.

Could it be I misjudged him?

"You're a nice person, Judy," he said. "You shouldn't be in here. Most of these women are no good. And the guys are creeps. You don't have to worry, though. I'll watch out for you."

"Thanks," I said, feeling a little guilty for thinking the worst of my big gentle Saint Bernard. "What'd you do, Hank?"

"I'm a florist."

Now I ask you, am I a judge of character? Afraid of this absolute honey of a guy?

"What do you do?"

"I'm a sculptress."

"Oh, that's nice," he said, wiping his hand on his shirt again. Were we going to shake hands once more or was this just in deference to my exalted station in life?

It was neither. He took out his wallet with his now clean hand and opened it, pushing it toward me.

"My mother."

Talk about your ugly old hags.

"Sweet face," I said.

"Yeah. That was taken a week before she dropped dead."

"Uh-huh."

"Just dropped dead in her sleep. Didn't suffer like most. Just dropped dead in her sleep."

Nice he might be, but a sparkling conversationalist he wasn't. I won't bore you with the next hour and a half. I found out lots of things about him; he was married briefly to a woman who was "no good" and ran off, which was just as well since his mother and she hadn't gotten along, he had been working on a scaffold and it fell, he sued, won and invested the money in a small florist shop, his childhood ambition, he was lonely but he had a cat and there was a whore in town he visited twice a week even though it cost too much and wasn't what he really wanted. And on and on and on until I thought I would literally drop dead just like his dear old mom.

So finally, having listened to the fourth volume of his fascinating life, I decided to take my ears back to the hotel and give them a well-deserved rest.

"Where you goin'?" he asked as I got off the stool.

"Back to the hotel. It was nice meeting you, Hank."

"Don't go, Judy . . ."

"Sorry, but I've got to get an early start in the morning and . . ."

"Don't go!" and his voice was insistent. The same threatening quality I'd heard earlier.

"Listen, I'd love to stay, I've really had a good time, but I'd better split now," I said and hotfooted it to the door.

I was in the parking lot halfway to my car when he caught up to me.

"What'd you have to go so early for, Judy?"

"I told you, Hank. I've got to get up first thing in the morning."

"We was having a good time," and he clamped his fingers around my elbow.

I was getting scared.

"Come on, Hank, be a nice guy," I said.

"What's the matter? Wasn't I nice to you?"

"You were swell, but it's late . . ."

"Come on back," and he started to pull me toward the door.

"Hank, don't do that. I've really got to go!"

He stopped pulling me and stood there in the half dark of the parking lot looking at me. He started to frown.

"What's the matter?" he said, and the threat was obvious.

"Nothing."

"You don't like me?"

"Sure I like you . . ."

"You talk to me all night and then you just pick up and walk out on me? You think that's fair?"

"I just didn't realize how late . . ."

"I said I'd watch out for you. You think that's fair . . ."

"Look, I'm really sorry that . . ."

"What's the matter? You mad because I didn't pay for your drinks?"

"Of course not . . ."

"That's all you want? Money? You like the other whores in that place? Is that what you're after? Money?"

"No! Really, Hank . . ."

"I got money!" and he reached into his pocket and took out his wallet. "Hell, I got lots of money!"

"I don't want money, Hank . . ." My voice came out trembling. "All I want is to go back to . . ."

"Here, you fuckin' whore!" and he threw a fistful of bills at me. "Here's your fuckin' money!"

He pulled me up against him.

"Please, Hank . . ."

"Fuckin' whore," he whispered, his face pushing into mine.

"I'm not! Please . . ."

"Come on, you fuckin' whore," and his tongue, his fat wet disgusting tongue, found my lips.

"Don't!" I screamed, and he released me.

We stood there in the dark, frozen for a moment before he spoke. And when he did, his voice was the most frightening sound I'd ever heard.

"I could kill you," was all that he said.

Neither of us moved.

Please, God, make him go away. Please, please, please . . .

He lifted his giant fist and pointed it at me.

"I could fucking kill you."

I didn't move. I didn't breathe. I didn't think.

The fist raised.

I closed my eyes.

And waited.

And then I heard his footsteps receding.

When I opened my eyes, I could barely make out his huge body going back into the bar, for I was crying. The money lay at my feet.

He would remember it was there. He would come back for it.

He would kill me.

I didn't move.

What would it feel like, that fist crashing into me? Like the car accident, or would I remain conscious longer? Would I feel the bones breaking this time? Would I see the blood on the ground, staining his money?

I don't know how long it took for me to come off the glandular high I was on and walk to the car, but by the time I drove out of that parking lot the shock wave had passed and I felt almost serene.

An hour and two Demerols later, the truth occurred to me.

He was sent there. For me.

The son whose mother had deserted him was sent to take revenge against another mother who had deserted her son.

An eye for an eye.

It made perfect sense.

KATE

By early evening, a vague uneasiness that had persisted all day became a full-fledged dread. Molly was in trouble; I sensed it, I knew it. The inevitable catastrophe that had hovered above us all these weeks had selected its victim and was descending on her, like a cloud of radioactive waste, and I was helpless to prevent it from striking her down.

We had been searching all afternoon and hadn't turned up a clue and now, the sun lowering, we were both near exhaustion.

"What do you say we look for a place for the night?" Charles asked me.

I looked over at him and could see the darkening circles under his eyes. He had been wonderful all day, taking charge, easing my tension, hiding his own.

I should have agreed, for his sake.

"Not yet, please. One more town?"

"Of course, dear," he said.

The sign ahead on the highway named two towns, Lee and Waterford.

"Which one?" Charles asked.

I silently prayed for a moment and made the choice.

"Waterford."

MOLLY

I finally rolled out of bed around one the next afternoon, got up for maybe a fat minute and then right back to the sack. I had had it. The thought of getting back in the car and driving to another town, calling another batch of hotels, the police, anybody at all, seemed like a death sentence.

I was through.

I lay there inhaling the poisoned air, staring at the network of cracks in the walls that looked like the varicose veins in some old lady's leg.

I knew I was dying.

No, not a real death, that would have been a privilege I wasn't entitled to. This was another kind. Death by choice. By not giving a damn.

If I could have stopped breathing at that moment and waited for the big fuzziness to come over me, I would have given thanks. But it wasn't going to be that easy.

Hell, I was going to have to sweat for it.

Demerols and gin? No. It wouldn't work anyway, not with the tolerance I had built up. And the indignity of waking up in a pool of vomit, still alive, still breathing, was too unfair. Wasn't it enough that I was willing to die, for God's sake?

And then I remembered him.

I could kill you.

Sure he could. Easy as pie.

I could kill you.

A couple of punches was all it would take.

I could kill you.

There in the parking lot, with no one to see us or interfere.

I could kill you.

One punch for Charlie.

I could kill you.

One for my mother.

I could kill you.

Another for George. And father. And Kate. And Alan.

I could kill you.

"Then do it already," I shouted at the room. "Do it already, you bastard!"

Now all I had to do was wait.

At nine o'clock I put on the one decent dress I had with me, fixed what was left of my face. Christ, the trip hadn't done my looks any good. I decided to make it easy on myself. I took one Demerol, just enough to soften the end, but not enough to chicken out.

Bob Randall

The end. Could anything be sweeter? Rest. Sleep. No feelings, no regrets, no punishment.

Hallelujah and amen already.

Fiften minutes later I floated into Louis's Place. Ah, that wonderful aroma of Piels and piss. Ah, that wonderful crowd of hatchet murderers.

I looked around for my own little executioner. Not there yet. But he would be, I was sure of it.

Lucky me, there was a small empty booth right in the middle of the snake pit. I slid in, ordered the usual and tuned in to the conversations around me.

". . . I don't give a fuckin' damn about him, you know what I mean? . . ."

I was a little woozy, but not too much. I'd be able to do what I had to do.

". . . Balls said the queen and the king laughed for he had two. Get it? . . ."

To flirt with that mountain of anger.

". . . What the fuck do you put in these, Louie? . . ."

And then to drop him.

". . . You don't like it? Take your fuckin' business somewhere else, you putz . . ."

To insult him. To enrage him. To force him to do what had to be done.

I toasted the end of thirty-nine years of crap.

"What's so funny?"

Someone was talking to me. I looked up. It was one of the local debutantes.

"Funny? Why?"

"You're sittin' there laughin', that's why. You smashed, honey?"

"Not yet, but I will be. Real smashed."

"Yeah, me, too. God bless booze, huh?"

"God bless it."

She slid into the booth opposite me. Just what I needed, a new friend.

"I seen you here last night," she started our little sorority meeting. "Listen, if I was you I wouldn't get involved with that one."

"Which one?"

"The tub of lard you was talkin' to last night. He's bad news, honey. Take it from one who knows."

"How can you say that? He seemed a perfect gentleman."

"Oh, he's perfect, all right. A perfect weirdo. You wanna meet somebody nice? Hey, Phil . . ."

"No, really, don't," I said, but he was already on the way. Another cripple-screwer? Why had it taken me so long to figure out how to attract the opposite sex?

"This here's Phil. She's . . . what's your name?"

"Selma."

"This here's Selma and I'm Ann. Park it, Phil."

Phil parked it. Next to me.

"What happened to your back, Selma?" Phil asked.

"Too much screwing," I answered, and my debutante friend doubled over.

"Ooh, I gotta remember that one. Too much screwin'!"

"There's no such a thing as too much screwing," Phil said, and gave himself quite a chuckle.

Boy, was this ever fun.

"I gotta remember that one," Ann repeated, just to make sure I knew I was being appreciated. "I gotta remember that one."

"I'll write it out for you," I said. "You do read, don't you?"

" 'You do read, don't you,' " she repeated and broke up again. "I gotta remember that one, too!"

I mean, can you believe this? There I am, preparing to meet my maker and these two nitwits are walking me to the graveyard!

"Hey," Phil says real urgent. "Balls said the queen and the king laughed for he had two. Get it, Selma?"

"Got it. Now how do I get rid of it?" I said, emptying my glass.

Well, that really tickled Queen Ann. This one was clearly hell-bent on having a good time. I could've killed her by reciting the alphabet.

"Who do you have to fuck around here to get another drink?" I said, a lot louder than I intended. Jesus, they were catching.

"Comin' up," Phil said, making a dash for the bar.

"Who do you have to . . . " she was already filing my latest *bon mot* away.

"You're a happy person, Ann, you know?"

"Listen, why not? You don't get nothin' for feelin bad."

Wisdom from on high.

"No? Sometimes you do. Sometimes if you fee bad enough you find the truth."

"What truth, honey?"

"Oh, just the truth. For every action there's a reaction. There's no reality except action. We're responsible for our actions. Stuff like that."

"Uh-oh, we're gettin' heavy," she said. "Hurry up with that drink, Phil!"

"Are you responsible for your actions, Annie?"

"I dunno. Maybe, I guess so."

"I'm responsible for mine, you know. Boy, am I. It'll all be okay, though, soon as I pay up."

"I don't know what you're talkin' about, honey."

"I know you don't. I'll tell you a secret. Neither do I."

And she laughed again.

Well, Phil returned with the wrong drink, which I drank anyway, and we continued our little party for a while. Then, suddenly, I wanted them to go away. He'd be there soon. If he saw them, he might not come over. He might mistake them for my protectors. He might not kill me.

"Go away," I said. "Go away."

"What, honey?" she asked.

"Both of you, leave me alone now. I don't have time for you anymore."

They just stared at me, nonplussed.

"Please go away before you ruin everything. Please!"

The woman got up without saying a word. I turned to the man.

"You, too. I don't want you."

"Come on," she said sullenly, and they both went back into the crowd around the bar.

"That one's crazy . . . " I heard her say.

Crazy? You don't know the half of it, sister.

Ten-thirty.

The bar's full. Big night. Lots of screaming. Laughing. The constant smell, worse each time someone opens the john door.

Four drinks down. A fifth in front of me.

Where the hell is he?

Get it over with, you fuck. You miserable degenerate fat pig of an avenging angel. *Get it over with!*

241

I'd drive into a wall and the hell with him, but I might lose my nerve at the last moment. Foot moving automatically to the brake without my consent. Shit. So drunk. Musn't pass out before he gets here.

Tease the bastard. Play up to him. Get him excited.

"You didn't really think I'd go to bed with you, did you? Jesus, God, look at you! You're revolting!"

Get here. Get here. Get here.

So drunk. So goddamned drunk.

Maybe too drunk.

I went into the john and vomited. Better. Much better.

And back to my booth to wait. The outcast, the condemned, the exiled.

Eleven.
He'll be here. He has to come.
What if he doesn't?
The car.
I can do it.
I must do it.

Eleven-thirty.
Someone at the bar is staring at me. No, not him. Not a candidate for executioner. He's dressed too well. Good-looking. Doesn't belong here, either. Has he come to die, too?

Midnight.
He's still staring. Is he going to try to pick me up? Funny. The poor sap. I'm not available, you poor sap. I die tonight. No time for playing games. Look somewhere else. Over there. There's a nice piece of

ass for you. Go get it. Go have some fun and let me die in peace.

Twelve-twenty.

"May I sit down?"

I look up and there he is. Goddamn good-looking.

"No."

"Why not? You've been sitting here alone for a long time," he says.

"Maybe that's because I want to," I answer.

He sits down anyway.

"Go away, fella. Nothing here for you. The lady's drunk, or couldn't you tell?"

"I could tell."

"Besides, I'm waiting for someone. A big guy. If he sees you here he might sit on you."

"I'll take the chance," he smiles.

"It's your funeral," I say, and then I start to laugh. "Correction, please. *Our* funeral."

"Are you all right?" he asks, touching my hand and looking like he cares.

"Compared to what?"

"I'm serious," he says, and I can tell he is. "You seem very upset."

"Me?" and I laugh again. "What on earth could upset me? I'm made of iron, haven't you heard?"

"No, you're not."

"And how would you know? Listen, if you really care, get me another drink, will you?"

"Haven't you had enough?"

"There's no such thing as enough. Hey, what are you, a priest or something? The Salvation Army send you?" and I look to the front door, which is opening.

"Just a friend," he says.

"I don't have any."

A man is coming into the place. A big man but I can only see his outline.

"Everybody has at least one friend."

Fascinating as his platitudes are, I'm still staring at the big outline.

"Yeah? You some kind of religious nut?"

"Maybe."

The outline heads into the crowd. Damn.

"Go write a book, your holiness."

The outline turns. Not my outline. Shit. I turn back. He's still there.

"What is it you want, fella?"

"I want to know why you're punishing yourself," he says, and I laugh after a beat.

"Oh wow, you're a shrink! A door-to-door shrink, what'd you know. Well, doctor, it all started in my childhood. My mother wouldn't warm my milk for me..."

The idea of putting the words "my mother" and "milk" in the same sentence gets me giddy. I mean, if it were up to her, I would've been weaned on gin. Like now.

"... And then my father, dear old dad, took one look at me and dropped dead..."

Even drunk I was making sense.

"... not to mention my husband and kid and my sister. Listen, Sigmund, do you notice the world is getting less populated? I mean it, they talk about your overpopulation, but I keep missing people, you know? Misplacing 'em, I guess. Hey, where's my drink? You getting me a drink?"

"How about coffee?" he says.

"What're you, kidding? Gin, sweetheart. Lots and lots of gin," and the door opens again. Just a couple this time.

"Later. I'll get you a drink later."

"Later I won't need one. Not once he gets here."

"Who?"

"Who? You're asking me who? The big fat messenger of God, you ditz. You're pretty dumb for a shrink, you know?"

He smiles at that. And I smile back.

"Listen," I say, "you wouldn't be into anything kinky, would you? I mean, maybe you could substitute for him."

"No. Nothing kinky."

"Well, in that case, bug off, cutie pie."

He just sits there.

"You still haven't told me why you're punishing yourself," he says.

"Listen, doc, my insurance doesn't cover this session."

"That's all right. This is a free introductory visit."

"Oh, yeah? Damn white of you, Sigmund."

Where the hell is he?

"Who are you looking for?" he asks.

"I already told you. Look, what's it to you? Why are you sitting here with me? There's a lot of action at the bar. See that one? Annie. She'll laugh at anything you say. She's easy. Go talk to her."

"I want to talk to you," he says.

If this is my knight in shining armor, he sure chose one hell of a time to show up.

"What first attracted you to me?" I ask. "My back brace or my dewy complexion?"

"You just seem to need help, that's all."

"Too late, sweetheart. Too late."

"No, it isn't too late," he says like he's sure. "It's never too late."

"Oh, Christ, another cliche from those gorgeous

lips. You oughta write a book. *Happy thoughts for the day.* You take one each morning with orange juice. Monday, let a smile be your umbrella, Tuesday, it's always darkest before the dawn . . . "

The door opens. Another mountainous outline. Him?

" . . . Wednesday, where there's life there's hope..."

"Don't you believe any of those?"

"Hell no."

The outline moves slowly to the bar.

"But like all cliches, they're at least part true . . ."

"God, you are so boring, buster," and I'm craning my neck to see the outline.

"I'm sorry," he says. "I don't mean to be boring..."

The outline turns. *It's him.*

" . . . I'm just trying to help . . . "

"Go away," I say, staring at my murderer who's looking around, adjusting his eyes to the dark.

"Please, let me stay . . . "

He's even more lethal-looking than I remembered. Good. I remembered Annie's words. *A perfect weirdo.* Good, better, best.

" . . . I just want to talk to you . . . "

He turns in my direction. I wave. He spots me.

" . . . just let me sit here and talk to you for a while . . . "

He turns back to the bar. Damn! He doesn't rush at me, fist up, screaming, cursing, swearing revenge. He just turns back to the bar. Oh no. No way, you son of a bitch. I'll get you.

" . . . sometimes it helps to have someone to talk to . . . "

I turn back to the guy at my table. He's chattering away. I want him gone.

"Get away from me," I say.

"Please," he says.

"All right, if you won't get away from me, I'll get away from you."

I slide out of the booth and rush into the mob at the bar, heading toward him. The other one follows me.

"Please, just let me talk to you."

"*Get away!*" and some of the people stop and look. He finally gets the message and moves away, slowly, to the other end of the bar. Good. I'm rid of him.

Crazy Hank is sitting nearby. I walk up to him.

"I've been waiting for you," I say.

"I don't want to talk to you," he growls.

"Aw, come on, Hank, don't be like that. I just want to apologize . . ."

He turns his gigantic face to me. Like a bull. Like a goddamn bull pawing at the ground.

" . . . you were right. I wasn't fair. But I'll make it up to you, okay? Okay, Hank?"

"I thought you were nice," he says in that thick slow-witted way of his.

"I am nice. I can be, if you give me a chance. Come on, Hank. I'll buy you a drink . . ."

Oh boy, I think, if I can just go through with this without puking again. If I can just tease this mountain of garbage without gagging and giving the whole thing away . . .

And the putz smiles at me.

"Better, Hank? Is this better?"

"Yeah."

I got him.

Two o'clock.

Old Hankey-boy and I are ripped. Really ripped.

He's told me about his goddamn mother a hundred times and all the while you can just see the hatred hidden behind the words. This one's a real woman killer. He just needs a little help, that's all. A little push.

Delighted to be of service, buddy boy.

Two-thirty.

I realize I'm stalling. He's made two attempts to get me out of the place and I'm stalling. I'm not ready.

"Tell me more about your sweet old mother . . ."

Quarter to three.

"Let's go, huh?" Hank says, his eyes bright red from the booze.

"Soon, sweetheart. Soon. I'm not ready."

Ten after three.

I'm ready.

Floating, blitzed, feeling nothing. Ready.

"Come on, baby," I say. "We can't stay here all night. Let's go."

"Yeah?" he says, and his fat lips curl upward.

"Yeah, killer," I say.

We stumble to the front door, supporting each other. Jesus, he weighs as much as a building. Good. It'll be over fast.

Outside it's dark. They turned off most of the parking lot lights. Not too many cars on the highway. Nice and dark. No one will see. Good.

First, get him really hot.

"I bet you're a fantastic lover," I whisper into his fat ear as we're stumbling along. "I bet you like to do a lot of wild things, huh?"

"Maybe," he says, smiling.

"Like what, baby? What'd you like to do that's really wild?"

"Anything," he says. "Anything you want me to."

"Yeah?"

"Yeah."

He's pulling us both toward the back of the lot where his car is parked.

"I like a lot of wild things," I say. "The wilder the better."

"Good."

"You think you can satisfy me, baby?"

There's no one around.

"Yeah," he says.

"I mean, 'cause there's a lot of guys who talk a good game but when it comes to action, they're nothing. Just a lot of mama's boys . . ."

"I ain't no mama's boy," he says, and that glorious threat is back.

You're doing great, Molly old girl. Keep it up.

"You know what a mama's boy is, Hank?"

"I ain't no mama's boy," he snarls again.

We are heading toward a lone car, way in back. No one could reach us there in time. Good.

"Let me tell you anyway. A mama's boy is nothing but a queer. A dirty little queer . . ."

"I ain't no mama's boy," he's chanting to himself.

"Sometimes they're real hard to spot, you know? Sometimes they're big and strong but underneath it, they're still little queers . . ."

"What're you talking about it for?" he says, mad.

" . . . sometimes they even get married, but it

249

never lasts because they're really queers, disgusting freak queers . . ."

He spins me round in the dark. Now I'm looking up into his face and even though I can't see it, I can feel the rage coming off it, like heat.

"What're you talking about it for?"

"What's the matter, Hank? Too close for comfort?"

"I ain't no queer!"

"No? I think you are!"

"I'll show you," he says. "You get in the car and I'll show you!"

"No! I changed my mind! I don't even care if you're not a queer! You're fat and ugly and disgusting . . ."

"What're you doing this for?"

"You're loathsome!"

"What're you doing this for?"

"You make me want to puke!"

I feel his hands on my arms, tight. His fingers are digging into me. They hurt! Oh, God in heaven, they hurt!

"What're you doing this for?"

"No!" I scream. "Don't! Please don't!"

His fingers are digging in harder. Oh, God, I was wrong! I don't want to die! I'm afraid!

"Please, don't! Please don't!"

"You fucking whore," he whispers. "I'll show you, you fucking whore!"

"No oh God no no no!"

"*I could kill you!*"

"No no no no . . ."

"*I could kill you!*"

And suddenly everything's white. Him, me, the ground around us. Everything's white.

My eyes close against the blinding light and then reopen.

It's a car. The headlights of a car. Right up against us.

"Get away!" he yells at the car. "Get away and mind your own fucking business!"

The car moves forward. He lets go of me and I stumble backward.

"Get away from me!"

And the car pushes into him. Pushes him back.

"Get away!" and he beats his fists on the hood. "Get away!"

The car moves forward and pushes him again.

"Get away from me!"

The engine gets louder and the car pushes him again. He beats at it, enraged, cursing, but the car moves forward, pushing him.

"Away!"

It knocks him down.

He's crying. Cursing and crying and beating at the bumpers.

And the car moves forward.

"You'll kill me!" he screams. "You'll kill me!"

The engine gets louder but the car stands still now, waiting.

"She deserves what she gets!"

And the car moves forward.

He gets to his feet, crying, cursing, shaking his fist at it.

And he stumbles to his car and gets in.

"She deserves what she gets!" he screams out the door.

And then he drives away. Away from me.

Safe. I'm safe.

The headlights go out and I'm standing in the dark again.

Safe.

A man touches my arm. But not like the other touch. This is gentle. This won't hurt me.

I look up at him.

The man from the bar. The man who wanted to help me.

He leads me toward his car. There's someone else inside. A woman, I think.

I go with him.

I want to go with him.

And then he says something and I don't understand.

"Let's go home, mother."

KATE

Molly was beyond understanding. She sat between us as we drove back to her wretched hotel, drunk, incoherent, exhausted from fear and remorse.

"I was afraid . . . I couldn't do it . . ."

"Shhh, darling," and I held her in my arms. "Later. We'll talk later."

" . . . why did you stop him? I wanted to die . . . Charles is dead . . ."

"No, Molly, he isn't. I swear to you he isn't."

"Yes, Charles is dead . . . Everyone is dead," and her head fell forward.

"Is she all right?" Charles asked.

"She passed out."

I lifted her head and stroked her hair as I had when we were children and the night frightened her. We drove silently, Charles and I, each in our own thoughts. Now that I had seen her, seen what I had done to her, I was more despairing than ever. And a new fear overwhelmed me. Even if I could explain the unexplainable to her, would it matter? Wasn't Molly right, after all? Charles was dead to her; the Charles she knew, the child she loved. I had taken him from her.

We pulled up to her hotel and Charles carried her to her room. She woke briefly as we put her to bed.

"Kate?" she called to me in a voice from decades ago. "Kate?"

"Yes, baby, I'm here. Go to sleep. I'll be here with you."

"I killed him . . ."

"No, darling. Charles is alive."

"No . . . I deserted him . . . I let him die . . ." and then, mercifully, she was asleep.

The next morning, we told her.

MOLLY

Oh, they told me all right. And told me. And told me.

Bullshit.

Insane, demented bullshit.

I sat there, between the two of them in some creepy diner listening to them go at it. Jesus, what the hell were they trying to do? I mean, I may have almost died yesterday, but I sure as hell wasn't born then. When they were finished with their little gothic tale, Kate was staring into her coffee cup, unable to face me. And the son of a bitch with her leaned back in his seat, like everything was going to be hunky-dory.

"What have you done with Charles?" I asked, and the hatred in my voice scared even me.

"Molly, we told you . . . " she started.

"Never mind that crap. Before I call the cops in here I want to know where Charles is."

My voice was low, tighter than a drum. No more screaming for little Molly. I had been through hell on a slow bus and every emotion had been burned out of me except hate. And there was plenty of that left.

"Is it him?" I asked Kate, nodding toward her boyfriend. "Did he put you up to this?" And then I faced him. "What do you want? Money? You bastard, where's my kid?!"

"Molly," Kate started in again, "I swear to you, he is Charles. I know how impossible this sounds . . . "

"Yeah? It sounds impossible to you too, huh? Then why the hell go on with it? What are you trying to hide with all this fucking mumbo jumbo?"

"Molly," he said, and I threw him a look that should have backed his blood up. "I can prove it."

"Yeah? Go ahead, you bastard. Go ahead and prove it."

"Do you remember Fire Island, three years ago?"

he asked, and he glanced over at Kate with a look that was supposed to be embarrassment. "Do you remember the night you were with your friend Gene?"

Sure I remembered it. The night Charlie saw his mother get laid.

"What about it?"

"I was there in the room. When you found me, you spanked me first, then you held me and asked me to forgive you. You said when I was older I'd understand, remember?"

The bastard. The clever, lying bastard. I looked over at Kate, who was busy pretending it was news to her.

"Charlie told you, huh?" I shot at her. "Charlie told you and you told this lying son of a bitch."

"No, Molly, I swear," and she looked like she was going to cry.

"Here come the waterworks, huh? Go ahead, Kate. Cry your fucking heart out. It's not going to change anything."

And she did. Nice and quiet, like her poor little heart was breaking. My sister the actress. My sister the kidnapper. My sister the God-knows-what.

"Please," she whimpered.

"Please what? Please forget I had a son? Please overlook that little detail?"

"Let me tell you other things," he said.

"Buster, you could tell me the fucking *Encyclopedia Britannica* word for word and it wouldn't make any difference."

"God . . ." Kate covered her face, still crying, and the bastard took her free hand and held it.

"I love you," he said to her, and it almost made me sick.

"Fine, terrific. You two love each other. Great. Now where's my kid?"

"Please give me a chance," the man said. "Please, Molly. For all of us."

"Charles couldn't have told me everything," Kate said between sobs. "He couldn't have told me his whole life!" and she looked at me as if her whole life depended on me.

Shit. Something flashed into my mind. A time when we were kids and I had tried to slide down the banister, only to fall off halfway down and bang my shoulder up pretty bad. I remembered Kate holding me, rocking me, telling me it would be all right.

Shit.

"All right, you're sure you want to play this little game?" I asked the guy.

"Thank you," he answered, like he was really relieved and it occurred to me that maybe he was an actor, too, like Kate.

He started.

I've never believed in miracles or God or heaven or hell or any of that crap.

But two hours later, sitting in that diner, hearing my son's life unfold in front of me, I didn't know what I believed in anymore. Except for one thing.

He was Charles.

KATE

Molly barely spoke the rest of the afternoon. We returned her car to a branch of the car rental outside Lee and the three of us started home. She sat in the back, staring out the window, occasionally looking at us with that same mixture of anger and suspicion. No more than we deserved.

And once, after hours of silence had passed, she leaned forward and touched Charles's cheek, quickly returning to the back window and her stunned immobility. Charles said nothing, made no attempt to help her, and my few attempts were rejected coldly.

"Molly, it'll be all right. You'll see."

"For whom?" she said bitterly, and I wondered if it ever would be all right for any of us again.

That evening, over dinner, the insanity came full circle. I was trying desperately to prove to Molly that something could be salvaged for us all, some vestige of a normal life. She was drinking heavily, looking from one of us to the other, then suddenly chuckling to herself and just as suddenly grim and removed.

"Charles and I have been discussing his education," I said. "I think we've come up with a pretty good plan," and my words sounded as idiotic to me as they must have to Molly.

"Do tell," she said.

"We're going to get a tutor for the basic stuff," Charles said. "Then on to a correspondence school."

She smirked into her glass. "How sensible of you both. How goddamn sensible," and she emptied her glass, refilling it from the carafe in front of her. "And exactly what field do you intend to enter, Charles?"

"It's a little early to decide that," he answered uncomfortably.

"Not at all, *son*," Molly chuckled again. "May I make a suggestion, as your *mother*?"

Charles's face hardened at that and I felt a sudden anger toward him for his lack of sympathy. How else could Molly possibly react?

"I think the biological sciences," Molly continued. "After all, it'd be a damn shame to waste all that expertise, wouldn't it? Don't you think so, Kate? Don't you think it would be a damn shame to waste all that expertise?"

"I guess so," I said, thoroughly humiliated.

"Or if not the biological sciences," Molly went on, "how about a related field? Why don't you open a freak show, Charlie? There's a lot of money in freaks. Of course it wouldn't be quite as prestigious for me. I mean, my son the scientist has a certain cachet to it, but my son the freak . . . well, whatever makes you happy . . . " and she patted his hand. "What more can a mother want than that her baby is happy?"

Charles withdrew his hand sharply and stood up.

"Excuse me," he said, leaving the table.

"Oh dear," Molly said, sipping her wine, smiling her angry smile. "He isn't touchy about his little . . .

peculiarity, is he? I mean, I certainly wouldn't want to offend him . . . "

"Molly, please. You're torturing us both."

"Am I? Oh dear, I suppose I am. How thoughtless of me. And how I do regret it. A thousand apologies, Kate. I humble myself before you and beg your forgiveness. I never was a good sport, was I? Well, I'll certainly make a concerted effort to mend my ways. I certainly will," and she started to laugh.

A couple at another table turned around to look at her and Molly met their stare.

"And how are you this evening?" she asked them, and they quickly turned away.

"You haven't touched your dinner," I said after a silence. "Don't you think you should eat something?"

"You're right, Kate, but not this. I'd like eye of newt, heart of bat, you know, all those delicacies you and Charles must be used to by now. Tell me, how *do* you prepare a dragon? Do you scale it with a fish knife?"

"God, Molly, please . . . "

"Or are you too full of your love to worry about food? Is your love the only food you need? That must be nice, Kate. I'm so happy for you both. So goddamn happy."

By the time Charles returned to the table, Molly was too drunk to go on with her attacks and we finished the meal as we began it, in silence.

That night I got my first hint that our odyssey, far from being over, was just beginning.

We had checked into two rooms at a Holiday Inn near Thompsonville. I planned to sleep with Molly, for the thought of her lying there in bed, imagining Charles and me sleeping together shamed me.

She'd need more time to adjust to that. Molly seemed surprised when I suggested we share a room, but she offered no resistance, merely saying coldly, "Suit yourself." No, it was Charles who was upset. When Molly went into the bathroom, leaving us alone, he turned to me.

"Why did you tell her that?"

"What?"

"That you'd sleep in here."

"Charles, imagine how she's feeling . . . "

"Please don't sleep in here, Kate. I need you with me," and I thought I saw fear in his eyes.

"Why?"

"I just do!" It was fear.

"Charles, what's the matter?"

"Please, Kate!" He sat on one of the room's twin beds, almost shivering with this new, inexplicable emotion.

"Darling, try to understand," I held him. "Molly's still furious with us. If we sleep together, with her in the next room . . . how can she tolerate that? We'll never win her over if we throw it up in her face all at once. We need to go slowly, for her sake. For our sake, too. You see that, don't you?"

He didn't answer at first, merely stared at the floor, troubled.

"I love you" I said. "But we've got to think of her, too."

Slowly, sadly, he nodded.

"All right," he said, and I looked into his eyes: the eyes of a frightened child trying to be brave.

"I love you," I said and, remembering his true age, I added, "I'll be right next door."

His half smile broke my heart.

Later I lay in the darkness, listening to Molly breathe, wanting to talk to her, not knowing what to say, knowing only that I must use this moment alone with her.

"Molly?" I said softly.

"What?" she answered, and her voice was mercifully without anger.

"I never meant to harm you."

Silence and then—

"I know."

"I love you and I love him and I don't know what to do."

"I know," came softly in response.

"There must be some purpose to all of this," I half said half prayed aloud. "Some decent purpose."

"Maybe there is," she said.

"We were so lonely, the three of us. Now perhaps we won't be. Do you think that could be it, Molly? Do you think it happened to save us all?"

"I don't know," and her voice was so filled with regret that I reached across the space between our beds and held my hand out to her.

"Hold my hand, Molly. Please?"

She did and we lay there in the darkness, sister next to sister, holding each other as we had from the beginning.

Later, her hand slid from mine and I heard her sigh to sleep.

Charles. One of my children was sleeping. The other needed me. I got up and put on my robe quietly. Surely there was something I could do to make it easier for him, too.

I left our room and went quickly to his, tried

the knob and found the door open. I went inside.

I heard it immediately.

The soft sound of whimpering.

I went to his bed and saw him in the half light, sleeping, his face tightened against some fearful dream, and I understood why Charles couldn't sleep alone. The child, still a child, was afraid of the dark.

I held him until the whimpering stopped, until his face relaxed and the dream was gone. It was near dawn when I went back to Molly's room.

An old familiar voice spoke to me as I slid into bed.

"Hello, Kate."

I closed my eyes and saw Alan sitting in the corner of the room.

"How goes it?" he asked, pleased with himself.

"Please, Alan, no sarcasm. You know exactly how it's going."

"Right you are, as usual," he said. "One of 'em drinks herself to sleep, the other cries himself to sleep. That's some job you're doing."

I opened my eyes, trying to will him away, and for a moment succeeded. I was alone with Molly, listening to the comforting sounds of her sleep. She, at least, was peaceful.

"Oh, what a tangled web we weave when first we practice to deceive," Alan reappeared, this time on Molly's bed, stretched out next to her, his long legs folded, so damned relaxed and smug. "You think you'll ever whip those two into shape?"

"Stop it, Alan."

"No, listen, I'm on your side, honey. I just get this funny feeling, you know, a kind of premonition? I see you playing nurse to those two for the rest of your life. That one," he indicated Molly, "a little old lady with a flask in her apron and the other one, this great huge lummox always crying and carrying on. I really feel sorry for you, Kate. I really do."

I turned my back to him only to see him sitting on the far side of my bed.

"Well, I suppose it's all for the best," he went on. "I mean, it's what you wanted, right? A real family? Well, you've got it now. In spades."

"Go away, Alan," I said wearily. "Go away and let me sleep."

"Sure thing, dearie. I only came here in the first place to tell you what you were already thinking."

"I was not."

"The hell you weren't. Come on, face it. I'm dead. I couldn't come up with an original thought if my life depended on it. Hey, that's a good one, huh? Nope, all I am is your mirror. You're so goddamn noble, you couldn't possibly feel any of this crap, so here I am to take the blame. Listen, I think I'm a hell of a scapegoat. I'm always there when you need me, God knows, the price is right, I don't eat much . . ."

Of course he was right. I turned my face into the pillow, flushed with shame but too exhausted to go on and Alan disappeared.

MOLLY

A little souvenir from Charlie's childhood made all the difference; it damn well saved me.

What happened was this: As a toddler Charlie was half mouse. He was always crawling into things to hide. Cupboards, closets, anything I forgot to shut he'd make a beeline for. Then, after yelling my guts out for him, I'd spot these two little blue eyes looking out at me.

He called it hide and seek. I called it a pain in the ass. Anyway, one day there's no Charlie around and I start the hunt.

"Charlie? Come on out, mommy's in a hurry."

Not a sound, but I know to listen carefully, 'cause pretty soon the giggling will start.

"Charlie, will you please get your butt out here?" Still no giggles.

"Charles, I'm not kidding around. Get out here!"

And then the telltale sound. This time, from the pantry closet.

"Honest to God, kiddo, one of these days I'm just going to leave you where you are. Fine by me if you wanna grow up in a closet..."

I opened the door and there he was, all scrunched up under the shelves, next to the vacuum cleaner.

"You found me!" he yelled.

"Yeah, yeah, get out already."

Well, he got out. A little too fast. As he stood up, without watching, he hit his head on the bottom shelf, which was just a plank held in place by a couple of pegs. The blow dislodged the shelf from the pegs and everything fell off, on top of Charlie.

Including a goddamn sharp serving fork which got him right in the back of the neck.

The point of this boring little story? Charlie had three small scars on the back of his neck from that little incident. Three dots.

The same three dots I found myself staring at, sitting in the backseat of the car that next day.

For some reason, even though I knew the man sitting in front of me was Charles, it took those three little dots to really get to me, to make me know in my gut that this was my own kid, the kid I'd been searching for, the one I wanted to die for.

I started blubbering like an idiot, my arms around him, kissing those three dots.

"I still don't get it," I said to Charles that night as the three of us sat in his hotel room. He was wearing pajamas, stretched out on the bed with me sitting next to him and Kate across the room. Goddamn, he was handsome. I never would have guessed he would grow up so handsome. "How the hell did it happen?"

"I don't really know," he said. "I just knew it had to happen."

"You mean you willed it?"

"I suppose so."

I glanced over at Kate, who was staring at me, hoping I suppose that I'd say something to comfort her, because despite my change in mood, she was still a wreck. For her sake I said, "Maybe it is a miracle."

"I know it is, Molly," Kate said. "I know it is."

"Yeah," I answered, but I still wasn't sure. I mean, how the hell can you understand a thing like this? I'd grown up with men walking on the moon, atoms being smashed, now they were even making clones, but this was still too much. This was . . . Christ, I had no idea what this was.

But he was so handsome. My kid was so handsome.

"Well, one good thing happened," I started to laugh, probably because I didn't know what else to do. "At least I don't have to live through your adolescent rebellion. Or maybe I already have, huh?"

I put my hand up against his cheek and smiled at him. God Almighty, it felt good to smile again.

He moved his head so that only my fingertips touched him and that embarrassed me so I let my hand fall in my lap. I guess I was coming on too strong. Sure, he'd need time to get used to having a mother around, at his age. But he'd warm up. I'd warm him up.

"Well," I said, getting up, "it's the sack for me. Sleep well kiddo."

He gave me a half smile and Kate got up.

"Listen," I said to her. "Let's not be silly. You sleep in here. I don't mind being alone."

"You're sure?" and she looked at me with a kind of melancholy gratitude.

"Yeah, yeah. I'll see you both in the morning."

I went back to my room and lay down on the bed, feeling a little proud of myself. Hell, at least I had come to my senses. I wasn't pissing on them anymore. And who knew? Maybe it was all for the best. Maybe what Kate said the night before about us all being alone and now having a second chance was right.

A knock on the door and Kate came in.

"My nightgown," she said, getting her suitcase and then she put it down and came over to me.

After a long hug, I finally said, "Go on, your boyfriend'll wonder what happened to you. Besides, my back can't take the pressure."

"I love you," she said, getting her suitcase.

"Yeah, yeah."

The next day was the marathon drive back to the house, just what the old back needed. But what the hell, suddenly I felt great. I sat up front, next to my beauty, with Kate in the backseat.

"Hey, who taught you to drive?" It suddenly occurred to me to ask.

"Kate."

"Really? A lousy driver like her? It's a wonder you got your license.

"Who's got a license?" Charlie smirked.

"Oh, shit. Slow down, kiddo." And then a hundred questions occurred to me. "How the hell are you going to get one? You need proof of age. Jesus, Mary and Joseph! How old are you?"

"My age is in the eye of the beholder," Charlie said, real cute.

"Go ahead, make jokes."

"He's ageless," Kate piped up. "Like the other eight wonders of the world."

"Oh, you two are adorable," I said. "How's he gonna get a license? How's he gonna vote? How's he gonna pay taxes? How's he gonna do anything?"

"We'll figure it all out, Molly," Charlie said. "Don't worry about it."

"I feel like a goddamn spy," I said, and they laughed. "Like you were parachuted in here from Russia or somewhere. What about Mars? You a Martian, cutie pie?"

"Could be," he answered.

"It figures. You were always a weird one. Hey, you remember the time you decided you were an artist and you waited till I was out shopping to do a little artwork?"

"Oh God," he laughed.

"What?" from Kate.

"Well, Vincent van Gogh here decided to give the world a new mural. Right on my dining room wall."

"In indelible markers, no less," Charlie added.

"I had to paint the whole damn wall," I went on happily. "And then of course the other walls didn't match and I ended up painting the whole damn room!"

"And I ended up standing for two days."

"Goddamn, you were a pain," and I tousled his hair. This time he didn't move away. Hot dog, we were having ourselves a good time.

"And what about the time I heard that dresses were getting shorter and I took the pinking shears to your best one?" he laughed.

"That I don't remember," I said.

"Sure you do. I cut half of it off."

"Go on."

"Don't you remember? It was your favorite dress; the purple one."

"You're crazy. I never owned a purple dress in my life. Purple makes me look jaundiced."

"What are you talking about? Of course you did.

A purple dress made out of some kind of shiny material."

"You must've dreamed it, kiddo," and I glanced over at him. He looked a little upset. "What's the matter?"

"Nothing, I was just sure I cut your dress," he frowned.

"So what's the big deal?" I said. "Maybe you did and I just forgot. Who gives a damn?"

Evidently Charlie did, because he pulled off the road in a few minutes and asked Kate to take over the driving.

I mean, talk about your delicate dispositions!

KATE

I drove for the next four hours during which the three of us altered dramatically. Before, everything had been gay. But then, as Charles grew sullen in the backseat, our moods, like dominoes, toppled. Mine first, as I recalled his whimpering in his sleep the night before. And finally, Molly, with no one to share her cheer, succumbed to the silence.

I wondered as she had why a simple childhood memory should upset him so.

And then I figured it out. Smug, amateur Freudian sleuth that I am.

Charles had dreamed it. It upset him, not because he thought it had actually happened, but because it brought back to mind a nightmare, the same kind of nightmare that made him whimper in his sleep.

He had cut his mother's dress. Her apron strings. His tie to her. And now he was motherless and alone.

In part his dream was true; in choosing to be an adult he had given up the mothering he still needed. But the other part was wrong. He was not alone. I was there and whatever he had given up for me, I would give back to him. It would pass, this fear. I would make it pass.

"Good work, Sigmund," Alan said, leaning over from the seat where he sat next to a sleeping Charles. "I'm very impressed."

"As well you should be," I answered from my pinnacle of smugdom.

"Only one thing, doctor. You've been sleeping with the guy for quite awhile. Have you ever heard him cry in his sleep before?"

"No."

"So how come, now, all of a sudden, he's in tears over no mommy?"

"I guess seeing Molly again brought it all back. Being with her made it all the more real and frightening."

"Goll-ding it, the woman's got all the answers," Alan said.

"You bet your late ass I do," I smiled.

"What are you smiling at?" a drowsy Molly next to me asked.

"At life, darling. At life."

Over dinner, our previous cheerful mood returned. I was thankful for that and even more thankful to see that Molly had only two small glasses o' vine. So much for Alan's fears. *My* fears. When we got back in the car, Charles took the wheel and I sat up front next to him.

"Wake me when we get to Paris," Molly said, stretching out on the backseat as comfortably as her back brace would permit.

"See you on top of the Eiffel Tower," I answered, leaning back and closing my eyes.

Warm. I felt so warm. I suppose it was the *three* glasses of wine I'd had with dinner. Charles had only one. Because he planned on driving. Smart of him. Responsible. Such an odd mixture of adult and child my lover had in him. My lover, I thought. Lover. Lover. Love.

And I was asleep.

I woke hours later, my head jerking forward slightly as the car stopped.

"We're home, sleepyhead," Charles called to me as I came slowly from what felt like a lovely dream. "Up and at 'em, ladies."

I half opened my eyes and saw his smiling face.

"What time is it?" I asked.

He glanced at Alan's watch. "Eleven-thirty. Let's go in the house."

I looked through the windshield.

"Which house?"

The car stood in front of an old clapboard two-story house I'd never seen before. In the moonlight I could see it was abandoned, the paint peeling in blotches, one of the shutters askew. The yard was overgrown as if it hadn't been tended in years.

I looked over at Charles who stared at it in disbelief, as if he, too, had just seen it for the first time.

"I must have taken a wrong turn," he said weakly.

271

"A wrong *turn?* Sweetheart, you took a whole wrong road."

"What's up?" Molly wakened. "We there?"

"Not yet," I answered her, still looking at a shaken Charles. "Go back to sleep."

He continued to stare at the house, and in the bright moonlight I could see the peculiar look on his face: the strange mixture of confusion and fear.

"Are you all right?" I asked.

"You drive," and he got out of the car quickly, hurrying around it as if he were actually afraid of the place. I slid behind the wheel and turned the ignition key.

"What's the matter with me, Kate?" he said as I backed up.

"Nothing, darling," I lied to both of us. "You're exhausted, it's dark, you just made a wrong turn that's all."

"That's not all and you know it."

"What else *is* there?" and I felt almost afraid that he would answer.

"I don't know," he said after a pause.

We said no more about it then, but as I pulled out of the driveway I saw Alan, standing by a maple tree in the yard, waving good-bye, a cruel smile on his face.

We were home in less than fifteen minutes, the clapboard house being merely on the other side of town.

We went into the kitchen, I made a pot of coffee and the three of us sat wearily at the table trying to keep our eyes open.

"Remind me never to get in a car again," Molly

said. "I feel like I spent the day in a blender, set at liquefy. I've got aches in muscles I didn't know I had," and she glanced over at Charles. "What's with you?"

"Just tired."

"Well, how about a weak little smile for the old lady before she crawls upstairs and passes out?"

He tried.

"You call that a smile?" Molly said. "You must be tired. Good night, kiddo," and she leaned across the table and kissed his cheek, getting no response. "Good night, mother dear," she said, feigning cheerfulness, and then a nod to me. "See if you can cheer up the grouch, sis."

When we were alone, I tried.

"I don't understand why you're so upset." This was said with a mock offhandedness that sounded as phony as it was.

"We shouldn't have come back here," Charles said.

"What? Why not?"

"There's something about this place, Kate. It's just not . . . healthy."

"That's easily remedied," I said. "We'll go back to the city."

"Do you mean it?" his face lit up.

"Of course. There's no reason to stay here."

"Oh, Jesus, sweetheart, I love you," and he took my face in his hands and kissed me. And kept kissing me.

"Charles, stop," I laughed. "You're getting me wet!" to which he started to lick my face. "Stop, you little puppy or you'll sleep outside in the doghouse."

"Come upstairs."

"What?"

"Upstairs, wench."

"Charles, I'm exhausted!"

"I'll wake you up. Come on."

"We've just driven for ten hours . . ."

"Come on, old lady."

"Old lady, my foot," I said gaily. "These are the peak years for a woman."

"Prove it."

An hour later, I had, but at a considerable cost. As Charles rolled off me, I thought I would faint from exhaustion. He, however, seemed wide awake, leaning on an elbow, looking at me lovingly.

"You're terrific in bed," he said.

"How would you know? You've never had anyone else."

"True," he smiled. "I'd never want anyone else."

"That's nice," and I rolled over on my side, away from him, and closed my eyes.

"How am I in bed?" he rested his cheek on top of mine.

"Oh, Charles, let me sleep. We'll talk dirty tomorrow."

"No, I want to know. How am I?"

"Oh, Lord . . ."

"Come on. Gentle, dominating, sensitive, brutal, animal, vegetable, mineral?"

"All of the above," and I yawned.

"Oh, that's nice. That's nice and romantic, isn't it?"

"I can't help it. Today was the Olympics. I'm beat."

A pause and then—

"You want to do it again?"

"Are you crazy? I barely lived through the last time."

"Let's do it again, sweetheart," and he pushed into me so that I felt his hardness.

"Charles, stop."

"Please?"

"Darling, I can't. I'm so tired I'm near tears."

"Okay," he whispered, kissing my cheek, and he moved to his side of the bed.

"Thank you," I said.

"It's only a temporary truce," he answered.

"God, I ought to have you spayed," and I dozed off.

As deep as my sleep was, the sound of Charles crying in the middle of the night still woke me. "Charles? Are you awake?" I said groggily.

No answer. Just the muffled sobs.

I turned to him and put my arm around him. "Charles, wake up, sweetheart. You're having a bad dream."

And a sudden lurching of his body. A shudder and a stifled scream.

"Charles, wake up."

More shudders and I became frightened. I turned on the bedside lamp.

"Charles? Charles, wake up." I shook him, to no avail.

His body was twitching violently, as if he were being struck.

"Charles, please wake up! It's Kate!"

Moans. Deep, profound, agonized moans.

The bedroom door opened and Molly stood there. "What's the matter?"

"It's Charles. He's having a nightmare and I can't wake him!"

"Don't try," she said, quickly going to him. "Charlie? Charlie, it's mommy, mommy's here . . ."

She pressed her body on his.

"You're okay, baby . . . mommy's here . . . mommy's right here with you . . ."

The moans started to abate.

". . . everything's all right . . . mommy's right here with you . . . mommy's not going anywhere . . ."

Whimpers now.

". . . mommy won't let anything hurt you . . . just calm down . . ."

His body started to relax, as if he could hear her from the depths of his nightmare.

". . . mommy's got you . . . everything's all right . . ."

His body went limp; he was panting.

". . . that's my baby . . . that's mommy's baby . . ."

The whimpering stopped.

". . . nothing's going to hurt you . . . go to sleep . . . nothing's going to hurt you . . ."

She kept chanting to him as I sat there, feeling useless and incompetent, and when his body finally relaxed completely and he was sleeping peacefully, she got up and came around the bed, and sat next to me.

"Don't try to wake him up when he has one of those," she said. "Just talk to him. He'll hear you."

"He's had them before?"

"Off and on all his life."

"Why didn't you ever tell me?"

"It's not something you brag about," she answered, her face filled with regret. "A little present from his doting mother."

"Molly, you can't blame yourself for Charles's nightmares . . ."

"No? Who then? The man in the moon?" and she was so wretched I took her in my arms. "Now you see why I wanted to cut out. I never should have had a kid. Some people aren't fit for it . . ."

"Stop it, Molly. You did the best you could. That's all any of us can do."

"Yeah," and she sighed, pulling away from me. "Go back to sleep." And then she got up but stopped at the door. "Maybe you can do a better job for him than I did. I hope to Christ you can."

"I'll try, Molly. I love him so much."

"Yeah. So do I, believe it or not. So do I," and she closed the door behind her.

I turned off the light and lay there, listening to Charles's even breaths. Molly was wrong; she took too much blame on herself. I knew she had never been the warmest mother possible, but she always fit into the normal range as far as I knew. She was concerned but self-involved, supportive but impatient. Surely other mothers were like that without torturing themselves over it.

Guilt. Our heritage, Molly and I. Unreasonable, self-destructive guilt.

I swore then, that the chain of guilt would stop with us. Charles would not suffer as the rest of us did. He, at least, would be free of it.

"Yeah?" Alan said, suddenly standing at my vanity mirror, studying himself in it. "How're you going to stop it?"

"By loving him."

"Egad, another case of Love Conquers All," he smiled into the mirror, cocking his head to one side, looking, I supposed, for signs of decay.

"Shut up, Alan, and go away. I'm tired."

"Then why did you send for me?" he said lightly.

"I didn't."

"Okay, okay, let's not go into that again," and he nodded to his reflection. "Not bad for a corpse. But seriously, Kate," and he was sitting next to me on the bed, "there are limits to what love can do. What about some nice newfangled drug therapy? Why don't you get the kid to a shrink? You can afford it. Just sell this dump. That is, if you can find someone pretentious enough to want it. I can just read the ad. 'Haunted house for sale. Complete with ghosts, regrets, memories, hallucinations, everything guaranteed to keep the conversation lively. Excellent opportunity for right ghoul.' Good idea, honey?"

"Yes, as a matter of fact, it's a wonderful idea," I said, realizing that it was indeed.

"Well, then, I've served my purpose. I might as well push off."

"Alan?" I stopped him midway to the door.

"Yeah?"

"Thank you."

"Listen, what's a dead husband for? Toodle, babe," and he was gone.

I'd talk it over with Molly first thing in the morning, I decided, rolling over on my side to face Charles. First thing in the morning.

I saw the outline of his face, peaceful now.

"Don't you worry, darling," I whispered to him. "We'll take care of you."

MOLLY

The next morning, I called Dr. Phillips in the city and got a big, fat scolding. Where the hell had I been? Didn't I know that cast should have come off a week ago? Didn't I remember him telling me the brace would have to be adjusted? Scold, scold, scold. I finally shut him up by agreeing to come into town in a couple of days and let him do his thing.

Ye gads, what is it with doctors? They must get a special course in med school. How to treat your patient like a child.

Screw 'em.

"Where's Charles?" Kate asked, coming downstairs.

"Out for a drive."

"Really? Where to?"

"Do I know? I'm just his mother," and I studied her face. "You look like you're ready for a nap."

"I'm ready for a grave. Any coffee?"

"Yeah, Charlie made a pot before he took off for parts unknown. Come on, I doubt that you can pour."

She followed me into the kitchen and I sat her down and got her a cup.

"Adrenalin," I said, handing it to her. "Speaking of which, I've got to go into town Thursday to get this damn cast off. Wanna come?"

"As a matter of fact, I want to *go*. So does Charles. We talked about it last night."

"What'd you mean, go?"

"We want to go back to town for good. Charles doesn't like the house and I don't really see any reason for hanging around, do you?"

I thought for a minute; hell no, they were right, what was the point?

"That only gives us two days to close up the place," I said, seeing myself vacuuming and dusting and covering everything with sheets and, oh shit, the work.

"We can manage," Kate said.

"Screw it. Let it just sit, dust and all. The raccoons can have it, for all I care."

"Do you mean that?" she asked.

"Which part? The dust or the raccoons?"

"Don't you care about the house?" and she looked anxious, like she had something on her mind.

"I don't know," I shrugged. "I never give it much thought."

"How would you like to sell it?"

I looked at her. She wasn't kidding.

"My, we're full of news this morning, aren't we? Why should we sell it?"

And then she lays on me the idea that Charlie should see a shrink and at fifty bucks a throw, five throws a week, that comes to more than we can manage comfortably, unless of course we sell the house, which none of us really want anyway and the market happens to be up and, oh boy, is she getting enthusiastic.

"Molly, he's the best candidate for analysis in the history of the world!" she said. "Just imagine, a logical, insightful adult mind just a few years away from his childhood! Think of the access he has to it!"

I plunked myself down at the table.

"It could make all the difference in the world to him..."

"But selling the house," I mumbled. I mean, we had grown up there and as much as I couldn't wait to leave the place, I couldn't imagine giving it up either. I had always run to it whenever things got tough, when George died, when . . . well, maybe it was time to stop running. Time to do something for Charlie besides rant and rail.

"I gotta tell you," I said. "When he starts analysis, I'm moving to Phoenix, at least till he's over the angry stage."

"Then you'll sell?" and she looked at me like I just told her she was elected first woman president.

"God, wouldn't it be something never to see these damn antique pieces of crap again." The idea was getting to me. Hell, Charlie had given himself a whole new life; why shouldn't we? "Sell it? I'll give it away," and I added, "for a price."

"Molly, that's wonderful!" and I got a hug for my trouble.

Well, then we sat there, planning the whole thing over coffee. Kate was really something. In her mind the dump suddenly became a stately home worth at least a quarter of a mill. And the junk inside? Hell, you'd think each piece was signed by Duncan Phyfe personally except for those Louis XIV made in his off time. By the time Charlie screeched to a stop outside, she was something like ten feet off the ground.

"Oh, darling, do I have news for you," she said as he came into the room. She was too high to notice he was dragging ass, but I wasn't. Not that he seemed tired but kind of depressed.

"We're all going back to the city Thursday and Molly and I have been talking. It seems to us . . ."

"Go back?" he said. "Why?"

She stared at him, taken aback. "What do you mean, *why*?"

"*Why* as in why rush back to the city?" he said, helping himself to a cup of coffee. "I just came from the most beautiful drive I ever had. The leaves are turning, it's absolutely fabulous out there. Why go back to the concrete and cement now?"

"But last night . . ." and Kate was nonplussed. I just watched.

"Last night I was exhausted from the drive and acting like a horse's ass . . ."

"You weren't *that* exhausted," she said like it meant something.

"Really, Kate," he said, sitting down next to her and brushing a wisp of hair from her face, "I think it'd be silly to miss the autumn leaves by rushing it. It's like *nature's palette* out there," and he smiled at the cliche. Smiled, but still looked depressed to me.

"Well, I give up," Kate said. "I don't understand you at all," this, with a pout.

"You don't have to," he answered good-naturedly. "All you have to do is love me."

Well, I was beginning to feel like a third wheel, so I said, just to remind them I was there before the lovey-dovey stuff went any further, "I still have to go to town Thursday. Anybody want to drive the gimp?"

"I will," Kate answered. "If we're going to stay here another week . . ."

"Or two," Charlie shot in.

". . . I'll need some things from the apartment. Honestly, Charles, I don't understand you."

"I love you when you sulk," he said, kissing her cheek.

"Please, not in front of the old lady," I said, and he leaned over and kissed me, too.

"There. Equal time," he said, and then, like an afterthought. "Oh, listen, you'd better rent a car."

"Why?" Kate asked.

"I can't stay here without a car."

"For one day?"

"For one minute. It's too beautiful out there. God, it's like I never saw the mountains before!" and with that he got up and swept out of the room, leaving Kate and me staring at each other.

"I don't think now's exactly the time to go into the question of analysis," I said after a beat.

Later that afternoon, Charlie took the car out again, presumably to cream over the scenery some more, and Kate wandered around the pond to where I was sitting, baking the old bones in the not-so-hot sun.

"I thought you were going with him," I said, which is what she told me a few minutes before.

"He didn't want me to," she answered, disgruntled as all get-out. "Molly, I don't understand what's happening to Charles."

"What's happening to him?"

"Well, his attitude about staying here for one . . ."

"You sure he said he wanted to go?"

"Sure of it? Molly, when I agreed with him, he practically . . ." and she broke off. "Yes, I'm absolutely sure of it. Not only that, but last night, when you were sleeping in the car, he drove us to the wrong house. I mean, he actually pulled into a strange driveway and

283

stopped the car in front of a house I've never seen before."

"So? It was dark, he was driving all day . . ."

"I know, I know," and she circled me and sat on the grass, pulling her knees up under her chin.

"You look like a kid again, sitting like that. I can just see you in a sweater set and poodle skirt," I chuckled.

"Be serious, will you?"

"Okay, but serious about what?"

"His mood changes, the way he changed his mind about going back to the city, his terrible nightmares . . ."

"Those he's always had," and I felt chilly. "Let's go inside."

Kate followed me into the house, complaining all the way, until I finally put a stop to it.

"Listen, I think you're making a mountain out of a molehill. If you're going to be upset, wait until there's something to be upset about, huh?"

"I guess so," she said begrudgingly.

She didn't have long to wait.

After dinner we sat around the living room and I sensed something in the air; equal parts Vivaldi from the old phonograph and tension from Kate. We hadn't said a word to Charlie about selling the house or what we planned to do with the money, and I guess she was working up her courage to lay it on him. At least that's what I figured when she got up and moved to another chair for the hundredth time.

"Will you light somewhere for good?" I said. "We're not playing musical chairs."

My little witticism earned me a pout.

And then, after a silence that lasted long enough

to resurface a small highway, Kate turned to Charlie, who was sitting on the couch staring into his glass of wine like he was reading tea leaves.

"Charles?"

"Uh-huh," he said, still reading his wine.

"Molly and I have decided to sell the house," and she looked at me like she needed help telling him, which I didn't understand. I mean, it was our house, wasn't it? What the hell was she afraid of?

I found out, real soon.

"What do you mean, sell the house?" Charlie finally looked up from the wine.

"We hardly ever use it . . ." she started with excuse number one. "And the truth is, it's too much for us, now that Sissy's gone," excuse number two came out. "Who needs it?" This last excuse came packaged with a little offhand smile, like it was no big deal, but Charlie didn't look like he was buying it.

"When did all this happen?" he asked, hard as nails.

"Well, we were talking this afternoon . . ."

"That's just great, isn't it?" and he slammed his glass down on the table in front of him hard enough to smash it. "That's just great."

"What's the matter?" I asked him.

"Nothing! Nothing is the goddamn matter!" and he got up and paced. "I just think it's terrific that you two decide these things without even consulting me. After all, who the hell am I to bring into your confidence? I'm just a ten-year-old kid, right?"

"Hold your horses . . ." I started, but he cut me off.

"You two decide we should go back to the city and off we go. You decide to sell the house and wham, bam, we're out . . ."

"Charles, honey," this time Kate tried.

"Did it ever occur to either of you that this is my house, too? I happen to be a member of this family or has everybody forgotten that?"

"Of course it's your house, too . . ." Kate whined, again sounding afraid.

"Then how the hell can you decide to sell it without consulting me?" he snapped at her.

"But you said you didn't like the house. Last night . . ."

"Never mind last night. I told you this morning . . ."

"I don't see why you're so angry . . ."

"Don't you? My *adoring* mother and my condescending love gang up on me? Don't you think that's enough to make me angry? . . ." Boy, he was really going full steam now, practically running around the room, shouting accusations at us. For my part, I was getting mad. Who the hell did he think he was, yelling at me like that? He might think he was grown up, maybe he was, but I was still his mother. And despite what he said, the house belonged to me and Kate to do with as we pleased, and we were only going to sell it to help him, the ungrateful little bastard.

Kate, however, had quite a different reaction. She sat there and took it. And took it. Then, practically on the verge of tears, she said—

"But we only wanted to sell it for you!"

That stopped him in his tracks. He answered nice and calm. And sarcastic.

"And how do you figure that?"

Kate didn't answer. I swear to God, she was too scared to answer. What the hell was going on here, anyway?

"We want to get you to a shrink." I was the one

who finally had the guts to say it. "Which, at this moment, I think is a goddamn good idea," I added, still steamed.

"A shrink?" he said like he never heard the word.

"An analyst," Kate finally joined in the act. "To help you, Charles. To help you adjust to growing up so quickly. To help you get rid of your nightmares . . ."

"Nightmares?" he asked like it was news to him. "What nightmares?"

"Oh come on," I said. "You've had nightmares all your life."

"When I was a kid! A kid! Damn it, when will you two realize I'm not a kid anymore!"

"Charles, you just had one last night," Kate whined.

He turned on her, mean as a snake. "What is all this bullshit about? I don't have nightmares, Kate."

"Yeah?" I jumped in. "Then it was some other guy who got us up last night, crying and screaming and kicking . . ."

"What?" and he seemed to soften a little.

"Some other guy who scared the shit out of us."

He just looked at me. Like I was talking Latin and he was busy translating.

"You had one the night before, too," Kate said gently.

He looked from one of us to the other, really stunned and then Kate went to him.

"Darling, it'll be all right. I promise you, it'll be all right."

He didn't say a word; just looked at us like he was figuring out who was crazy, him or us.

And then, without a word, he walked right out of the house.

KATE

Molly was wrong; I wasn't afraid of Charles. I was afraid for him.

I caught up with him by the pond. He was staring into the water, deep in thought. Neither of us spoke for several minutes and then he turned to me.

"There is something wrong with me, isn't there?" and his voice reminded me of the Charles of months ago.

"No, darling, not really. But you've been through something extraordinary. It's foolish to think it wouldn't have an effect on you."

He turned away, back to the water and said, "All right, if you think I should see an analyst, I will."

"I think it could help. I wouldn't have suggested it if . . ."

"*All right*," he interrupted, walking away from me toward the house. "Let's not belabor it, okay?"

I remained outside alone. And then I remembered the last time I had tried to force Charles to see a doctor.

The time he first ran away.

The next morning, Molly and I were due to drive into the city; over breakfast I tried to convince Charles to come with us.

". . . but you'll enjoy it. You can go to a movie while Molly and I . . ."

"Kate, will you knock it off? I'm not going. I've got things to do."

"What things?" I asked innocently.

"What are you, the local inquisitor? Can I please have some privacy around here?"

"I'm sorry," I said, and, glancing at Molly, saw that she was glaring at him, just spoiling for an argument. "Molly," I said, to avoid one, "we musn't forget to go to the apartments. We'll need some heavier clothes."

"You bet," she said, distracted from him. "God, it'll be nice to wear something different. I'm gonna burn all the stuff up here when we get back. Especially that little beige number that makes me look like a . . ."

"Excuse me," Charles said, getting up from the table and leaving the room, almost, it seemed to me, in disgust.

"We better sell this place quick," Molly said, looking after him. "The sooner he gets to a shrink the better."

An hour later, we were on the road home.

Home.

I hadn't realized until that moment how much I had missed the city and my life there. Everything had changed so completely, so quickly. And now it seemed so long since I'd been home. So terribly long.

I dropped Molly at her doctor's office and went to my apartment.

Opening the door, the melancholy swept over me. The hall table was piled high with mail, those pieces they hadn't bothered to forward to me at father's house.

Two copies of *Gentlemen's Quarterly*, Alan's subscription. Ads, bills, letters, some for him, some for us.

I ran my hand over the surface of the table, noting the familiar feel of it. We bought it in an antique store in Greenwich Village barely a year ago. I remembered us standing off in a corner of the shop, plotting like thieves.

"Alan, it's four hundred dollars!"

"I don't care. Honey, look at it. It's gorgeous."

"I know but it's not real. Four hundred dollars for a reproduction?"

"Look, the money's going to go anyway; why piss it away on dinners out? Come on . . ."

He was such a child when he wanted something.

"I'll tell you what," he whispered. "I'll get him down, okay? If I get him down fifty bucks, what do you say?"

"What can I say? You're going to buy it anyway, even if he ups the price. I know you when your heart's set on something."

"And with the fifty I save us, we'll go shopping."

"God, Alan . . ."

"God, Kate," and he winked at me and sallied forth to do battle with the young man who ran the shop.

Four hundred the price was, four hundred the price remained, but the table did not.

I went into the living room. I'd forgotten how pretty a room it was. There were still ashes in the fireplace from the last cool day of spring.

"Alan, you're not going to make a fire?"

"Sure, why not?"

"Darling, it's June, that's why not. It's not cold enough out."

"So put on the air conditioner."

"You're a total cuckoo, you know?"

"Right. Come on, sit and perspire with me."

I slapped the couch pillows and saw the dust billow up. Before we came back, I'd have to get a maid in there. *We.* Who were the *we* who were coming back? Charles and I? No, I wouldn't think about that now.

On the mantel, the collection of elephants, our little herd, stood firm, guarding the place, tusks up, facing the front door for good luck. Where had we heard that?

"You've got to have them facing the door for luck," Alan's cousin Clare said.

"Don't be silly," Alan answered.

"Kate, talk to him. He knows I've always been a closet psychic. I'm telling you both, they have to face the door with their little tusks up, otherwise it's doom and destruction, destruction and doom . . ."

We finally gave in, to shut her up.

The piano was open. Damn. Dust on the sounding board. I ran my fingers over the keys. One maid and one piano tuner.

I wanted to come home, to clean and tune and put my home in order. My life in order.

The corner lamp didn't go on. That's right, I'd forgotten the bulb blew once upon a time.

I tried another lamp. It worked. The table was so dusty, the little French clock unwound, standing there dumb, the cigarette box half filled, the cigarettes crackled with dryness. Kent Light, my brand, Marlboro, Alan's. Dry. Dead. Useless.

I avoided the bedroom.

Caked toothpaste on the bathroom sink.

"Jesus, Alan, will you please clean up the sink after yourself? There's blobs of shaving cream and toothpaste all over it."

"Sorry, Harriet Craig," he had called in from the bedroom, months before.

"It isn't funny."

"Sue me for divorce. Irreconcilable sloppiness."

The hamper was still open; I could see a shirt of his lying in it. I remembered taking things out of it, packing them to take to father's house. Alan's things. The real Alan, not the Alan I conjured up in my madness.

The final blow came in the kitchen. I opened the refrigerator, to see what food had spoiled in my absence. There was something wrapped in wax paper; I opened it. Half a sandwich from the corner coffee shop. A bite taken out of it. The mouth print, the teeth marks still in the stale bread. Alan's.

I quickly packed the clothes I needed and left.

Molly was waiting for me in front of her apartment house.

"God, you're taking enough," I said, noting the suitcases.

"Listen, if you'd been running around all summer in a hospital gown and a few dresses, you'd be a clotheshorse, too."

We got into the car and started the long drive back.

"What'd the doctor say?" I asked, and she held up a castless leg.

"Quite a gam, huh?"

"For crying out loud, I didn't even notice. That's great."

"And, if you could see beneath my jacket, you'd note the new, lighter back brace. Very *in* this season, very now and with it."

"That's wonderful."

"Thanks," and then a pause. "By the way, sis, you look like shit. Was it rough?"

"Nothing a good old-fashioned suicide wouldn't cure."

"Not funny, kiddo. One near calamity in the family's enough."

"I'm sorry, I'm not thinking," I said, slightly surprised at my own insensitivity, but no more than slightly.

"I know," Molly said thoughtfully. "I had a little scene at my place over Charlie's old toys. They were all over the place."

A flush of guilt and then, "God, Molly, I am sorry. I'm so incredibly selfish . . ."

"Knock it off. Neither of us is up for the Eleanor Roosevelt Award this year. Anyway, I told the super to gather it all up and send it off to Goodwill. I doubt that Charlie'll have any use for the stuff now."

We turned onto the highway in silence. I assumed we were both back at our apartments, putting to rest our past lives.

Later, turning into the road that would take us to the house, I felt a new regret; that I was returning at all. Returning to Charles and what seemed to be an endless future of scenes, arguments, moods. But I did love him and that wasn't such a terrible price to pay for love, was it?

I still didn't know the answer to that question as I pulled the rented car into our driveway, and saw that my car was missing.

"Charlie must be out kissing trees," Molly said.

He didn't return until nearly seven that evening. Molly was upstairs napping and I was reading in the living room when I heard the car pull up. He came through the front hall on his way to the kitchen and I called to him.

"Hi, nature lover."

No response, as he entered the kitchen and closed the door behind him. I got up and followed him. As I entered the room, he was at the sink, washing his hands.

"Hi, darling."

He didn't turn, didn't speak.

As I approached him, I saw the muddy water; his hands were covered with soil and he was scrubbing them fiercely. Then I saw his face. The almost mesmerized look on it.

"Charles?"

He glanced at me and smiled.

"I found it."

"Found what?"

"What?" and he seemed to see me for the first time. "Kate, I didn't hear you come in."

"I know you didn't. I called to you twice. Look at that mess," and he seemed upset that I had seen it. "What did you find?"

"Nothing."

"What do you mean, nothing? You said you found something."

294

"Did I?" and the falseness of his smile struck me. "It doesn't matter."

"Tell me what you found, Charles," and I tried to say it lightly.

"You have a cuticle brush, honey?" he ignored me.

"Charles . . ."

"Later, sweetheart. I'll tell you later. Right now I need a cuticle brush. Be a good girl and get me one, will you?"

"I don't feel like being a good girl when you keep secrets from me . . ."

"All right," and he left the sink. "I'll get it for myself." Just before he pushed the swinging door open with his back, he smiled at me, this time, a genuine smile. "Don't be silly. Everything's great," and he left the room.

Great? Everything was dreadful. And getting worse.

That night, in bed, I tried once again to get the truth from him, and again met the same offhand but firm resistance.

"Don't be a nosy-body, sweetheart. Come here and let's make love."

"No, I'm not in the mood," and I rolled over to face away from him.

"You're not going to go into one of your pouts, are you?"

"I'm not going into one. I am in one."

"Silly."

"That's what you get for keeping secrets," I answered from the center of my pout. He put his arm around me and cupped my breast in his hand. "Don't do that, Charles."

"Shhh . . ."

"And don't *shhh* me. Take your hand away."

He fondled it.

"Charles, that's my body and I don't want it touched right now."

He put his cheek on mine.

"Yes, you do," he whispered seductively.

"Charles . . ."

"Yes, you do."

I pushed his hand away angrily and he rolled away from me.

"Okay, if that's the way you want to be, but you're missing out on a good thing. I'm terrific in bed, remember?"

Sadly enough for me, I did.

Hours later, the nightmare struck. The worst ever. I tried to soothe it out of him, but when the spasms increased, when he seemed to be jolted by them from one side of the bed to the other, I screamed for Molly. She had no better luck than I did; indeed, it took both of us, holding him as hard as we could to keep him from falling off the bed.

And then a horrific scream and he was awake; wide awake, staring at the both of us.

"What? . . . What's going on?" he asked.

"You had another nightmare," Molly answered, wiping the perspiration from her upper lip. "Jesus H. Christ, did you ever."

"What do you two do," he said, "work in shifts around the clock?"

At first I didn't understand what he meant, the sarcasm of it evaded me.

"If I can't get any privacy in this room," he continued, looking at me, "maybe I'd better sleep somewhere else."

The suddenness of his attack on us, the sheer lunacy of it prevented either Molly or me from reacting.

Charles got up and reached for his robe.

"First one of you is at me all night to tell her something, then you join in to spy on me while I'm asleep . . ."

"What in God's name are you saying?" Molly said, waking to the attack.

"I'm saying I don't like being watched like I'm some kind of freak . . ."

"Are you crazy?" she started to shout. "Are you fucking out of your mind?"

"If I am," he snapped back, "it's the company I keep," and he left the room.

Molly looked at me, stunned. "What the hell? . . ." and she bolted for the door. "Wait a minute, you! Wait a goddamn minute!"

"Molly, don't!" but it was too late; she was already shouting at him in the hallway.

"You think I like getting up in the middle of the night and wrestling with you?"

"Sure. I think you love it. I think it makes you feel like a sacrificing mother, that's what I think. A real martyr."

"Are you crazy?"

I got out of bed, shivering, afraid to get between them but knowing I must.

"If I am, you're the one who did it to me. My own loving mother ..."

I saw Molly first: outraged, stunned. And then Charles: enjoying every moment of it.

"You bastard!"

"Molly, please ..."

"You ungrateful little bastard!"

"Ungrateful? For what?!"

"Charles, don't ..."

"Keep out of it," he said.

"Charles," I pleaded, "we love you!"

And he laughed. "Love? What the hell would you two know about love? Just look at the two of you. Sisters in your fucking self-indulgent misery. Don't you think anybody else has ever suffered? Don't you think anybody else has any complaints except you two self-pitying bitches?"

"You go to hell," Molly started for her room.

"I'm already there," he answered.

It was madness. Madness.

"Charles, she's your mother!"

"*She's not my mother*," and he raced down the stairs to the front door. "Just because she gave birth to me doesn't make her my mother. You have to earn that."

And then the two doors slammed shut, one after the other, leaving me standing there, shaken, not knowing what to do, to whom to go. When I heard the car start up outside, I went to Molly.

We wept together.

MOLLY

It must have been around dawn when I heard him call me.

"Molly? Molly, wake up."

I opened my eyes and there he was, sitting at the foot of the bed. I swear, I almost threw up my hands to defend myself but then I got a look at him. He wasn't there to fight.

"Molly, I'm sorry," he said.

"Yeah?"

"Yes."

I studied his face and decided he meant it.

"What the hell was the matter with you? Kate and I were just trying to help you . . ."

"I know, I know."

". . . and you turn on us like some kind of maniac. Jesus, Charlie . . ."

"I know, I'm sorry," and he touched my hand.

I didn't mean to, but I found myself taking his big hand in both of mine and squeezing it, trying to tell him I loved him. I guess he understood, because he put his other hand over mine. We sat like that, holding on to each other, me fighting the need to cry, him not saying anything.

"Listen, kiddo, I did the best I could raising you. I know it was a crapped-up job, but it was the best I could manage. I had a mother, too, you know."

"Yes, I know," and he suddenly looked weary. "It wasn't your fault, Molly. No matter how you raised me, it wasn't your fault. We are who we are."

"Or who we're forced into being," I said, and he took his other big paw and stroked my cheek with it. "I love you, Charlie. I wish all this crap was over."

"It will be. I promise you. It'll be over soon."

And, thinking he meant the shrink, I lay back on my pillow but held on to him until he gently took his hand from mine and left.

Over soon? I didn't know about that. Shrinks can help, but not overnight. No, I thought, we're going to be tiptoeing around Charlie's emotional droppings for quite awhile yet.

Well, the next day, Charlie's pendulum swung a full hundred and eighty degrees. Talk about your Jekyll and Hydes. But at least it was Jekyll's turn, I thanked God. Over breakfast, Kate and I were treated to such relentless good cheer from him I began to wonder which was worse, the screaming or the stand-up comedy. I mean, Jack Carter served up with my first cup of coffee in the morning is not my idea of heaven. But if he wanted to make up, the least I could do was let him.

"Ladies," he said, beaming at us, "I've got a great idea. This afternoon, I'm going to take you both for a ride to see the scenic splendors of the great autumnal phantasmagoria."

"Oh, please," I said. One thing I didn't need was to gape at a lot of trees.

"I'd love to," Kate chirped, sitting on top of cloud nine with her feet dangling in the sky.

"You, too, Molly," Charlie said. "You've been cooped up in the house too long."

"Who's been cooped up? I've been in cars for weeks. Count me out, I just wanna find a soft spot and leave my derriere print on it."

"No, you're coming and that's that. We're all going to have some fun around here from now on."

"Listen, kiddo, one man's fun is another woman's pain in the butt. You two kids go and have a good time. Bring me back a leaf."

"Kate, will you talk to her?" he said.

"Well, if she doesn't want to go . . ."

"But she's got to go. Molly," and he turned the baby blues on me, "I've got a lot to make up for. Give me a chance."

Like I said, if he wanted to make up.

"All right, all right, but a short ride. I get hives from too much beauty."

A couple of hours later, our tour guide was rhapsodizing over a bunch of flaming trees on top of a local mountain.

"Let's drive up and get a closer look," he said, and Kate turned around and smiled at me, happy as a pig in shit.

"Boring," I said, and boring I meant. I mean, if you've seen one tree et cetera.

But as usual, I was wrong. The view from the top was sensational. It even got a rise out of hardhearted Hannah here.

"Let's get out and walk," Charles said.

"Riding, walking, pretty soon he'll have us running up and down like mountain goats."

Which is exactly what happened.

Charlie spotted a path through the woods to the top of the mountain and no amount of pilling from me would get me out of climbing it with them. So, trouper that I am, I soon found myself dragging ass up the goddamn mountain.

We got to a level spot just about the time my feet gave out.

"Rest stop," I called out, sitting on a rock. "You want me to climb higher, you get me a ricksha and a Jap."

They came back to where I was sitting and Kate found herself a rock. Charlie, however, was too elated to sit down.

"Just look at it!" he said. "Isn't it incredible?"

"Breathtaking," Kate agreed.

"Like a goddamn picture postcard."

"Oh, Molly, you're a curmudgeon," Kate said.

"Thanks, I take that as a compliment."

Well, they let me sit for a while, just long enough for the ache in my bad leg to start to go away, and then we trudged on. Through hill and dale, over ridge and deer crap, till we got pretty high up and even Kate succumbed to fatigue.

"Listen, Charlie old boy, may I remind you that what we climb up we've also got to climb down?"

"Molly's right, darling. Let's start down."

"I'm out with a couple of old ladies. All right, geriatrics, let's start the descent."

So we started down the frigging mountain, which was only a little easier than climbing up it. Oh boy, visions of hot tubs and soft chairs were dancing in my head. We took a new path down, because God forbid Charlie should miss a new vista or two, and we came upon a pretty steep stretch, going down the side of the mountain and as far as I could tell, leading to a sheer drop.

"You're not getting me to go down there," I said. "I may smell like a mountain goat, but that's as far as the similarity goes."

"Oh come on," Charlie said. "Look, there are flat rocks all the way down. It's like a staircase."

"Molly's right, that's too steep an incline."

"Will you two stop? I'm right here with you. Besides, it'll cut a half hour out of the climb."

"God help us," I said as Charlie took my hand and we started down it. Real slow. He was right, the rocks made it easier, but Charlie didn't. With those long legs of his, he took the rocks two by two, with me holding on to him for dear life, lagging behind a step. Then, halfway down, he let go of my hand.

"Wait a minute," he said. "There's a little clearing here. Rest stop number two."

We stepped off the trail, carefully, and all three of us sat on a fallen tree. My feet were two symphonies of aches and don't ask about my back.

"If we ever get back to civilization," I said, "I'm going to cement myself to a chaise and never move again."

"Make that two chaises," Kate agreed.

"Old, older, oldest," Charlie boy said.

"Blow it out your ass," I answered, always the lady.

After too few minutes, Charlie hustled us back to the path, the three of us took hands like kids crossing the street, and we started down, again with Charlie taking the rocks two at a time.

"Slow down, kiddo," I said. "You're yanking my arm."

"We don't have all day," he answered. "After this mountain, there are a few more on the itinerary."

"Why don't you just take up bowling or something to work off your boyish energy?"

And then it happened.

One of the stones must have been loose because as I stepped on it, it gave. I wasn't holding Charlie's hand at that moment and suddenly I felt myself lurching forward. I don't know how long it takes a person to formulate a thought, but in that hundredth of a second I saw myself falling down the rest of that path and right off the mountain. A goner.

Thank God Charlie reacted like lightning and got me by the arm. Thank God.

"Are you all right?" Kate's voice was really petrified.

"Yeah, yeah, queen of the klutzes is all right."

"It wasn't your fault. The rock was loose."

"You'd better hold on to me," Charlie said.

"Well, I would if you didn't walk so damn fast."

We inched our way down the rest of the mountain, my heart smack between my dentures. Never in my life did I ever see a sight as welcome as that car.

KATE

Molly was still badly shaken when we got back to the house. I helped her inside while Charles parked the car.

"There's mail," she said, stepping over it on the

hall floor. "I'm gonna go upstairs and lie down for a while. You want to bring me a cup of tea?"

"Of course, dear."

I picked up the few letters and glanced at them. A bill for Molly from the hospital, a letter for me forwarded from my apartment, an ad . . .

And a letter for Charles.

I studied the latter, wondering who on earth would be writing to him. The envelope was small, invitation-sized. There was no name on the return address, merely the initials E.H., written in a somewhat feminine hand and a local return address.

"Put some honey in it, will you?" Molly called from the top of the stairs.

"Of course," I answered, putting the mail on the hall table and going into the kitchen.

As I waited for the water to boil, I heard Charles come into the house. I wanted to call to him, to ask him about the letter straightaway, but I remembered his anger about lack of privacy and decided to wait. After I'd brought Molly her tea and seen to it that she was comfortable, I joined Charles in the living room. He had made a fire.

"It's a little chilly," he said.

"Yes," and I looked into the fire and saw the envelope and card that had been inside it, both turning black in the flames.

"You got a letter," I said.

"Yeah, I saw. It's the one you're staring at in the fire," and he stretched out on the couch.

"Who was it from?"

"A stamp company."

"A what?"

"A stamp company. You know, two hundred

foreign stamps, only ten cents. From a matchbook."

I looked at him and felt myself blush against his lie. He smiled in return.

"I was only that high when I sent for it," he said, holding his hand up at his previous height. "But I don't think I'm interested anymore. Collecting stamps is too sedentary for a middle-aged man, don't you think?"

"Yes, of course."

He lied well, casually and offhandedly, as if he were used to it.

I sat down across the fireplace from him and weighed my reaction. To confront him with his lie would surely lead to a scene, but to ignore it would widen the gulf that was already forming between us.

"I love you," I said, for that seemed to be the only solution.

"I know."

"Do you love me?"

"What a silly question. What do you think?"

"I don't know," I answered.

"Come here."

I went to him and allowed him to kiss me, all the while feeling the insincerity of his kiss, the strain of it. Another lie.

"I've got to go out for a while," he said abruptly.

"Where?" and I wondered if my voice were trembling like the rest of me.

"Just out. I'll be back soon."

I didn't argue the point; actually I preferred it that way. It would give me time to compose myself, time to decide whether or not to face him with his lies.

"All right," I said. "See you later."

I did indeed see him later.

It was in town, several hours from then. I walked all the way, Charles having taken the car as usual. I was in the supermarket, pushing a cart, happy to be a part of a normal everyday scene once again, when I saw Charles through the window of the market. He was walking down the street, deep in conversation with a woman. I hurried to the window and watched them until they turned a corner. She was a few years older than me, dressed in that typically bland country way. She wasn't pretty or even attractive but I felt a wave of jealousy nevertheless.

Was the letter from her? Was that why he had to rush out of the house?

I remembered my cart, sitting by the checkout counter unattended.

In a few minutes I was walking home, laden down with a bag of groceries and a hundred doubts.

He lied to me. Over and over again. Was anything ever the truth? Was our love the truth? If not, what was it he wanted from me?

An old loneliness returned.

"Well, maybe it was too good to be true," Alan said, walking alongside me. "You shouldn't have expected to replace me so quickly. I always felt the period of mourning was a little rushed, didn't you?"

I refused to answer, hoping that the self-mocking fantasy would go away.

"I mean, there I was barely embalmed and you were already cavorting with him, letting him kiss you, having little dates with him . . ."

"Please, Alan. Please. Not now."

"Face it, honey, there's something wrong with him. To be frank, I'm a little scared for you. Who the hell knows what he's capable of?"

"What does that mean?"

"It means that a guy who can go from ten to forty in a couple of months can do anything he sets his mind to."

My shudder was dispelled by the honking of a car horn. I turned to see Charles approaching.

"Need a lift?" he called out of the window.

"Tell him you'd rather walk," said Alan.

I opened the car door and slid in, leaving Alan standing on the road, shaking his head in disgust.

"Busy little housewife," Charles said, starting up the car.

We rode in silence for a moment and then I couldn't bear it anymore.

"I saw you in town," I said, not meaning to say anything at all, but needing so badly to dispel Alan's fears for me.

"Did you?" he answered flatly.

"Who is she?"

Silence.

"Who is she, Charles?"

"Just a woman I met. Just somebody I was talking to, that's all," and his face hardened. A bad lie, that.

"Was the letter from her?"

He stared ahead out the windshield and his eyes were filled with anger.

"I told you who the letter was from. Let's not make a federal case out of this, huh?"

"The letter had a local return address. Since when is there a stamp company in this town?"

"Since when do I have to answer to you?" he said, his voice constricted with resentment.

"Charles, why are you lying to me?"

"All right," and he pulled over to the side of the road and stopped the car. "I'll tell you. I met her the other day in town," and I could feel my heartbeat. "The letter was from her. She invited me to lunch, that's all. She's just a friend. Just a local yokel who's nice to talk to and doesn't treat me with the kind of condescension you do. She doesn't see me as a ten-year-old nitwit the way you do. I'm allowed the privileges of adulthood with her . . ."

"I don't condescend to you!"

"The hell you don't. You treat me like a fool. You *inform* me that I'm going back to the city, that you're selling *my* house, you treat me like a fool a hundred times a day. I'm a man, Kate. A man doesn't like to be treated like a fool, so I made a friend. Somebody who respects me, who thinks I'm pretty smart and worth listening to . . ."

And all the while he talked, I relived the past few weeks. My nagging at him over his driving or drinking. My instinctive resentment whenever he made a decision. *My* decision to sell the house, to put him with an analyst . . .

He was right.

"Oh, Charles, I'm so sorry," and I was crying.

He put his arms around me.

"Don't cry, sweetheart," he said, my *old* Charles said. "Maybe you couldn't help it. It wasn't so long ago that you had to treat me like a child because I was one. It takes a while to break that kind of habit."

"I'm sorry."

"Okay, stop crying. It's okay."

"But it isn't okay . . ."

"We'll make it okay," he said, and I looked into his eyes and saw the love I needed. "And don't be jealous of her. You're the only one I love, you know that."

"Do you, Charles? Do you love me?"

"Silly," he said, and he kissed me.

And I believed him. I believed him until that night in bed.

I was hungry for him; hungry in a way I hadn't been in weeks. He was my lover again. I was safe again.

I was lying in his arms, feeling the warmth of his body, his scent, his strength.

"Make love to me, Charles."

He kissed me and his hand moved to my breast, brushing it gently, stroking it. Oh, God, I thought, thank you for this. Thank you for him.

I reached down beneath the blanket to hold him and we lay there loving each other.

But he was flaccid.

I kissed him passionately and pressed up against him but in a while I knew it was no use. I relaxed a bit; perhaps my overzealousness had inhibited him. But the lovemaking slowed and finally stopped.

"I'm sorry, darling," he said in the darkness.

"Don't be silly. We have a lifetime to make love," but I felt saddened and cheated.

"I'll wake you up early in the morning," he said.

"Yes. Please."

But in the morning, Charles was gone and Molly in a rage over him.

MOLLY

You bet your ass I was in a rage. What happened was this: His Majesty deigned to, come downstairs a little after nine. I was in the kitchen mixing pancake batter, not exactly a crime, right? Well, His Royal Highness thought it was.

"None for me," he said, gulping his coffee. "I'm going out."

"Oh, come on, Charlie, one little pancake couldn't hurt. I put blueberries in 'em, how can you resist?"

"I hate blueberries," king of the grouches said.

"What're you talking about? You love blueberries."

"Loved. Past tense. Now I hate them."

"Excuse me for living."

"You're excused," and he finished his coffee.

"Listen, so I'll pick the blueberries out," I said, doing the mother bit.

"I don't want pancakes, Molly," and his voice had an edge. "I told you, I'm going out."

"Where are you rushing to?" I said, beating the shit out of the batter instead of him.

"Hey," he said pointing a finger at me. "A little privacy, huh?"

"Don't point, it's not polite. Besides, who's invading your goddamn privacy? All I asked is where you're going."

"None of your business, *ma*," he said, real sarcastic.

"Listen, give me a chance, will you? I'm on a time lag. I still think I'm your mother."

"You still think I'm a kid."

"Here we go again," I moaned, creaming the batter.

"Nope. This time, here *I* go," and he waltzed out without so much as a good-bye.

Well, I stood there, taking out my anger on the goddamn pancake batter, and I started to get really steamed. This I didn't need. The smart ass repartee, the now-you-see-me-now-you-don't routine, the I love you-I hate you crap. This I definitely didn't need.

By the time Kate came downstairs, I was carving those pancakes up like they were Charlie himself. It's a wonder I didn't cut right through the plate.

"What's the matter with you?" Kate asked, sitting across the table with a cup of coffee.

"Nothing. Nothing's the matter except that boyfriend of yours."

"Where is he?"

"Who the hell knows? *Out*. That's all the answers I get around here. 'Out.'"

"What did he do now?" and Kate looked like she didn't really want an answer so I didn't give her one.

"He's just a royal pain in the ass, that's all. I'm sick to death of those goddamn moods of his."

"He's been under a strain . . ." she started, looking the coffee in the eye, not me.

"*He's* been under a strain? And what have the rest of us been under? A hair dryer?"

"Be patient, Molly. He'll come out of it."

"Yeah, if we live long enough. Look, I've been

thinking. Let's get the hell out of here and back to town, huh? He must've had enough of the great outdoors by now. Besides, I'm getting the heebie-jeebies sitting around this place."

"All right," she said after a beat. "I'll talk to Charles later."

"Yeah, yeah, by all means get His Majesty's consent," and she looked kind of ashamed. "I'm sorry, Kate. You know me, my mouth's my biggest part. I know you love him and you don't want trouble, but I really think we should get moving on selling the place and getting the hell out of here."

"I'll see the broker this afternoon."

"Terrific. But you'll have to walk. Guess who has the car as always," and that started me on another tirade until I saw how unhappy I was making Kate and I finally shut my trap.

KATE

Later I walked into town and visited the local realtor. It was a one-woman office, presided over by a Mrs. Dreighton, a remarkably attractive woman for that neck of the woods, I thought. We discussed the house, which she knew, the acreage, the plumbing and heating of which I knew next to nothing. Sissy had always managed those things. And then, when the phone rang and occupied her for several minutes,

I looked around at the office. It was like Dr. Shiff's; simple, unassuming, smaller than I would have expected. *Functional.* Lord, I thought, would anyone ever want our massive house? They'd better have a dozen children.

"Here," she cupped her hand over the phone's mouthpiece and handed me a small loose-leaf book. "Look through. It'll give you an idea of pricing."

I flipped through the book of houses for sale, studying their photographs and prices. They were, for the most part, normal homes. Three or four bedrooms, ranch or split-level, forty to sixty-five thousand dollars generally. Ordinary, nonspecific houses for ordinary nonspecific people. A few Victorian monsters were there, but their prices were considerably lower than I imagined they'd be. Eighty thousand. Sixty-seven five. A hundred and twenty five. A good deal lower. I checked the estimated heating bill of the largest. No wonder it was underpriced.

And then I turned a page and saw a house I knew. A clapboard, two-story house. The one Charles had driven to the night we first came back. The one that seemed to frighten him. I read about it. The Pratt house. Up for sale for three years. Reason for sale, owner transferred to Washington, D.C. Condition, good inside, needs work outside. One and a half acres. Oil heat. Underground septic system. Four bedrooms, two full baths, one half. Asking price $47,500, down from $55,000.

I stared at the photograph. In daylight, there was nothing extraordinary about the house; as a matter of fact, it was if anything drearily usual. Perhaps that was why it hadn't been sold.

"I think we might start your place off at a hundred forty-five, if it's in good shape," Mrs. Dreighton said, hanging up the phone.

Charles was still out when I returned to the house, and Molly's mood hadn't brightened any. I suppose the estimated value of the house, so much lower than we originally thought, didn't help her. After lunch she said she was tired and went upstairs to nap. I sat alone in the living room, thinking of Charles. Was he with his new friend, his *platonic* friend who didn't condescend to him? Or was that all a lie, too? And what about his sudden love of nature? An obvious lie. How was I to sort the truths from the lies, coming as they did, one upon the other? And what was the point of them all; what was he hiding?

The ringing of the hall telephone interrupted my tirade of questions. A woman's voice spoke to me.

"Is Charles there?"

"No, I'm sorry. He's out. Can I take a message?"

"You sure can," and the voice was angry. "You just tell him that Elizabeth called and that I'm going to be busy from now on. You just tell him that."

"I'm sorry, I don't understand."

"He will," and she hung up.

Elizabeth. E. H. The friend who treated him so well, so much better than I, didn't want to see him anymore.

I couldn't wait to tell him.

I got my chance later that afternoon when Charles entered the house, or rather slammed into it, passing the living room without so much as a hello, and went straight upstairs to our room. In the hours between his phone call and abrupt reappearance, I

315

had time to think, and the thinking led to resentments that flowered into a full-blown fury. I would have it out with him, finally. Molly was right, his moods were intolerable and his lying outrageous.

I fairly flew up the stairs after him.

He must have sensed my mood, for as I entered the bedroom, he glanced at me, his expression nearly as angry as my own, and he said—

"I don't feel like talking, Kate."

"Really? Well, I feel like talking."

"Then go talk to Molly. I'll see you later," and he turned his back on me.

"No, I don't think so," I answered. "Just this once I think it's what *I* feel like that matters."

He turned around and seemed genuinely surprised. Lord, I thought, how long have I been giving in to him? How long has it been since I made demands of my own and didn't treat him with the kid gloves he didn't deserve?

"All right, what do you want?" he asked.

"Me? Oh, I don't want a thing. I'm here to serve you, didn't you know?"

"Sarcasm doesn't suit you," he said, again turning his back on me.

"Doesn't it? What suits me, Charles? To accept your rudeness without resentment? Your lies without question?"

"What lies?" he asked defiantly, back to me.

"I don't know. I don't know how many of the things you've told me are lies. I don't know where you go, what your relationship is with that woman..."

"Oh, Jesus... I told you, she's just a friend."

"Not anymore she isn't," and the words felt glorious, like weapons.

"What do you mean?"

"She called while you were out."

"What?" and he turned around. He seemed almost frightened. "What did she say?"

"Very little, actually, but I'm afraid you've lost a friend. She said to tell you she was going to be busy from now on."

He started to pace, literally wringing his hands in front of him. "What did you say to her?"

"What could I say? What business is it of mine?"

"What did you say to her?" and he took a step toward me.

"I told you, I didn't say anything. I just took the message."

"You must have said something to her!" and he continued to come toward me, his expression changing from fear to anger.

"Charles . . . " and I backed up.

"What did you say?" he caught me midarm and pulled me toward him. "Tell me exactly what you said!"

"I didn't say anything! You're hurting me, Charles! Stop it!"

He released my arm abruptly and started toward the door.

"Who is she, this friend of yours that you're so worried about losing?" I called after him.

He ignored me and left the room. I followed, standing at the top of the stairs, watching him go.

"Who is she, Charles?"

"None of your business!" He approached the front door.

"Are you having an affair with her?"

He wrenched the door open and turned to look

at me, a look of pure disgust. And then he was gone, the door slammed shut after him.

I heard the echo of the slamming door many times before I realized I was trembling and turned to go back to my room. Molly was standing in her doorway, staring at me.

"What the hell is happening?" she asked.

"I don't know," I answered. "But I mean to find out."

That night Charles didn't return to the house. I went to bed, miserable, confused and frightened.

And I dreamed.

A dream so monstrous that only now in retrospect can I admit to it.

I was in the gazebo once again, looking out over the lake, waiting for a boat that was to bring me something important.

"I'm worried for you," I heard Alan say, but when I looked around I couldn't see him.

"Alan?"

"I'm here, honey. Over here."

I searched for him but couldn't see him.

"Go back to the house, Kate. It's dangerous out here."

"I can't. The boat will be here soon."

"You don't want that boat."

"Yes, I do. I've been waiting for it for a long time."

"Your mother used to clean up the boats in the pond," he said, and then there was mother, up to her waist in the water.

"If it comes, I'll get it," she called to him. "Don't worry about that. She won't get away with a thing, not with me around."

"Mother? Mother, help me. Alan says I'm in danger."

"Well, he should know," she answered. "The dead always know these things," and she started to walk out to the center of the lake.

"Mother? Don't take the boat away, please . . ."

"Good-bye, daughter. Good-bye, whatever your name is."

I saw the water rise around her.

"Mother, please . . ."

"Good-bye for the last time. Take care of yourself. We all have to take care of ourselves. Nobody else will do it for us . . ."

"Mother? Mother . . ."

And she kept walking deeper and deeper into the water until her head disappeared beneath it. Her hair floated on the surface for a moment and then quickly vanished.

"You're frightening me!" I called out to the eddy where she had been. "It's not fair to frighten me!"

And then I was on the mountain, walking behind Charles and Molly. I saw Molly slip. I saw the earth beneath the rock, fresh and black, as if it had recently been overturned.

"Don't fall, Molly," I called to her.

"Why shouldn't I?" she smirked at me. "You fell, didn't you? You fell for him hook, line and sinker."

Then I was in the kitchen watching Charles wash the soil from his hands.

"I found it," he said.

"What? What did you find?"

"The dress I cut. Molly's dress. I found it under the rock, isn't that funny?"

"No, it isn't funny. You're frightening me, Charles."

"Am I?" and he washed his hands. "That's too bad, Kate," he turned and smiled at me; a smile so filled with danger, so cruel and monstrous that I began to back away from him.

"Don't go. I love you," and he held out his hands to me, his dirty hands, but it wasn't dirt on them now. It was blood.

I woke in a near panic.

The room was still and dark, it must have been around three in the morning. I lay there, panting against the remembered terror, listening to my own exaggerated breathing. And then I heard his. I turned my head and saw Charles sleeping next to me.

Smiling.

"Alan? Alan, where are you? Please come to me! Please, Alan!"

"It's okay, I'm here," he was sitting directly next to me, his arms around me.

"God, Alan, I'm so frightened!"

"I know, baby. I know."

"The rock . . . the ground under it looked like it had been . . ."

"I know."

"And the day before . . . I saw him in the kitchen . . ."

"Shhh, calm down, Katie. Just calm down."

I held tight to his arms and he seemed more real to me at that moment than Charles did; more real and safe and welcome.

"Do you think he tried to kill her?" I said, finally forcing the thought out into open. "No, that's ridiculous," and I waited for him to answer. "It is ridiculous, isn't it, Alan?"

"I don't know, honey," and he was on the other side of the bed, studying Charles's face. "What the hell is he smiling at?"

"But why? Why would he want to kill Molly?"

"A holdover from childhood?" Alan answered, staring at Charles. "Most kids want to kill their parents at one time or another, but they outgrow it. Lover boy never had the time to outgrow it," and he leaned in to Charles, face to face with him. "Is that it, kid? Are you a great big lethal baby?"

"But he couldn't have," I tried to reason in the midst of my panic. "He caught her!"

"Maybe he changed his mind," and Alan was back sitting on my side of the bed, stroking my hair.

"Alan, what's happening?"

"I don't know, baby, but you're going to have to find out, to protect Molly and yourself."

"Me? He wouldn't hurt me. He loves me," and I felt the bruise on my arm Charles had inflicted earlier. "What should I do?"

"Maybe his girl friend knows something. What was her name?"

"I only know her first name, Elizabeth, and the last initial, H."

"What was the return address on the envelope?"

"It was around here . . . I don't remember."

"Try and think, honey."

I lay there trying, Alan stroking my hair, calming me, loving me.

"Old Creek Road! It was Old Creek Road!"

"Good girl," and he started to fade.

"Don't go yet, Alan, please. Stay with me."

But he was gone. I rolled over, my back to Charles, to his monstrous smile, and I tried to force sleep. I would have to get up earlier than he did. I would have to take the car before he did. To Old Creek Road.

Old Creek Road was poorly named. If there had been a creek nearby, it had long since dried up, and the land had been parceled into small, suburban lots. The houses were like most of those in Mrs. Dreighton's book: Small, ordinary dingy. I drove slowly down one side of the road, looking at the names on the mailboxes, searching for an H.

Leavy ... Barrow ...

The sun shone brightly but my mood of the previous night lingered and the dread blocked out the sunlight.

Richmond ... Melnick ... Reish ...

Was it possible that Charles wanted to harm Molly or had the dream unsettled me to the point of lunacy seeming real?

Norris ... Weiss ...

Murder? No, not possible. Unthinkable.

Hampton.

The house was like the others that surrounded it, innocuous.

I stopped the car and got out.

By the time I rang the front doorbell, I was out of breath, wanting to run more than to find the truth.

An elderly man opened the door.

"Yes?" he said, without smiling.

"Is Elizabeth here? May I speak with her?"

He looked at me suspiciously and then—

"There's no Elizabeth here. You're sure you got the right address?"

"No, actually I'm not sure."

"There's no Elizabeth here."

"I'm sorry," and I started back to the car, relieved.

What would I say to her if I did find her? I didn't know. I hoped that she'd say something to me. Something to explain where Charles went, why he had been acting the way he had.

I prayed it would be something as ordinary as the neighborhood I was driving through. As simple and straightforward and safe.

I got in the car and started it up.

Two blocks later, I saw her.

She was walking down the street carrying a shopping bag. At the sight of her I clutched; I pulled the car to the curb and stopped.

She went into a small yellow house half a block from me, and I sat behind the wheel, again breathless, again wanting to run.

I didn't.

I pulled the car up to the front of her house and got out.

An ordinary house. Painfully ordinary. Surely there was nothng in this house that could harm me.

I started toward it.

And I saw the name on the mailbox.

In a moment I was behind the wheel again, pulling the car out as fast as I could, racing away from it, trembling and near terror.

The name on the mailbox was *Harley!*

I drove home in a frenzy, reliving my mother's crime over and over again, seeing Sissy in the kitchen, sobbing as if it had just happened.

She must be his sister, this woman Charles was seeing. The sister of the boy my mother had . . .

Why had Charles sought her out? What could he possibly know about a murder that happened so many years ago? I hadn't told him. I hadn't told Molly. I hadn't told anyone, and yet Charles was somehow involved with her. How could it be mere coincidence that out of all the people in town he had chosen to befriend the Harley woman!

I swerved onto the shoulder of the road, not paying any attention to my driving. I slowed down then, and the panic started to lift.

Sissy! She was the only person other than myself who knew. But why on earth would she tell Charles?

Yes, of course. To punish him. To show him the madness that streaked through our family. To show him that his own change was as evil as what mother did.

Yes, of course that was it. Sissy and her damned Bible, so ready to damn the innocent, so self righteous and serene in her one decent church-going dress. Sissy had told him.

But why had Charles befriended the boy's sister? Could it be that he was taking on the burden of mother's guilt; trying to make it up to the sister for her loss?

That would explain everything. His wanting to stay in the country, to be near her, his sudden anger at the responsibility he was taking on himself, his resentment against Molly, who was protected from the crime that he sacrificed himself for.

But he mustn't do this! It wasn't his fault!

As I pulled into the driveway of our house, I saw Charles standing on the front steps, waiting for me. He came up to the car and around to my door.

"Thanks a lot for taking the car without checking with me," he said as I got out.

"What?"

"I've been sitting here twiddling my thumbs waiting for you," he said angrily, and pushed past me to get in the car. He held his hand out for the keys.

"Charles, I have to talk to you."

"Just give me the keys, will you?"

"Charles ..."

He snatched them from me.

"Charles, please. I have to talk to you!"

He started the motor.

"I don't feel like talking," and he pulled away from me.

"It's not your fault," I mumbled to the back of the receding car.

I waited hours for Charles to return. I said nothing of what had happened to Molly, who was, as usual, in a fury over him. Charles had come downstairs to find that I had taken the car; he was angry and resentful. An argument ensued when Molly reminded him that it was, after all, my car. That's why he was waiting outside for me, as far from Molly as he could get.

Soon, I thought, as she railed against him. Soon we'll put everything right and leave this town and its hideous secrets.

It was after four when I could wait no longer. I started to walk to town, to see Charles, and a new fear occurred to me. What if he told the Harley woman what Sissy had told him?

A fantasy presented itself as I hurried along the country road.

It was a town somewhere in the South. A neighborhood near the outskirts. Small, undistinguished houses, many in disrepair. An elderly woman lived in one of them. About eighty. An alcoholic woman who clung to remembrances of past respectability. My mother. I saw her there, in that godforsaken house on the outer fringe of nowhere. The police car pulled up outside. They took her from the house. She was wild with fear.

I shook the fantasy off, realizing that I was shivering, from it as well as from the coolness of the autumn air. The trees on either side of the road on which I walked were already fading; the bright yellows and reds took on a somber tone that would soon enough give way to the browns of winter. We would be safe by then, safe in the city and we would never return. Eventually I'd tell Molly about our mother. Later, when she was stronger, when life was back to normal for all of us.

It took the better part of an hour to reach Old Creek Road and the sun, starting downward quickly, sent out a pale, almost surreal, light, placing elongated shadows on the narrow sidewalk. The yellow house was just ahead of me, still innocuous, still harmless. I looked for my car parked outside it, but it wasn't there. I decided to go up to the house anyway. If Charles wasn't there, perhaps she knew where he was.

It took several minutes for her to open the door. She stood there, looking at me questioningly. She was plainer than I recalled, she wore no makeup, her graying hair was pulled back and secured by a rubber band.

"What do you want?" she asked when I hesitated.

"I'm Charles's aunt," I said. It was the first time since his change that I had referred to myself in that way and I felt as though I were lying.

"You're his *aunt?*" and she smiled at that, showing a row of nicotine-stained teeth. "Yeah, so?"

"I was looking for him."

"Believe me, this is the last place you'd find him."

"Why is that?"

She half closed the door against me. "Look, if he sent you here with more lies, forget it. I'm not buying whatever it is he's selling and I told him so. If this is some kind of swindle, you're barking up the wrong tree," and she closed the door.

I stood there, stunned for a moment, and then I rang again.

"I told you . . ." she said as she opened the door.

"Please, I don't know what you're talking about. What lies? What did he tell you?"

"You know what he told me," she said suspiciously. "All that junk about my brother."

My God, he did tell her!

"You'd better tell him to stay away from me," she went on. "Otherwise, I'll put the police on him."

"Please, you mustn't!"

She eyed me suspiciously and then—

"Why? Has he done this kind of thing before? Is that why you came here, to shut me up?"

"But what has he done? I don't understand . . ." and I was shivering.

"You know."

"But I don't! I swear to you I don't!"

She looked at me for a moment then, and seemed to soften.

327

"All right, maybe you don't, but your nephew, if he is your nephew, got himself a nice little racket going. You know the kind. He looks up funerals and then goes to see the widows to get money their husbands supposedly owed him, that kind of thing."

I stared at her as if she were mad.

"But I'm not as dumb as he thought I was," she continued. "That cock-and-bull story about my brother . . ."

"He said your brother owed him money?" I asked.

"No, I used that as an example," and she lost patience with me. "Look, why don't you just ask him what he said, huh?"

"No, please. Please tell me. What did he say happened to your brother?" and I clasped my hands together to prevent them from trembling.

"What do you mean, what happened to him? He said he *was* him."

"*What?*" and my fingernails dug into my palms.

"Sure, my long lost brother. I don't know what he had in his mind. Maybe that I'd sign over the house to him or something. I just laughed at him and when he kept insisting, I got mad. I told him to stay away or I'd call the police. Now I'm telling it to you . . ."

"He said he was your brother?" I stammered.

"That's what he said, but it was too stupid to believe even for a minute. Hey, are you all right?"

I don't know what the look was she saw on my face that made her ask, but at that moment I realized with certainty that something even more horrible than I'd imagined was starting.

"Are you all right?"

328

"I . . . I . . . "

"You're not going to faint, are you?"

"No . . . no . . . please, could I have a glass of water?"

Something dark and beyond understanding was coming toward Molly and me; something I was helpless to stop.

She took me into the house, through a small drab living room spotted with crucifixes and a print of the Madonna to a large kitchen filled with the late afternoon sun. An elderly woman sat staring out into the backyard and as the daughter got me a glass of water, I studied the mother. *His* mother. Her pain and loss had not diminished through the years; they were still there in her eyes that never turned even to glance at the intruder in her home. Could she still be waiting for her son to return, I thought?

"Drink this," the daughter handed me a glass and as I drank she took a photograph from the windowsill next to her mother and held it up before me. An old family photograph. Father, mother and two children. A girl, about ten, plain then as she was now. A boy, slightly younger, perhaps a year, redhaired and freckled, plain as his sister.

"You tell me how that kid could grow up to look like your nephew," she said, returning the picture to her mother who glanced vacantly at it and then back out the window. "But he certainly went to a lot of trouble to con me. He said he even went back to our old house, looking for us, then he checked the phone book . . . "

I didn't hear what she said after that. I was walking away quickly, through the living room, where the Madonna stared at me, and out the door, terrified to hear any more. The last sound I heard from the yellow house was the slamming of its front door as I reached the sidewalk and started up the street. I didn't think. I couldn't. It was madness.

I had walked a few blocks when I heard a car's horn behind me. I turned to look.

It was Charles. He had seen me come from her house.

I started to run.

He pulled the car up beside me and hit the horn again several times.

I didn't look at him. I ran.

And again the car pulled up just ahead of me and the horn sounded.

I ran past it.

In a moment, I heard him drive in the opposite direction.

I stopped running, out of breath, aware that the few people on the street were looking at me, and I walked on, looking straight ahead.

I was afraid of Charles. Afraid of him!

He said he was her brother!

He had gone back to their old house, that was what the sister said. Was it the house he had driven us to the night we returned? The house that seemed to terrify him so?

I was a few blocks from the realtor's office. As I hurried up the stairs, Mrs. Dreighton was already locking up.

"Hi," she said. "You caught me just in time."

"Mrs. Dreighton, would you do me a favor? There's a house I saw in your book. Could I see it again, please?"

"Sure. Is anything the matter?"

I realized what I must have looked like; out of breath, hair wild from running, obviously frightened.

"No, I'm all right. Please, the book?"

"Sure," she said, opening the door.

I went to her desk and got it.

"Would you like something, Kate? A cup of coffee?"

I didn't answer her. I was too busy searching for the clapboard house amid all the others. And then I found it. The Pratt house.

"Could you find out who owned this house before the Pratts?" I demanded, holding the book out to her.

"Sure, it must be in the files. Listen, are you sure you don't want something? A cup of coffee?"

"No, please. I don't have time."

She took the book from me and went to a large filing cabinet in the corner of her office as I sat there, still unable to think, still unable to put the mounting pieces together. In a few minutes she said, "It belonged to Richard Harley. He sold it to the Pratts in fifty-four. As a matter of fact, I think he bought another house through this office, but that was before I worked here. Let me take a look . . . "

"A yellow house on Old Creek Road," I said getting up and hurrying to the door.

"Kate? Kate, are you all right?"

But I didn't answer. Outside, the sun was nearly over the rim of the hills and it was cold. I doubled my sweater in front of me and walked into the wind, unconsciously choosing a path homeward.

He said he was her brother.

Her brother who died thirty years ago.

Her brother who would have been about forty; the age at which Charles stopped growing.

He found their house without knowing what he was doing.

Once he found it, he became moody and hostile to Molly and me. Perhaps he even . . .

Molly! Was she alone with him?!

Oh no, God, please no!

I ran on, near tears, the wind opening my sweater and flapping it on either side of me, like the hysterical wings of a frightened bird.

I saw the rock, the soil beneath it, the muddy water in the kitchen sink . . .

Please, God, don't let this happen!

. . . I saw Charles twisting and jolting in his sleep as if he were being hit and dragged by a car; my mother's car . . .

Things like this don't happen!

. . . Charles in the gazebo, months ago, starving. . .

God help us!

. . . Charles smiling in his sleep . . .

Molly! Molly run!

MOLLY

I was in the kitchen when Charlie came in, looking worse than I'd ever seen him. At first I thought he was sick, but as he slumped down at the table, I realized he was just exhausted. Shot.

"Sit down, Molly," he said softly. "It's time."

"Time for what?"

"To talk."

"Yeah? What're we gonna talk about?"

"Me."

"Sure, the favorite topic around here," I said, still mad as hell at him.

"My name is David Harley," he said, real low.

KATE

I could run no further; I ached from it. It was dusk and the shadows of the trees on either side of the road met in the middle; I stepped over them wearily, near exhaustion.

I knew it was true.

They were sitting at the kitchen table when I arrived at the house; just sitting there, both looking weary and drained. But for the moment, at least, Molly was safe.

"You know, don't you?" Charles said as I came up beside Molly and put my hand protectively on her shoulder.

"Yes."

She looked up at me and snorted a short derisive laugh. "Welcome to the nuthouse, Kate. I'd like you to meet . . . what did you say your name was?"

"David Harley," he answered.

"Yeah, that's right. David Harley," Molly went on, and she seemed dizzy from it all. "Sit down, Kate, and I'll fill you in."

"You don't have to," and I sat next to her, drawing my chair close so that I could put my arm around her.

"Oh yeah, I better," she went on. "Believe me, it's one hell of a story. Straight out of Edgar Allan Poe. The only thing we're missing is the fuckin' raven . . ."

I took her hand.

" . . . yeah, so, it goes something like this," she turned to him, "correct me if I screw it up, huh? It's not the easiest story in the world. Anyway," and back to me, "it seems I never had a kid. Not my own, anyway. What I gave birth to was somebody else's kid. You got that? It gets better, I promise you . . ."

"Molly . . ."

"No, let me finish, Kate. The kid I gave birth to, the kid that wasn't mine, remember, was actually killed years ago. He was run over. Now we get to the good part," and her eyes glowed red as if she might cry. "Take a guess who ran him over."

"Mother."

The look on her face, a mixture of grief and amusement, vanished and she stared at me. Then, after a moment, she said, "He already told you?"

"No. I knew."

She smiled. "Great. Now I not only have a ranting lunatic for a son, I've got one for a sister."

"He's not your son," and the words, spoken as tenderly as I could speak them, stunned her. Molly stared ahead blankly; the same look I had seen earlier on the face of Charles's real mother.

"Let me explain, Molly," I said, and as I told her of the day that Sissy and I sat at that same table, a day that now seemed decades away, she continued to stare, numbed by the apparent lunacy of it. I told her of our mother and the house where Charles had lived one lifetime ago, of his sister and his mother who still sat, looking out vacantly, waiting for him. And if Molly understood, she was beyond acknowledging it. And then, having completed my insane rhetoric, I looked at Charles's face directly for the first time. But where I had expected the glare of a demon was only the sad, regretful look of a man; a man who was in as much pain as we were.

"When did you find out?" he asked.

"Today. And you?"

"I don't know when I first realized it," he answered sadly. "I've been piecing it together for a while."

"Yes, I know."

"But David Harley is dead!" Molly suddenly shouted. "He's dead!"

"No, Molly," was all that he said, and he tried to take her hand, but she refused. "Poor Molly. We've asked you to believe in so many impossible things. I suppose one more doesn't matter. Yes, I was dead, but then I was alive again. I don't know how. I don't even remember when it first occurred to me that I was somebody other than I'd always thought I was. One day I just ..."

"Kate, make him stop these lies!" Molly pleaded with me.

"It's the truth, darling," I took her in my arms. "God help us, it's the truth."

She put her head on my shoulder as she had

done a thousand times when we were children and as I stroked her I turned back to the man who had once been my lover and who, I knew certainly but without fear, would soon be my executioner.

"How did you know, Charles?"

He smiled at me tenderly, this creature who had recently been the center of my life and would soon be the end of it.

"It was a slow awakening, Kate. Very slow. It started when I changed. At first I thought I had changed for you. It seemed to be a great thing born out of a great love . . . "

Yes, that was how I had seen it. A miracle of love. But of course, we were both wrong.

" . . . but then other thoughts came to me. I wasn't the Charles that had been, certainly, but was I Charles at all? Or was I someone else entirely? So many memories just out of reach . . . memories that couldn't have been Charles's . . . even death . . . "

"God," Molly whimpered.

"You remembered death?" I asked, myself growing numb from the fear that was starting in me.

"A blackness only. I was part of a blackness. Not in it, part of it. There's a difference."

Molly trembled. "Don't, Charles," I pleaded. "Don't frighten her."

"I don't want to," he answered. "I don't want to frighten either of you. I love you both. I swear that's true, Kate. I do love you both."

He swears, I thought. The devil swears but by what?

"And yet you've come back to harm us?"

He looked at me in surprise.

"Harm you? What are you talking about?"

"Surely it's obvious," and though I meant to protect Molly, at that moment I needed to hear the truth out loud before the nightmare end started. "Our mother ended your life . . ."

"And Molly gave it back to me," he said.

"For what purpose, Charles? Why are you back from the dead?"

"I don't know," was all that he said. "Not yet."

"Then let me help you figure it out. You're here to kill us both. To kill the children of the woman who killed you," and having said it, finally, irretrievably, I knew it was the truth.

"No!" He went white.

"Charles, you already tried once!"

"What are you talking about?"

"That day on the mountain, the rock was dug loose . . ."

"I didn't! I swear I didn't!"

"And the day before, you washed the soil from under that rock from your hands, right here, right in this room . . ."

"No!"

"Yes, I saw you!"

"No, Kate," and his voice was near breaking. "It was the soil from my grave!"

We froze.

MOLLY

I don't know how long it took me to pull myself together. Listen, I'm not proud of it, but at that moment, I just couldn't face it. Personally, I never bought any of it. David Harley back from the grave? Sure, and pigs fly. What I had to deal with here was worse. Charlie and Kate were crazy, that was all there was to it. They were both plain nuts.

Anyway, I pulled myself together.

And it was lucky I did, for Kate had had it. She just sat there, her head in her hands, gasping for air. And Charlie? Charlie was worse off. He just stared at the table, thinking God-knows-what. The room was pretty dark now, for they'd been going at it for quite awhile. I got up and turned on the overhead lamp and the two of them looked like scared raccoons caught at the garbage in the light of a flashlight.

Anyway, remember me, I'm the one who cooks when she doesn't know what else to do? I figured this was definitely a time when there was nothing else to do, so I suggested we eat something. Nobody objected and though nobody agreed either, I got some cheese and bread out of the refrigerator and made sandwiches. I mean, talk about your insanity! Here my son tells me he's somebody else, my sister tells me our mother killed him before he was even born and what do I do? Spread the mayonnaise. And I called them crazy?

Needless to say, nobody ate, but we did get down some tea, in almost total silence. Once, Charlie looked over at Kate and said, "I'd never harm you." And that was the evening's conversation.

God, if you're up there, enough's enough.

KATE

But enough was not quite enough. One more night to get through; this night just past, for it's dawn now as Molly and I sit here telling you our bizarre story.

A few hours ago, satisfied that Molly was sleeping and that Charles had no immediate intent of harming her, I slipped out of bed and came downstairs. I found myself sitting in father's wingback chair, thinking. We had to leave, Molly and I, before Charles could realize his terrible destiny. But what would he do without us? Even in that moment of grievous fear I worried for him. And loved him still.

A sound at the doorway. I turned to see Charles standing there.

"Kate? Can I talk to you?"

Was this it, then? The start?

"Please, Kate?"

But there was no threat in his voice; just the same weary resignation.

"Yes, come in."

He sat on the couch across the room from me.

"You look exhausted," he said.

"I am."

"Yes, of course," and he looked around the room as if he were seeing it for the last time. "I won't harm you," he said, without looking at me.

"Yes, you will, Charles. You have to."

"Why?"

"Because it's your destiny."

We sat silently for a long time, he, staring at the room, me, looking at his still handsome face, remembering the first time I'd seen it there in the gazebo.

"Can't one change one's destiny?" he asked finally.

"I don't know. Can you control your rages? When you attacked Molly after your nightmare, could you have controlled that?"

Another silence and then—"I love Molly."

"She doesn't think so," I answered.

"I know. I gave her a hard time. Maybe part of the reason I did was that somewhere in my mind I knew I wasn't her son."

"I think I should take Molly away from here," I said.

"Away from me you mean."

"Yes."

And a final silence after which Charles got up and walked to the doorway.

He turned before going upstairs and said the last words I ever heard him say.

"I love you, Kate."

I sat there, in the hardness of my father's chair,

in the hardness of the legacy he and mother had bequeathed Molly and me.

I love you, Kate.

Had anyone ever truly loved Kate? Alan, perhaps, for a while. Charles? I did not know.

It was hours later, near dawn, that I awakened next to Molly. I heard the echo of a sound; a moan, perhaps, or had that been dreamed? I looked at Molly, who was still sleeping that impenetrable sleep of hers, and slipped out of bed quietly. Outside our room the house was still but it was stillness left over after something has imploded; could it have been Charles? I went to his room and listened at the door. Nothing. And nothing downstairs in the living room or the hall. Or the kitchen. At first.

And then I saw the envelope on the table in the dimness. My name was on it, written in a child's handwriting. A familiar child's handwriting. The sound I had heard focused. It was the car, starting up, pulling away. I opened the letter.

Dearest Kate,

A few minutes ago I stood by your bed and watched you and Molly sleeping together, peacefully. Please believe me, I'd never willingly do anything to disturb that peace. I've come to love you both too much for that. But what you said must be true. My destiny must be to harm you both. You were right about the rages, you know. I don't think I can control them. And so the only thing I can think of to do is to go back where I belong before anything more terrible happens. We've all been through a monstrous time, but it's over now. By the time you read this letter, it'll be over for me, and soon, I pray, it'll be over for

*you both. Go back to your lives, dear Kate and Molly.
Go back to your lives and forget the Charles that
never was and the David that never should have been.
Both of them loved you with all their hearts, even if
they did put you through hell. Please forgive them.
They never meant to.*

Charles.

I stared at the terrible words, trying to understand what they meant. And then I knew.

"Molly, get up! Get up, for God's sake!"

She moaned and turned away from me.

"Molly, please! I need you!"

"What?" she said, and her eyes foreshadowed the
terror that was to be.

"It's Charles! He's going to kill himself! Hurry,
please!"

"My God, what's happening?"

"I'm going down the road to try to borrow a car,"
I said, wrenching a dress from my closet with such
force that I snapped the plastic hanger in two. "Quickly, get dressed!"

The heritage of death, always a part of our lives,
was near again. But this time, I would prevent it. I
had done this to Charles; I had determined his cruel
destiny and I would prevent it.

I raced from the house, Molly's voice calling to
me in unrecognizable words.

The nearest neighbor was two blocks away. As
I ran, I cursed the distance. Who were they, these
people in the white clapboard house that had always
stood far enough away from father's house to be
impenetrable? I vaguely remembered the sound of
children from another time, but of course, they would

be grown and gone by now. Gone to safe lives, unlike the madness that grew up near them.

The house was dark when I reached it; it seemed I had pounded on the door endlessly before a window, directly above me, turned yellow.

"Who's that?" a woman's voice called to me.

"It's Kate from up the road," I answered stupidly, as if she would remember.

The head disappeared and the window turned black; but then another window, beside me, glared.

The front door opened slightly and a face, now too old to be judged man or woman, looked out at me suspiciously.

"Yes, it's you," she said, satisfying herself. "What's happened, child?"

Child. I thought I heard a hint of honest concern; had it always been there, just out of reach?

"There's been an accident," I lied or foretold. "Please, Mrs. . . ." and I had no idea what her name was.

"Emily," she said, her voice hoarse with sleep but surprisingly sweet.

"Can I borrow your car? Please?!"

She shuffled into action, throwing the door open wide and hurrying into the darkness of the house.

"The key's in the kitchen, child."

I followed her inside, through the living room filled with photographs of the children who were now gone, past love-worn furniture into the kitchen.

"Is it your sister?" she asked, searching the cupboard counter.

"Yes . . . I've got to get her to the hospital."

"Oh, dear," she muttered, coming up with the keys. "Hurry, then. The car's out front. Hurry!"

I kissed her quickly. "Emily, thank you."

"Call me later, I'll be home," she said, half pushing me toward the living room.

Outside, I found, instead of an ancient wreck of a car, a brand new Toyota, the incongruity of which struck me as I turned on the ignition and heard the strong, confident purr of its motor. Was this, then, what had been happening around me without my knowledge? People growing old, living normal lives, buying new cars, untouched by the dreadful fates I knew to exist? You, too, will grow old like them, I swore to Charles. You offer me your life. I offer it back to you.

Molly was hurrying down the road as I drove toward the house; she was dressed, but in her daze she had put on a robe over her clothes.

"I read the letter," she said, getting into the car. "I still don't know what the hell's going on."

"Just pray, Molly. Pray we can find him."

"Where are we going?"

"To the mountain." The mountain Charles had taken us to. The one he seemed to know. To be drawn to.

We drove silently through the blue-black of predawn, and, not daring to think of what might lie ahead, I conjured up the only person who could understand; the only one who had seen it all with me.

"I think you're making a big mistake," Alan said, leaning forward from the backseat.

"I don't want him to die."

"Would you rather die in his place?"

"If I have to. I'm responsible for this, Alan. I helped him when he changed. My mother killed him."

"The sins of the mother, huh? Babe, turn back. No matter how you feel about him, he's still a demon."

"No, he isn't."

"Then what would you call him? Misunderstood?"

"Please, Alan, I'm so frightened. Please help me."

"I'm trying, babe, I'm trying. What about Molly? You're playing Russian roulette with her life, too."

I glanced over at Molly, who was deep in her own thoughts, and wondered if George, too, were back. Would he be warning or comforting her?

"Jesus, Kate," Alan sounded petulant, "he as much as admitted in the letter that it's you or him. Why the hell are you trying to save him?"

"Nobody's going to die," I answered, mindlessly.

"Sure, and we're all going to live happily ever after."

I pressed on the accelerator in response.

"You're going too fast." Molly woke from her silence. "Slow down. We can't help him if we get killed."

"Nobody's going to get killed," I repeated.

We were still several miles from the mountain and it finally occurred to me that there was no real reason to assume he'd go there. Unless . . . and a thought so bizarre occurred to me that I pushed it out of my mind immediately. And as if he could read my thoughts, Alan said,

"Why are we going to the mountain?"

"I think that's where he'd want to die."

"Why?"

"Because I think that's where his grave is," I admitted, pushing harder on the accelerator, watching the needle reach sixty.

"Slow down, for crissake," Molly said.

"Returning to his grave?" Alan said, and then snorted. "We are getting Poeish, aren't we?"

345

"I suppose," and the needle hit sixty-five.

Two miles to go. Perhaps less.

"Jesus," Molly muttered, seeing the needle.

I imagined myself finding Charles. He was standing on top of the mountain, facing a deep precipice as I reached him. His eyes were filled with tears as I pleaded with him.

Seventy.

It was difficult to persuade him not to do this terrible thing but I won out in the end and we went home together, the three of us. Triumphant.

A mile to go.

"For God's sake, will you slow down?" Molly snapped, and I obeyed.

Ahead, the mountain came into sight as we swerved, too quickly, around a turn in the road. The gold glow of dawn sat on its peak.

"The sun's coming up," I said, mindlessly.

"Since when does it come up in the north?" Molly answered.

Oh, God, no!

The road up the mountain was steep and twisted. I took it as fast as the four-cylinder car could manage, painfully slow for me, terrifyingly fast for Molly.

"Jesus Christ, Kate, are you trying to get us killed?"

No one will die! No one will die!

"Slow down!"

"I can't!"

No one will die!

The glow was gold and red. Too harsh for the rising sun. Too cruel for anything but fire.

"What's the matter with you?!"

"Alan!" I pleaded, but he was gone and I was too frightened to conjure him back.

"Kate, please . . ." Molly went on at me but I only heard my own prayers, my own hysterical pleadings. Don't let this happen; oh God, let me be in time!

I was not in time.

The car was on its side thirty feet off the road, down into the woods. It burned with a terrible black smoke, its upturned wheels melting, making puddles of molten rubber. The smell of hell.

"Oh my God . . ." someone said.

We stood at the top of the mountain, looking down on the spectacle.

"Oh my God . . ."

And then I was running toward it.

"Kate! Kate, don't! . . ."

The heat made a wall around the car; a wall to keep strangers out, to lock Charles inside.

"Charles!"

"Kate! Come back!"

"Charles!"

The door of the car was open and from outside the wall I looked in; the front seat was ablaze but empty. I ran around the car, as close to the wall as I could before the searing heat claimed me, too. Still no one there.

"Kate!"

I looked around wildly; perhaps he had crawled out of the car before it caught fire. Perhaps he lay near, alive.

No one will die!

There seemed to be an entrance into the woods; broken plants, trampled undergrowth. I started toward it.

Please, God, please . . .

We could make it right. We could love each other

enough to make it right. We needed the chance. We deserved the chance.

Please, God, please ...

"Kate!"

I was right; there was a path. I hurried onto it; brambles scratched at my legs, an overhanging branch slapped my forehead.

We could make up for father and mother and George and Alan and all the curses that followed us and all the lost chances for love and all the failures and all the torments ...

I saw Charles.

He was lying face down in a small clearing directly ahead of me. I stood motionless, waiting for him to move.

He didn't move.

"Charles, my sweet baby Charles," I said to him. "Please, Charles, please ..."

And I went to him. I sank down to my knees and took him in my arms, rolling him over, cradling him.

"Please, Charles, wake up. It's Kate. Wake up ..."

And his head lay to one side in my lap. Awkwardly to one side. Impossibly to one side.

"My baby ... my baby ..."

But the horror was not yet over. Not quite over. I started to drag Charles out of the woods. To bring him home. To bring back what was left of my sweet Charles. And then I saw it. He had been lying on it.

And I started to cry.

It was the half unburied skeleton of a child.

My other Charles.

MOLLY

I didn't see any of it. Kate wouldn't let me. She came out of the woods, more dead than alive herself. I got her in the car, afraid to ask any questions, already knowing the answers, and brought her home. And this is where we've been, sitting here in the kitchen, watching the goddamn sun come up, trying to figure out what the hell to do. My kid is dead, if he ever was my kid. I'll be damned if I know. And as for getting back to my life, like Charlie said, what the hell is it? Except just to sit here and wonder if it was my fault. If I'd loved him better maybe none of this would have happened. He could've stayed Charlie and grown up and had some kind of a normal life. Who knows, maybe there's a David Harley in everybody just waiting to get out when the going gets tough enough. Maybe that's what being crazy is all about.

Anyway, for what it's worth, thanks for listening to our troubles. I know it was no picnic. As for me, I think I've said just about all I have to say. Except I did the best I could and that's all anybody can do, isn't it?

KATE

Of course it wasn't Molly's fault. If blame is to be given, give it me; I'm the one who aided Charles in his terrible change. I'm the one who helped end his life a second time.

If there is any hope to be found in our odyssey, it's that Charles is at peace now and his death is cleaner than it had been before.

And perhaps Molly and I have undone what our mother did so long ago.

That could be it, couldn't it?

OUTSTANDING READING FROM WARNER BOOKS

THE EXECUTIONER'S SONG
by Norman Mailer   (80-558, $3.95)

The execution is what the public remembers: on January 17, 1977, a firing squad at Utah State Prison put an end to the life of convicted murderer Gary Gilmore. But by then the real story was over—the true tale of violence and fear, jealousy and loss, of a love that was defiant even in death. Winner of the Pulitzer Prize. "The big book no one but Mailer could have dared . . . an absolutely astonishing book."—Joan Didion, *New York Times Book Review.*

THE GLORY
by Ronald S. Joseph   (85-469, $2.75)

Meet the inheritors: Allis Cameron, great-granddaughter of the pioneers who carved a kingdom in southern Texas. Go with her to Hollywood where her beauty conquers the screen and captures the heart of her leading man. Cammie: Allis's daughter, who comes of age and finds herself torn between a ruthless politician and a radical young Mexican. They were the Cameron women, heirs to a Texas fortune, rich, defiant, ripe for love.

THE IMAGE
by Charlotte Paul   (95-145, $2.75)

The gift of sight came to Karen Thorndyke as the bequest of an unknown man. His camera, willed to the Eye Bank, enabled the beautiful young artist to see and paint again. But with that bit of transparent tissue came an insight into horror. With her new view of life came a vision of death.

CRY FOR THE DEMON
by Julia Grice   (95-497, $2.75)

Where the lava flows and sharks hunt, Ann Southold has found a retreat on the island of Maui. Here the painful memory of her husband dims, her guilts and fears are assuaged, and she meets a dark man who calls to her—a man who wants her more than any man has ever wanted her before. Out of the deep, a terror no woman can resist . . . CRY FOR THE DEMON.